TOURNAMENT OF SHADOWS
IV

FEINT & DOUBLECROSS

TILLY WALLACE

Cover design by Aero Gallerie

Editing by Moonshell Books

Proofreading by Ellison Lane (Kat's Literary Services)

To be the first to hear about Tilly's new releases and exclusive offers,
sign up at:

https://www.tillywallace.com/newsletter

ONE

Late Autumn, 1788
London, England

There cannot be another Nereus.

When Seraphina Winyard first read that warning on Lord Branvale's ensorcelled paper, it made no sense. Nor could she see how it had any relevance to her. And yet men had used those words to wrap her magic in chains. Now, snippets of information gleaned over the preceding weeks had begun to snap together like a mosaic. The picture that time slowly revealed made her skin crawl with foreboding.

She plumped up a teal brocade cushion and lay back on the settee in her little parlour. Eyes half-closed, she stared at the night sky she had painted on the ceiling and tried to unravel a tangled history.

In mythology, Nereus was the child of Mother Earth and Old Man Sea. In the context of the secret message sent to Lord Branvale, she believed it referred to the child of two mages. Yes. Those words tasted true as she mouthed them. The warning implied that shadowy forces sought to ensure she never took a male mage to her bed and birthed such a Nereus.

A snort huffed through her. They could have simply sat her down and requested that she not conceive a child with one of their number. Although when she looked around the council table, they didn't even have to ask such a thing. There were probably tens of thousands of men in England she'd prefer for the task before she became desperate enough to consider a fellow mage.

Should she even be inclined to procreate.

But why exactly did the council want to prevent such a pairing? Apart from the obvious, in her opinion. Of those who had reached adulthood, none of them even remotely appealed as a potential lover. Lord Pendlebury made a fine friend, but she had no desire to peer beneath his clothing. As for the others... a shudder ran through her body.

From talking to the Crows, she had learned that Mother Nature imposed a limit on their numbers, just as she did with her mages. Twelve mages. Three Crows. Neither could create greater numbers of their kind than that first spontaneous appearance. But the

Crows were different in an important way—the women gifted their magic to the next generation when the girls were ready.

If what Sera had discovered held true, any child she conceived by a mage or an Unnatural would wield their own unique magic, rather than being a powerless second generation. Not to mention that child would be able to transfer their ability to one of their descendants when they were ready to give it up. The same cycle could occur over and over, throughout her line, with no waning of their magic.

Yet Mother Nature still maintained some control over such offspring. Sera couldn't mother a dozen (nor did she want to!) and create her own powerful army. So why was such an outcome so feared that, for centuries, the council had stopped girl babes from drawing breath? Given the nature of society and the rules imposed on women, she suspected there was a darker truth behind their actions: Men baulked at the mere idea of powerful women controlling which of their blood descendants received magic.

A cold shudder worked down Sera's spine. If two mages produced a gifted child of similar ability to its parents, then the bestowing of their power was no longer subject to the random whims of chance. Magic would pass from one generation to the next with absolute certainty. Families could build political power on such a base, knowing they would always have a mage among them. Would children of a given bloodline vie to be that chosen one? Would they kill for it?

She let out a slow breath and, across the plaster ceiling, games between descendants played out to find the most worthy to receive an ageing mage's magic. Like the battles of ancient gladiators.

"I'm not sure that would be an improvement over the current situation," Sera whispered. Perhaps Mother Nature really did know best by ensuring that mages appeared spontaneously and unpredictably.

Another thought crammed itself into her whirring mind. What of children with a mage father and an Unnatural mother? Such couplings must have occurred throughout their history. But how to find out? Lord Pendlebury might assist her in finding more. She would also study the old genealogies for clues. There was one name she was determined to find, to see how the magical book treated such a mage—Morag, mother of the Crows.

The modest blue enamelled mantel clock chimed the hour. Morning had slid past while she'd been engaged in her silent contemplations.

"Bother." Yet again, she had too much to do and too little time. Instead of interfering in her life, mages should direct their energies toward the problem of cramming more hours into a day. Although which was worse—mages meddling in women's affairs or having the ability to control time and alter past events?

"Elliot! I need a hackney!" With a brush of magic, she made her request echo throughout the house. There might yet be time for a quick trip to mage tower before she was expected at the Napier residence in Mayfair for her visit with Kitty.

Footsteps stomped up the stairs. Then the footman appeared in the doorway, still clutching a piece of toast. Apparently, she had disturbed his breakfast, which meant he must have risen late.

"I'm short on time. I'll finish dressing and need a vehicle ready outside by the time I come down." She rose and headed for the door. That morning, she had descended the stairs in a robe to take breakfast while sorting out her correspondence.

"Challenge accepted," he murmured, after swallowing his mouthful. He rushed out the front door and down the steps.

By the time Sera had donned a gown appropriate both to visit her friend and to wander the dusty hidden library, and Vicky had pinned up her hair in a loose style, Elliot stood by the door once more with a grin on his face. Out in the street, a hackney waited to take her to the tower.

"How did you manage that so quickly?" she asked.

Elliot winked, then broke into laughter. "He heard you one street over and was on his way here when I encountered him. You ever thought that summoning one directly might be handier than hollering at me?"

Sometimes she forgot how powerful her commands could be when projected by a push of magic. How many other vague requests meant for her staff alone were being trumpeted across her neighbourhood? Elliot was right, though—reaching out to a driver with magical tendrils was more efficient than sending the footman to chase one down.

On the ride out to the tower, Sera chatted with the driver and determined he was more than happy to answer any summons, should he be in the area. Probably the fee out to Finsbury Fields and back made it worth his while, as it saved him from finding a succession of smaller rides around London to earn the same amount.

Outside the tower, her oak sapling had shed its leaves in preparation for its first winter. The tree would go dormant and await the spring for its next burst of growth. The green lawn spread at its feet, and no doubt upset the long-standing test for admission to the hidden library. The council would need to create some other pointless test to torment young mages, now that she had caused the grass to grow all on its own.

Inside the tower, her footsteps echoed on the stone stairs as she journeyed deep into the chill earth. At the wrought-iron gates to the library, Sera whispered the spell to the entwined ouroboros snakes. With a slither, they untangled their bodies to allow the door to swing open.

"Thank you," she murmured as they locked together again behind her.

From what she remembered of Erin the Crow's tale, Morag had been born sometime in the fifteenth century. The current edition of the mage genealogy sat on its rosewood stand, illuminated by a soft amber orb. To either side stretched an angled shelf housing the older editions. Each large volume was given sufficient space that it could be opened and read where it lay, as the old books grumbled if they were moved. It didn't take too long to find the one she needed.

Sera summoned a stool, sat before the dusty book, then carefully lifted the thick cover. As she thumbed the heavy pages, a trickle of excitement wound through her. How would the book record the magical, shape-shifting daughters of a mage?

Page after page was crammed with the spidery lettering and straight lines of each long-ago mage's offspring and the outline of their lives. Births, marriages, deaths, and a few words as to the type of aftermage gift they'd inherited from the mage. The next turn of the page revealed only the soft, grainy hand-made paper. Two sides were almost entirely blank, except for the brief entry near the top of the left-hand side.

Morag Haynes
21 February 1450 – 11 October 1520

Sera traced the name with a gentle touch. This was no girl mage snuffed out before she reached adulthood, like all the other female names she found. Often there were only a few days separating the dates of birth and death. Morag had lived a full seventy years. Yet no births, deaths, marriages, or any other details appeared under her name.

In Europe, women mages lived in isolation,

engaged in scholarly pursuits, and never married or had children. Their pages would appear similar to that of Morag. But the lack of detail didn't fit with the story of the mage bearing children to her shifter lover. The two pages should have been crammed with the details of her descendants for the seven generations the book tracked.

There were two possibilities why they were not. First, that Erin's tale was simply that, a story or family myth. Obscured by time and retelling, someone had added the embellishment of a mage being the matriarch of their line. Second, the book might have refused to recognise Morag's love match with a shifter, and their children, which contravened the Mage Council's rules.

Sera straightened her spine and stared at the book and its scant details. Morag had lived a long life for those troubled times and the council's horrific policy of not allowing magic to flourish in *inferior vessels*. Considering the prevailing environment when she was born, Erin's claim that an elderly mage had spirited the babe away to allow her a chance to grow to adulthood seemed plausible. Sera's father, after all, had threatened to hand her over to the gargoyles for her safety.

Then her thoughts turned to the negotiations between her father and Lord Rowan. Branvale had sworn a blood oath in return for having his marriage to an Unnatural erased. The fact that the genealogy had recorded the marriage in the first place proved that the book itself had no prejudices against whomever mages chose to love, marry, or have children with.

Given what Sera knew of events from Erin, and the evidence that the genealogy's magic recorded everything, left a third possibility.

Someone had erased Morag's offspring from the book.

Lord Rowan had drained himself to exhaustion to remove the record of a failed marriage. What would it take to erase the records of three gifted daughters? More than one mage. Three at least, if all the magic in one mage was needed to coerce the book into removing just one entry. The blank page suggested that an entire council of powerful men had drained themselves to keep the secret that a woman had bested them and found happiness outside of their rules.

With reluctance, Sera rose to her feet and closed the book. Time ran through her hourglass and she could ponder the mystery of Morag's blank pages on her way to Kitty's home. So far, Sera had plenty of ideas but little hard evidence of what had happened long ago, who or what Nereus was, and how either might impact her.

How would she prove any of her theories? She most certainly was *not* going to get herself and Lord Tomlin drunk enough to perform an intimate act so that nine months later she could announce, "Aha! Just as I suspected."

But until a theory was tested, it was merely a hypothesis. What if she found proof of Morag's descendants being erased from the genealogy? If more than one mage had been drained, such an event might have been mentioned in their histories. Ideas spiralled inside her, each sparking another until the fire grew and fuelled her determination to uncover the truth. Locating Lord Branvale's Unnatural wife was another possibility. Or simply asking Lord Rowan.

Had the time come to negotiate handing over the Fae bracelets, in return for the old mage's divulging all the secrets her mind itched to know?

Perhaps.

Two

Later that same afternoon, Sera sipped tea in Kitty's parlour while a rare foul mood unfurled over Hugh. The surgeon ignored the plates of sweet and savoury treats laid out on the table. Instead, he crossed his arms and huffed, his eyebrows pulled so low they nearly joined in the middle.

"Why is it that you ladies are allowed to go off on adventures, and I must stay here?" With narrowed eyes, he glared at the fireplace.

"Because there are many in London who rely upon you and your medical skills. Would you leave your patients unattended for a week?" Sera reached out and patted his arm. She managed to keep a sympathetic look upon her face, even though the situation amused her immensely.

Contessa Noemi Ricci, her companion Vilma Winters, and the latter's mother were returning to

Mistwood Manor to end the very ill Vilma's life before the tumours snatched her away from them. Vilma would breathe her last in her own bedroom at the beloved old house. Then she would awaken as a vampyre. Kitty and Sera had a role to play in the process and would follow the group in another carriage, as they only intended to stay for two nights before returning to London. They wanted to celebrate the chain of events that had bound the four women together.

Hugh exploded with curiosity and excitement about the transformation, and Sera wondered that if they tortured him for any longer, he might stamp his foot so hard he would break through the floor. Noemi and Vilma had already agreed that he might join their party. The surgeon had proven his worth with the pivotal role he had played in freeing Meredith, the former Lady Hillborne, from Bedlam.

Kitty glanced at Sera, then schooled her features in a stern expression. "Well, Hugh, I think that if you could find another doctor willing to undertake your rounds before we depart tomorrow, then you may join us."

The surgeon leapt to his feet with such force that the heavy armchair rocked back, slammed to the floor, and quivered. Hugh disappeared out the door at a run. Kitty and Sera shared wide-eyed looks, but before they could speak, he reappeared in the doorway gripping the jamb with both hands. "Apologies, ladies. I shall find a stand-in immediately and be ready to join you in the morning!"

His last words drifted from the foyer as he left, his footsteps scrabbling over the tiles in his hurry to leave and ask a fellow physician to tend any patients needing closer attention in his absence.

Sera erupted in laughter at his eagerness and Kitty chortled until they both struggled to draw breath and had to wipe tears from their eyes.

Kitty leaned back on the settee and placed one hand over her chest. "That was fun."

"But so unkind. We shouldn't use his enthusiasm as a weapon against him." Only now did Sera consider whether it might be cruel to poke fun at the gentle surgeon.

"I only tease him because I like him. He is a good man and they are in woefully short supply." Kitty waved a hand, dismissing Sera's concerns. "Besides, when I offer myself as breakfast to Vilma, it will reassure me to have both you and Hugh there."

Sera's humour dissipated as she considered that serious topic. They discussed the matter heatedly enough that Mr Napier enquired whether the two friends had had a falling out. They had to reassure him that they merely argued over which school was more deserving of Kitty's patronage, and he left the room with a chuckle and a shake of his head.

It seemed obvious to Sera that Hugh should be Vilma's first meal because of his size and strength. Kitty pointed out that she would rather have him present in his medical capacity, not playing the part of a fried kipper. If something went awry during the feeding, Hugh's surgical skills might be required. Noemi had whispered of the slim possibility that Vilma might become ravenous and unable to stop herself. In which case, they would have to forcibly remove her from Kitty's vein.

The thought of Vilma inadvertently draining Kitty or tearing her friend's flesh had ended their disagreement. Sera would have begged Hugh to attend if there was even the most remote chance her friend would need his assistance.

"I must return home and advise Lord Ormsby I will be absent again this week." Sera rose from the settee.

"How is he taking his loss?" Kitty referred to the amendment to the Mage Act which the Speaker of the Mage Council had championed in Parliament.

Had Lord Ormsby succeeded, it would have classified women mages differently to their male counterparts, and imposed additional close supervision over women mages until they reached the age of thirty. The amendment also sought to give the Speaker of the Mage Council the power to appoint an appropriate guardian for any woman mage; she had to comply or face *seclusion*. A polite way of saying *interment at the Repository of Forgotten Things*. Thankfully, Mr Napier's campaigning among his powerful friends had resulted in the amendment being defeated, and the Mage Act stood unaltered with all its glorious gender-neutral language.

14

"He is taking it badly. But there is little he can do—and the more he scowls at me, the bigger my smile becomes." Sera's tasks in her official capacity as a mage couldn't get any worse. She had been ordered to clean drains, remove refuse, and generally get her hands dirty. While she would never tell the council so, she enjoyed plodding through fields and rivers. Not so much the drains, though. Magic could do little to dampen the smell of human effluent, but it gladdened her heart to help those so often overlooked.

"You are free, Sera, with the same rights and freedoms as all the other mages around that table. There is nothing he can do to you now." Kitty rose and accompanied her friend out to the foyer.

Sera kissed her friend's cheek. The council had been rendered impotent to act against her, unless she broke the rules that applied to all mages. As an Englishwoman, she was still subject to the dictates of her king, but surely Queen Charlotte would moderate any outlandish demands King George made? Especially if the queen succeeded in being named Regent in the current political arguments that consumed everyone's attention.

With her rights upheld, Sera hoped whoever lurked in the dark and sought to control her would give up and fade back into the shadows. A grain of worry remained inside her, though. Until she knew the whole truth, she would never truly be free. Every day she waited for her mysterious correspondent to deliver what she needed in order to cross Shadowvane into the Fae realm, but they never appeared. She was tempted to reply to the ensorcelled note with a reminder.

"I will see you in the morning. I am sure Hugh will be ready bright and early." Sera took her leave.

They planned a small celebration at Mistwood to mark the ownership of the house returning to Vilma and her mother, and to toast Vilma's new life with Noemi. Aware of the pain and sacrifice Meredith had endured as the wife of Mistwood's unlawful previous owner, Vilma and Noemi planned to visit the Crows' Nest (as their secluded estate was called) to ensure the former Lady Hillborne and her daughter had all they required for their new life. Noemi would care for them, as she did for Vilma and her mother.

Back at home, Sera nibbled on a biscuit as she dealt with pressing matters. The plate rattled as the rosewood box on the desk vibrated for several long seconds. Then it fell still and a thin strip of golden light shone from under the lid. With one hand, she flipped the box open and withdrew the sheet of paper. It contained a summons, not from king or council, but from Lord Rowan.

She held the page in one hand and with the other, placed her half-eaten biscuit on the plate. She didn't want to visit Lord Rowan. Well, she did, and she didn't. There were matters she wanted to discuss with the far more experienced mage. But she knew the price that would have to be paid—handing over the Fae bracelets that had the power to control others. Hugh had hidden them at her request and she was disinclined to have them returned to her just yet. She had numerous draw-ings of the runes worked into them to study and no pressing need to hold the original items.

An itch at the back of her mind cautioned her to keep hold of the pieces and not surrender them. Not yet. She waited for a compelling piece of bait from Lord Rowan that she couldn't refuse. What tasty secret would make her hand them over? There were so many to pick from. The name of Branvale's anonymous corre-spondent. Full disclosure of why there couldn't be another Nereus. Information about whether or not male mages could father magical offspring with Unnat-urals. How to find her former guardian's wife.

Oh, yes. That last secret intrigued her the most. Who and what type of Unnatural was she? Had Bran-vale spurned her on their wedding night because he'd learned of her Unnatural state and that legally, they could not wed? And yet the mage genealogies had recorded the match, so clearly the book had no problem recognising a diverse range of matrimonial partners. Or was it because a mage was forbidden to father children with an Unnatural? Which had the greater effect on Branvale—his personal opinion of Unnaturals, or the dictates of the council?

Sera stared out the window as she considered, and discarded, several possible replies to Lord Rowan. Eventually, she wrote a carefully worded reply to the former Speaker of the Mage Council. She informed him that regrettably, she was unable to comply with his request due to a pressing matter taking her away from

London (again). She closed by saying how much she looked forward to discussing many topics with him on her return, particularly that of Lord Branvale and the circumstances surrounding how she had come to be placed under his care.

Let the highly respected grandfather of her friend Lady Abigail Crawley tell Lord Ormsby about the bracelets if he wanted. In return, Sera would innocently let slip about the erasure of Lord Branvale's marriage. She would wager Lord Ormsby didn't know about that. It raised the question of what other secret bargains Lord Rowan, the previous Speaker, had struck with his mages to ensure their compliance with his orders?

To keep Elliot occupied while she was away, Sera had a number of tasks for him to perform in her absence. Chief among them was distributing the glow lamps she had made for the most needy. Sleep had been sacrificed to brew the delicate mist that produced the light, but she would have plenty of time to doze in the carriage on the way to Mistwood.

Elliot was also to keep his ears open as to the reaction of the everyday Londoner to her Nyx persona. While the initial furore over her royal performance had abated, she wanted to know if she had laid to rest old superstitions about witches or blown upon the embers. She walked a dangerous line and recognised that many might now fear her. But the lower classes saw the work she did around the city to ease their lives, and she hoped they would view her as one of them.

The next morning, their two carriages left London on the dot of nine. The lead vehicle held Contessa Ricci, Vilma, and her mother, Lady Hillborne. Inside the Napier family carriage rode Kitty, Sera, and a grinning Hugh. He had found two young doctors to take over his rounds while he was away, and they would consult with Lord Viner, Hugh's mentor, should anything arise beyond their experience. Even though it pained him to leave those who needed him, he simply refused to miss the opportunity to see the vampyre transform her orchid into one of the undead.

As they travelled away from London, Sera reached into her reticule and pulled out a small piece of jewellery. She held it out to Hugh. "I have crafted you a mage silver ring, Hugh, to make it easier for us to contact each other."

He took the ring, which resembled a tiny metal bone. "How does it work?"

"If it vibrates, I am thinking of you. If you need to contact me, touch the ring and think of me. Then I can use my magic to find a bird to convey any message." The more the little avian messengers permitted her to use them, the more her skill grew.

The surgeon slid the ring onto his little finger, whereupon it adjusted to the correct size and the ends of the bone touched to close the circle. "Thank you."

After an uneventful and bottom-numbing journey of two days, they arrived at a very different Mistwood. The gloomy cloud and low-hanging mist of their previous visit was replaced by the pale caress of a low autumn sun. The dull grime that clung to the unusual dark stone used to build the house had peeled away to show glimpses of something like obsidian. Mrs Pymm, the housekeeper, stood on the front step, her smile beaming so brightly it would chase away any cloud if there had been one. As the footman helped down the older Lady Hillborne, the housekeeper rushed forward.

"Oh! Lady Hillborne, you cannot imagine how pleased I am to see you again." Then remembering her manners, she curtseyed.

"Don't go starting that, my old friend. My heart is full of joy to see you and this house again." Lady Hillborne linked arms with the housekeeper.

Natalie Delacour, the gargoyle who was also Sera's aunt, emerged from the archway, dressed in her long split skirt and waistcoat, the sleeves of her shirt rolled up despite the chill in the air. She nodded to Sera.

"How did the current Lord Hillborne take his departure?" Sera asked.

Nat's shoulders heaved with laughter. "I'm surprised you do not already know. He screamed loudly about Miss Winters and her mother cheating him out of his inheritance."

Kitty snorted. "Let him cry like a baby all the way to Yorkshire. He still has the title and the entailed lands. Which Father tells me are located in a particularly cold and desolate spot, where it rains almost year round."

"Did he leave without difficulty?" While Sera had

wanted to see the look on his face, it was better this way and reduced the distress to Vilma and her mother.

"No. But he is gone, and no damage was done to Mistwood." The gargoyle refused to be drawn any farther on Lord Hillborne's histrionics. From the grin on her aunt's face, Sera hoped it had involved the gargoyle *woman*-handling Lord Hillborne into a carriage.

"Thank you, Mrs Delacour, for ensuring that Mistwood remained undamaged." Vilma offered her thanks for the role the gargoyle had played in evicting the previous unlawful tenant.

"What do you make of Mistwood, Nat?" Sera wondered if the gargoyle could sense what made the manor so different from any other building.

Nat patted the ebony stone of the exterior wall. "Gargoyles have lived in this spot for centuries. They built the manor. I hope Miss Winters appreciates it."

Vilma laid a hand over Nat's large one. "I treasure Mistwood and what lies at its heart."

Nat huffed and patted Vilma's frail hand. "Good. Mistwood likes you. They are happy now."

Noemi tucked Vilma's hand into the crook of her elbow, and Kitty and Hugh followed them up the steps. Sera watched the others, heads bent together as conversation and laughter flowed out to the lake.

"Give Father my love. We shall detour on our way back to London to see him." Sera hugged the gargoyle. With her role over, Nat wanted to return to her quiet life working as a mason alongside Sera's father.

Nat stepped out onto the drive. There, she puffed out her chest, and her form blurred as though an artist made a hurried drawing in charcoal. Her size enlarged as stone coated her limbs and monstrous wings sprouted from her back. Transformed in mere seconds, in her Unnatural state Nat stood much taller and broader than Hugh. Skirt, shirt, and waistcoat were carved into her stone body. Her wings unfurled and she jumped to the sky. In a few heavy strokes, she disappeared among the clouds.

"I wish I could fly," Sera murmured. She focused on the spot where Nat had vanished for a quiet moment, then retreated inside Mistwood.

Vilma had paused on the threshold, one hand pressed to the aged timber. "I have returned, my friend."

Sera crossed the foyer and stood in the middle of the tile with closed eyes. She let magic trickle through the floor and spread through the house. This time, the soul of the old home rose up to greet her, rubbing against her like a cat that had missed its owner. A far different response to the sadness-filled entity she had discovered on their previous visit.

Vilma is restored and will always be with you, she told Mistwood.

The soul of the house wrapped her in a warm embrace, which she took as thanks, then it sank back into the depths. Opening her eyes, she found Hugh peering at her with a curious look.

"The house is happy to have Vilma and her mother back," Sera said.

That dug his frown deeper. "The... house?"

"Yes. Did I not tell you that some ancient entity resides at the heart of Mistwood?" She bit back a laugh at his wide-eyed response.

He stared at the ceiling as though it might rap him on the head for not paying attention. "The house is alive?"

Sera considered her answer. "I'm not sure I would say *alive*, exactly, but it has an awareness."

"Mistwood has a soul." Vilma joined them, a flush of colour to her cheeks at being once more in her childhood home. Then pain bloomed. She sucked in a breath, and her knees buckled.

Noemi took her arm, worry ploughing across her forehead. "Tonight. Yes?"

Every day, Vilma faded a little more. Pain filled her eyes, and she struggled with each breath. Only the desire to claim Mistwood as her own had kept her going. That and a need to sign all the legal paperwork that would secure Mistwood in perpetuity.

Vilma's eyelids fluttered closed, and she leaned heavily on her companion, but she breathed a faint, "Yes."

THREE

They ate supper early, using exhaustion from their journey as an excuse to retire early. Lady Hillborne, oblivious to Noemi's true nature and unaware that her daughter would die that night, kissed Vilma's cheek and retired to her rooms. Vilma had reclaimed her old bedroom, the one previously occupied by Noemi that looked out over the lake.

Kitty and Sera sat by the fire. Hugh paced, casting glances at the two women sitting on the bed. Noemi had loosened the blood-coloured velvet drapes from their ties, so that they partly enclosed the bed.

"You will wear a hole in the carpet, Hugh. Do sit down," Kitty said at length.

"Vilma is willing and Noemi has explained the process to her." Sera wondered if he might try to intervene, unable to sit back while a life was snuffed out as he watched.

He ran both hands up over his face and through his

hair, then dropped into a chair beside Sera. The leather emitted a puff of air as his bulk deflated it, rather like a surprised person spitting out a mouthful of water.

"But... what if something goes wrong? Or she changes her mind partway through?" He curled his hands into fists, then uncurled them to fidget with his new ring, spinning the mage silver bone around and around.

"What if we delay even another day, and death snatches Vilma due to the tumours? You were surprised she endured the entire trip here," Sera reminded him gently. She had wrapped the room in a protective spell so no one would overhear or burst in uninvited.

Vilma stretched out on the bed, and Noemi adjusted a pillow behind her. Then the vampyre gathered her companion in her arms and bent over the exposed neck. A sigh and then a soft moan came from the ill woman.

"It's rude to watch," Kitty murmured. She set up a chessboard to distract them.

Sera had never been as good as her friend at the game of strategy, so she enlisted Hugh to partner her. Two to one, they might have a chance against her dear shrewd friend.

"Didn't you say the contessa usually only takes a small portion from Miss Winters?" Hugh cast a glance at the embracing couple.

"Yes. The equivalent of only a finger or two in a glass, Noemi said." Sera slid a pawn forward. For a change, she played the white side while Kitty took the dark. Ironic that the *good* side would still most likely lose.

Kitty ignored her pawns and instead moved her knight to the centre of the board.

Hugh contemplated the pieces and nudged Sera's hand towards the bishop's pawn. "But it requires a great deal more than a mean pour of liquor to drain a person. A woman of Miss Winters' size and build could contain as much as four quarts. What happens if Contessa Ricci enters some sort of blood lust and cannot stop? Such as she cautioned might happen with Miss Winters in the morning?"

Sera opened her mouth to answer, shut it, and glanced at Kitty. They had planned how to stop Vilma if she drank too deeply of Kitty; they hadn't pondered what draining her companion would do to Noemi. How strong a magical net would she need to cast to restrain a rampaging vampyre and protect her friends and the staff?

"Oh, don't look at me with that face, Sera. I don't know the answer. Tomorrow we might discover that two vampyres can drain the lot of us, including the servants and horses, and we will all either live forever or become compost for the vegetable garden." Kitty advanced a pawn two squares.

There was a terrifying outcome. Sera wondered how her friend could concentrate on the game and not worry they had set in motion a course of events that might quickly spiral out of their control.

The faint sucking stopped, and Noemi laid Vilma's

still form back against the pillows. When Hugh rose from his seat, she held up one hand to halt him. "Do not approach. It is... intoxicating... to drink so much. I cannot remember the last time I took so much from someone."

"Are we in danger from you?" He voiced in a low tone the question that pressed on their minds.

"Only if you make a sudden move towards me or her." Noemi tilted her head back and drew deep, even breaths, even though her lungs did not require it.

Sera wondered if it was some control exercise, similar to the way she counted to ten when her anger flared. A tactic that didn't always work for her. But Noemi had decades of experience in reining in her baser instincts.

After a few minutes stretched into what felt like hours, Noemi turned to stare at Hugh. The darkness drained from her all-black eyes, to reveal the whites and her grey irises once more. "It has passed. Pain at taking my beloved's life has washed away the compulsion."

Sera fetched a bowl of water and a cloth before approaching the bed with a slow tread. She held out the wet cloth to Noemi, who used it to wipe a trace of blood from her lips. "Is she...?"

"Soon. Her stubborn streak is strong, and it clings to life, even though death is inevitable. When I feel that her heart is to beat its last, it will be time for the next step, when she will sup from me." Noemi passed the cloth back to Sera and leaned close to Vilma, listening to the faint beat in her companion's chest.

Sera placed the bowl by the bed within reach. Noemi pulled down the shoulder of her gown and drew her nail across her flesh, creating a bright red slash. Cradling Vilma in her arms, she held the other woman's face to the trail of blood.

"If her heart no longer beats, I wonder how Miss Winters can drink? There must be some compulsion triggered by the vampyre blood that trickles over her lips. Or it might possess some magnetic quality." Dear Hugh. He could not help speculating even as he watched.

This part took several minutes. Vilma's lips were pressed to the wound. The movement of her throat as she swallowed was almost imperceptible. Noemi hummed a haunting tune as the dying woman drew forth the blood. Then Vilma slumped in Noemi's arms. The vampyre lowered her companion against the pillows and placed a kiss on her forehead. Vilma's skin was pale with a tinge of blue, her lips verging on purple. No breath rose in her chest. The contessa used the damp cloth to gently clean blood from the other woman's lips and chin.

Finally, she wiped her hands before tossing the ball of fabric into its bowl. "It is done."

Hugh approached the bed and studied the prone woman. He glanced up to seek permission from the woman on guard. "May I?"

Noemi nodded and rose to her feet.

Hugh performed an examination of Vilma, flexing her arms and wrists and splaying her fingers over his large palm. Then he pressed both hands under her chin. Leaning down, he rested his ear upon her chest. Lastly, he placed two fingers on her neck.

"Miss Winters has passed," he murmured, glancing at Sera and Kitty.

"What happens now?" Sera directed her question to Noemi.

"We wait. It will take some hours for my blood to spread through her body and for the transformation to seep into her flesh, bones, and organs." Noemi stretched her arms up and rolled her head to and fro. Then she returned to the bed, lying next to Vilma.

The game of chess was now abandoned. Sera took off her boots and curled up in the armchair, resting her head on its arm. Kitty fetched a book, but held it open in her lap, her face turned aside. Hugh sat on the window seat, arms crossed as he stared at the bed, accustomed to keeping an all-night vigil at his patient's bedside.

Despite her awkward position, Sera managed to snatch a few hours of sleep. She stirred to find the faintest touch of pink blushed the sky. Her body ached from being curled up all night and someone thrown a blanket over her. For a moment, she wondered what had pulled her from sleep. Then a murmur came from the bed.

The dead woman had roused.

Sera swung her feet to the floor and reached out to shake Kitty. Her friend had slept with her face pressed into the wing of the armchair and, when she turned, she had a faint imprint on her cheek. Hugh was already on his feet and crossed to stand by the bed as his dead patient... sat up.

"I am thirsty, Noemi. My throat is so dry," Vilma rasped.

"I know, *cara mia.*" Noemi slid off the bed.

"Breakfast is served," Kitty muttered as she approached.

Vilma adjusted her pillows as they gathered round. Sera thought death suited the other woman. Her skin no longer had the blue tinge of other corpses, or the pallor of illness, but the lustre of a pearl. Even her lips were pinker and dawn light caressed her hair and turned it to spun gold.

Noemi stood and gestured for Kitty to sit on the edge of the bed. "Katherine will offer you what you need, Vilma."

"I do not want to hurt her." Vilma gazed at her protector as her hands hovered by Kitty's outstretched arm.

The old vampyre stood close to her new creation. "Remember, Katherine is your friend, and you would never hurt her. You must only drink a little to finish your transformation. Afterwards, you may have your fill from the bottles we brought with us."

Sera curled her hands into fists, her palms heating with pooled magic. While she trusted that Noemi had the situation in hand, she was poised to protect her friend if need be.

Hugh leaned on the bedpost and tried to appear

unconcerned. But the tight set of his shoulders gave away the fact that he, too, was ready to pounce if Vilma could not stop. He held a pocket watch in one hand.

"One minute, Mr Miles. No longer," Noemi said.

She had suggested they time Vilma's feeding, to ensure Kitty did not lose too much blood. Hugh had done some calculations about blood flow and the effect on the body, and settled on one minute as being permissible.

Kitty glanced at Sera, then addressed Vilma in a soft tone with only a tiny hint of a tremor. "I am willing, Vilma, and know you will not harm me."

Vilma nodded and took Kitty's arm, holding one hand over the heel of Kitty's palm and the other by the elbow as though her forearm were a large piece of corn. She hesitated a moment, then lunged and bit down.

Kitty cried out, and Sera jumped. Hugh surged forward, but Noemi held up a hand. Before Sera could swipe the vampyre out of the way, Kitty's cry of alarm changed to a quiet moan, and it became clear her friend was in no immediate danger.

Everyone stilled, the room silent except for the tick of Hugh's watch and a gasp from Kitty.

"Time," Hugh called after sixty seconds, and snapped the watch shut.

Noemi placed a hand on Vilma's bent head. "That is enough, *cara mia*. Bite your tongue like I showed you, so that your blood will heal the wound. You do not want to leave Katherine with a scar."

Being an obedient pupil, Vilma did as instructed.

31

When she lifted her head, her blue eyes had turned a deep violet. She licked her lips and released her hold on Kitty's arm.

Kitty rose from the bed and Sera rushed to her friend. She held out her arm for Hugh to examine.

"I am not harmed." Kitty reassured Sera with wonder. "There was a brief moment of pain, as when a splinter enters your skin when you pick up a piece of wood. But I suspect it was surprise that made me cry out, not any real pain. Then... well... let us simply say it did not hurt."

Colour rose in Kitty's cheeks and Sera tucked away her friend's reaction to discuss much later, when they were alone. From what she had observed, the feeding appeared to be pleasurable to the party offering up their vein. Examining the spot on Kitty's inner wrist, Sera marvelled that apart from a slight red patch, which was already fading before their eyes, there was no mark or scar to hint at what had just occurred.

"You have still lost an unknown quantity of blood, Miss Napier. I could only estimate how much Miss Winters might have been able to drink. You must have some sweet tea and breakfast to restore you." Hugh's concern was for his patient with a pulse. The one without a heartbeat was being tended by her creator.

"I will fetch breakfast." Sera opened the door to find the young maid, Truby, at the end of the hallway.

The girl stood at the edge of the barrier Sera had created, her eyes wide and her bucket of kindling clutched in both hands. "I was going to set the fire, milady, but my feet won't move, no matter how hard I try."

"My companions did not want to be disturbed after our tiring journey, so I created a shield to give them privacy." Sera waved her hands and pulled down the barrier. "Since you are here, I can offer a trade. I will revive the fire in Miss Winters' room, if you would tell the kitchen we need tea and a breakfast tray, please." Sera took the bucket from the shocked maid.

Before she could protest about a mage dirtying her hands with ash, Sera adjusted her features into that of a fellow maid the girl would recognise. In a moment, Jones, an identity she had assumed on her previous visit, winked at her frozen companion.

Truby gasped. "You!"

Sera grinned. "Yes. I am a maid sometimes, a mage at others. I came here under disguise last time to find out what really happened to little Hannah." Then she leaned closer and whispered to Truby, "I told you that I would ensure Lord Hillborne never harmed you again."

Truby's eyes widened. "You didn't... how...?"

"Magic." Sera placed one finger to her lips. Then she turned the maid around and pointed her back down the hall. "Now, tea for three and a small bite to eat, if you would, Truby. And if you could please ask Cook to have a hearty breakfast ready for us downstairs, Mr Miles has rather an appetite."

Not long afterwards, a maid and Truby returned with tea trays holding enough for three and a plate of warm scones with clotted cream and blackberry jam.

Sera and Hugh fussed over Kitty. Then, once they had drunk the tea and polished off the scones, Sera insisted they go downstairs for breakfast. Vilma remained in her room with Noemi, needing time to become accustomed to her new state.

Lady Hillborne joined them at breakfast, saying she had been unable to sleep, but only picked at her food.

"Vilma will be well. She simply needs a little longer to recover from the journey," Sera reassured the worried mother.

"How we love this place. Vilma's one wish was to... pass here." Lady Hillborne pushed her plate away and picked up her teacup. Unshed tears shimmered in her eyes, as though her maternal love sensed her daughter had not made it through the night.

"I saw Miss Winters this morning, Lady Hillborne, and I believe she will be much revived by suppertime," Hugh said between mouthfuls of sausage.

"How it eases my mind to have you here, Mr Miles, but I do not think even you can work a miracle and remove the tumours inside my darling girl." Lady Hillborne stared at the wisp of steam curling off her cup.

"Miracles can happen, and do not discount the effect Mistwood has on Vilma," Sera murmured.

By dying on her own terms, Vilma now had centuries of living before her.

"I hear Vilma intends to write a novel?" Kitty filled the silence and soon they had Lady Hillborne out of her despondent mood and chatting about the sadly neglected state of Mistwood's library.

That day Kitty, Sera, and Hugh kept themselves occupied by exploring the manor and poking into dark corners. When the gong rang for dinner, they waited at the bottom of the stairs in the foyer. None of them had seen Vilma all day, as Noemi had kept them away. Kitty gripped Sera's hand as the couple descended the stairs. Where once Vilma had appeared frail, her beauty now radiated an ethereal lustre. The blush pink gown she wore was the perfect final touch to transform her into a fairytale princess. Noemi beamed and happiness radiated from the two women.

"Oh, Vilma! Why—why—what miracle is this? You are simply stunning," Lady Hillborne cried, rushing to embrace her daughter.

Vilma reached out to wipe a tear from her mother's eye. "You do not have to worry about me anymore, Mother. I believe Mistwood has indeed wrought a miracle."

Lady Hillborne cupped Vilma's cheek. "Let us pray this recovery lasts a little longer. I could not bear to lose you just yet."

Hugh bent his elbow, inviting Sera's hand. As the only man present, he could claim the honour of escorting her to the dining room.

That evening, dinner was lively, with much laughter. Afterwards, Vilma took everyone to the library to show her mother where her father's will had been concealed. Noemi threw back the shutters to let in the moonlight, and Sera crafted a glowing orb to hang in the middle of the room.

When tiredness finally snapped at Sera's mind and limbs and she had to seek her bed, it was the early hours of the morning. As Sera left the library, Vilma sat in the window seat with a journal open on her lap, gazing out at the lake. Sera wondered what writerly inspiration the new vampyre would find in the water that seemed to contain a thousand stars.

FOUR

Two days later, Sera heaved a sigh as she crossed her own threshold back in Soho. She had witnessed a marvellous ending to her mission at Mistwood, and she couldn't wait for Vilma to pen her gothic novel.

Elliot took her cloak and hung it on its hook. "Nothing much happened while you were away. Still no sign of our watcher and I handed out those lanterns like you asked. I've kept my ears open. Folk are divided —some think you're bloody terrifying, what with having those crows yank out souls and a dragon the size of a building climbing out of the Thames." He fell silent and waited.

Blast. Sera swatted a strand of hair away from her face. "I will take that as an *I told you so* and promise to listen to you next time." At the time, the banquet had seemed the perfect opportunity to demonstrate the extent of her power.

He huffed. "It's not all bad, though. Others are pointing out that your crows only went after the toffs and it won't take much for folk to claim you as their own. You're the first mage any of them can remember to get your hands dirty and rub shoulders with them. Personally, I think if you could get them to stop stabbing each other in dark alleys, that'd be real magic." Elliot picked up her trunk and swung it up on his shoulder.

"I'll do what I can, where I can." While it was well and good for the council to send her to tend drains during the day, they also needed to address crimes committed at night.

Sera had raised the subject before and Lord Ormsby had replied that they were mages, not the constabulary. Once she had given the issue some thought, Sera would approach the topic from another angle. Lighting would be a start. Most criminals preferred to hug the shadows. If they provided people with well-lit walkways as they returned home, that would surely reduce thefts and attacks.

The cynic in her thought it suited the aristocracy to let crime fester in the poorer neighbourhoods. If common folk were fighting among themselves or simply struggling to survive, they weren't eyeing up the nobles and demanding an equal say in the running of the country.

The next day, Sera donned her favourite dark green riding habit and had Elliot hire a horse. She would head out to Finsbury Fields and mage tower. After so many

days crammed into a carriage, she wanted the somewhat fresher air (if London could ever be called fresh)
of being on horseback.

Inside the tower, she waved a hand to open the
doors of the meeting room and took her place at
number six on the circular table. Most of the other
mages present nodded in greeting. Lord Pendlebury
called out a cheery hello. From farther around the
table, Lord Tomlin narrowed his gaze at her with a cold
glint in his eyes. Since her public defeat of him, their
relationship had slid from cool associates to a festering
animosity. If he thought to cow her with his foul mood,
he would be disappointed. She found his response
amusing. He resembled a child sulking because they'd
lost a promised treat. Sera clasped her hands together
to stop herself from creating a hat-sized thundercloud
to drizzle rain upon him.

Lord Ormsby wore a face as unhappy in defeat as
that of Lord Tomlin. Both men had probably shared a
few drinks in the Speaker's office to grumble about
troublesome women.

"I assume you are back in London for at least a few
days, Lady Winyard, before gallivanting off somewhere
else?" Lord Ormsby glared at her over the rims of his
glasses.

"I thought you understood the reason for my
absence, Lord Ormsby? I had hoped that since the
demise of Lady Hillborne, her spirit might finally
reveal her missing daughter's location. I could not
search for the girl from London. Alas, I have to report

that I failed." She dropped her gaze to her lap with the last word and drooped her shoulders. Throwing Ormsby a bone of defeat to gloat over always improved his mood.

He huffed a distinctly satisfied noise. "You had already failed in your assigned task. I cannot understand why you went back, only to fail again. That will be noted in our records."

Was that a note of glee in his voice? She dared a glance from under lowered lashes. Yes, there was a smirk on his thin lips.

"No more unauthorised trips outside London, Lady Winyard." His pen scratched over paper.

"We do serve all of England, not just London," Lord Pendlebury said. "The use of our skills sends us to the far-flung corners of these isles and we are often absent from this council table. I have been set a task that will soon send me to Scotland. I find I am quite looking forward to it. It has been some years since I had a good bite of haggis."

Lord Ormsby muttered under his breath, but it sounded remarkably like an old dog growling in a corner. The normal mage business passed without further incident, the Speaker making much of writing that Sera had failed in her task to locate the missing Hannah. Twice. Then correspondence and magical matters were discussed and any pressing tasks allocated. Lord Tomlin was given a noble client with an infestation of pixies in their rose garden. The pesky folk needed to be relocated to a more suitable woodland.

Sera tried not to pout. How she would have loved that assignment, her days spent wandering a grand estate and studying their trees to find a new home for the tiny mischievous folk. If she recalled her lessons correctly, they had a rather nasty bite if stirred up. Pixies were best treated like a wasp nest—with respect and from a distance. No wonder the noble wanted them evicted from the gardens close to the house.

"Lady Winyard, your skills are required in Southwark," Lord Ormsby said. "A man was attacked and killed last night. From reports of those who discovered him, they say it was an *inhuman* assailant. From the nature and extent of the injuries, the doctor suspects a rogue lycanthrope." He tore off a page and, with a push of magic, sent it sailing across the table to land before her.

Sera scanned the details of the attack and the location. It appeared to be a working-class area soaked in crime and misfortune. On the positive side, it lay not far from Vauxhall Gardens, a place she longed to visit at night to see all its wonders and entertainments.

She grinned. "Of course, Lord Ormsby."

To herself, she added, *Only too happy to undertake the dirty work at night that these men are too afraid to touch.* The task gave her the perfect opportunity for an adventure—one suited to her magic, Elliot's cunning, and Hugh's brawn.

"If it is indeed an Unnatural, the creature must be

41

caught and dealt with. There are books down in the library about the beasts and their habits. I am sure you will want to study for this task so you don't *fail* to capture the thing." The Speaker gathered all his papers together and shuffled them into a tidy pile—his cue that the meeting was concluded.

Sera ignored the deliberate snipe at her skills, since she had in reality succeeded in finding Hannah. No one would prise *that* secret from her. "Will it be interred at the Repository of Forgotten Things? I would like to see the place." The mere name aroused a ghoulish curiosity in her. What was imprisoned within its walls? And where was the shadowy prison?

"It's not Bedlam, Lady Winyard. You don't pay a coin to tour the cells and gape at the inmates." Lord Ormsby pushed back his chair and the other mages rose.

She would not be deterred so easily. "If I am to capture this creature, would it not be prudent to show me where I am to deliver it? Or shall I bring it here?"

The Speaker uttered a startled sound as though she had dropped the raging lycanthrope in the middle of the table. Then he glared at her. "Find it and secure it first. Then send word, and we will take it from there." He nodded and strode from the room.

Sera folded the sheet of paper and stuffed it into her reticule. Now she had an added incentive to hunt down whatever had killed the poor man: the opportunity to peer inside the Repository.

First, Sera had to find Hugh—a process made easier now that he wore a mage silver ring.

She guided the horse towards the centre of London and once the city pressed on her, she halted. After slipping off her gloves, Sera wrapped her fingers around her ring and pictured the surgeon in her mind. The ring tingled as it connected with the one on his hand. Letting her mind soar, the pull of Hugh's ring acted like the needle on a compass. Sera found a pigeon perched on a building close to where the signal pulsed in time with his heartbeat. With the bird's permission, Sera joined with its mind to spy out the exact location of the surgeon. The pigeon fluttered to a nearby window and peered in.

She could see Hugh's broad back, but he appeared rather busy with a vomiting child while a distraught mother held a bowl. She asked the bird to fly up to the roof, where she could look about to determine Hugh's rough location. After thanking it, she separated from the pigeon. Sera returned the horse to the mews, then hailed a hackney to take her in the required direction. The slow journey gave her ample time alone with her thoughts.

In the East End, she paid the driver and continued on foot, scanning buildings to find the one where the pigeon had landed on a ledge. However, things looked different from ground level than they did from a bird's-eye view. Wary eyes regarded her as she passed, no doubt wondering what a well-dressed woman was doing alone on their streets. On a whim, Sera let a trail of ebony mist punctuated by glittering stars follow in her wake. The night sky slowly faded away after several feet.

The path she left was a subtle clue to her identity, and a warning not to try something stupid on a mage. It was at times like this that she wished for eyes in the back of her head. She could only defend herself against a blow she saw coming. With that in mind, and not being without sense as to her surroundings, Sera crafted an invisible shield around her that would act as a warning should anyone think her an easy mark.

"You lost, Nyx?" a boy called out. He had been following her, trying to catch stars that burst apart and dissolved in his hands like dandelion fluff. Obviously he didn't fear her sending a crow to tug out his soul.

"I'm looking for Mr Miles, the surgeon. Do you know of him?" She took in his grubby face and bright eyes. A smart one, on the lookout for a way to earn a coin, and bold enough to approach not only a mage, but the night witch to boot.

The lad pointed across the street. "Oh, yes. He's in there." Then the hand turned palm up.

"Thank you." As had become her habit, Sera crafted one of the magical red balls with extra bounce and tossed it to the boy.

A brief scowl crossed his face. He had sought money, not a toy, but curiosity made him drop the ball to the hard surface of the road. It bounced far above his head and the scowl turned into delight. Three other boys rushed after him, elbowing each other as they tried to catch the ball as it plummeted back to the ground before spinning skyward again.

Sera crossed the street as the surgeon emerged from the tenement. She hailed him and waved. "Hugh!"

The tight lines at the corners of his eyes crinkled into a smile on seeing her. "Sera. I'm sorry I could not answer your summons. I was busy."

She pointed up at the cluster of birds on a rooftop. "I saw, thanks to a pigeon. How fares the child?"

Hugh shook his head and stared up at the building. "If the lad survives the night, he will recover."

A pang shot through her heart at the possibility of a life snatched too soon. "Is there anything that can be done for the family?"

He scrubbed his hands over his face. "They're a close bunch in there. The neighbours have rallied around them."

"If you have any time to spare, I am in need of your professional expertise." Her task could wait a few days. The man was already dead, unlike the boy.

"There is little I can do here for the next few hours. I'll return this evening. You may have me for the afternoon, if I can be of assistance." He fell into step beside her as they headed along the road.

"I am to investigate an attack on the south bank. Apparently, a man was killed last night, and the attending doctor thought either dogs or a lycanthrope. Would you be able to accompany me to meet him and discuss the injuries?" She first wanted to ascertain if an otherworldly assailant was responsible for the crime.

"Of course. I could do with a drink and something to eat first, if you don't mind. It's been a long day. I was summoned before dawn and had no chance for breakfast." He gestured to a tavern on the corner. The doors were shut tight against the creeping autumn cold, but light and laughter escaped the cracks around the windows.

She murmured her consent, and he shouldered the door open. People turned as they entered, the glint of suspicion in their eyes. Then one raised his hand in greeting to Hugh and said something to his companions. Murmurs of recognition flowed through the crowd and distrust was replaced by welcome.

Hugh approached the bar and ordered two pints of ale and a bowl of stew with bread for himself. They found a table in a corner, where Sera wrapped her hands around the pewter tankard. People barely glanced their way and she found an odd comfort in their easy acceptance of her presence. Not everyone ran in terror from her. Or perhaps they knew she only sent her crows to pluck the souls from aristocrats.

"Do you know much about lycanthropes?" Hugh asked as he waited for his meal.

"Very little. After we have spoken to the man who examined the deceased, I will do my own research in the mage library. I wanted your opinion first, in case this is merely a terrible case of a roaming pack of wild dogs." If the assailant was lupine and not canine, she would ferret out any volumes in the library devoted solely to the study of that sort of being. She had only a limited knowledge of the folk who could shift into wolves, gleaned from general works on Unnaturals.

Hugh's meal came, and he dipped a chunk of bread in his stew, swallowing it before speaking. "If they are like wolves, they tend to form packs. There could be more than one?"

The idea sent a shudder down her spine. There would be panic on the streets if a pack of enormous wolves were hunting in London for sport. It would, however, make them easier to spot and capture. "Lord Ormsby thought a rogue shifter, perhaps one who has been ejected from his pack for some reason."

Hugh drained his tankard like a man who had spent all day labouring in the hot sun, and then waved the barmaid over to replenish it. "But it is all conjecture until we ascertain how the man died."

"Hence the reason I sought you out—to determine cause of death." She extracted the sheet of paper and smoothed it on the table before Hugh.

He read the notes while finishing his lunch, tearing off hunks of warm bread to swipe through the stew, then folding them into his mouth. "The description of lacerations and excised flesh does seem to hint at something not human."

After he had finished his meal and second ale, they left the tavern to find a hackney to take them to London Bridge. They walked across its length, the waters of the Thames swirling around the brick arches that supported it. The sky darkened and more rain threatened to fall as they stepped onto the south bank.

Sera stopped a man pushing a barrow. "Do you know where we might find Doctor Emmery? He has rooms somewhere around here."

"Five Foot Lane." The man gave directions, and before too long they stood on the path outside a tidy looking establishment.

A sign attached by the front door had the words DOCTOR EMMERY painted in black on a white background, with a few artistic spots of red. Sera leaned closer, hoping it was paint and not the result of someone spattering the sign with their blood on the way past. The door swung open and a woman emerged with a baby swaddled against her breast.

Hugh caught the door before it swung shut and they entered the dim interior, neither of them wishing to loiter on the step as rain began to fall. Voices came from the open door to one side, where a parlour had been turned into a surgery. Mismatched shelves were wedged in against one another on one wall, crammed with jars, bottles, and baskets with unknown contents. A strip of fabric escaped from one, indicating it held bandages. A man sat at a desk by the fire, scribbling notes on a piece of paper.

A woman swept the floor as she gave the doctor orders. "You still haven't fixed the leak in the kitchen," she grumbled as she made a pile of dust.

The doctor tossed his pen to the desk and scrubbed his hands over his face. "I keep telling you to find a builder to fix it. I'm a doctor, woman. I can't stitch up the roof."

FIVE

H ugh and Sera exchanged amused looks. Apparently there were troubled waters in the doctor's household. Then Hugh coughed into his hand. The woman tightened her grip on the broom, then made a show of sweeping her pile to one side where they wouldn't walk in it.

Sera swirled a finger and created a tiny vortex that guided the pile into a waiting dustpan. "Doctor Emmery? I am Lady Winyard. The Mage Council set me to investigate your deceased victim."

The doctor's head shot up, and the weariness around his eyes faded. "Excellent. The case is dashed odd. I've never seen the like. People are nervous to think such a creature is lurking in the alleys waiting to feast upon them."

He pushed back his chair and walked around his desk.

"This is Mr Miles, a surgeon. I have asked him to accompany me for his expert opinion on injuries." Sera rested one hand on Hugh's arm.

The doctor stared at Hugh for a long moment. "I have heard of you, *Mr* Miles." He stressed the form of address. "You did not attend university."

Hugh stiffened beside her. "No. While I attended some classes, I did not complete a course of study to earn the appellation *doctor*. My mentor, Lord Viner, oversaw my education and engaged what private tutors I needed."

The doctor huffed. "You'd be the better for it, no doubt. You learn quicker what to do when you have a man bleeding all over you."

"There is much to be said for practical experience," Hugh agreed.

Doctor Emmery chuckled. "The chap is here still. There doesn't seem to be any family to claim him."

"I will not take up much of your time, as I am sure you are busy. I can conduct my own examination, if you don't mind, and leave the man exactly as I found him." Hugh prodded the man along.

The doctor rubbed the back of his neck and before he could answer, the front door banged and a child's cry drifted into the room. A harried-looking woman appeared in the doorway. She carried one child on her hip, led another by the hand, and a third clung to her skirts.

"Have a seat, Mrs Malone. I will be with you and

your brood directly." Then he gestured for Sera and Hugh to follow him.

The doctor led them down the hall and out the rear of the building. Across a packed dirt yard stood a low-roofed building constructed from chunky slabs of stone. He swung the thick door open to reveal a storehouse. "Do you require a lantern?"

Sera rubbed her hands together and crafted a bright white orb. "No, we shall make do. Thank you." She also had two glow lamps in her satchel. Magical light balls were fine until she got distracted, forgot to maintain them, and plunged herself into darkness.

She set the orb to hang in the centre of the room, then drew out the lamps for additional illumination. In the middle of the chill room sat a pine box atop a table. An image flashed through Sera's mind of Hugh lifting Meredith from a similar box. But she would not be restarting this person's heart.

"Let's have a look at him." Hugh withdrew a pocket knife from his jacket and wedged the blade under the lid. Bit by bit, he prised the tacks loose. Then he lifted the lid free and placed it on the ground. "I will need your help to remove him for a proper examination. If you don't mind."

Sera wrapped the corpse in a magical net and lifted him free. The body hovered above the table as Hugh slid the coffin out of the way. Then she lowered the man to its surface.

"Thank you," Hugh murmured, his attention focused on the deceased.

He worked quickly, undressing a man somewhere in his early thirties with curly brown hair and a lanky build. Sera offered magical assistance to aid in stripping sleeves from arms when the corpse resisted Hugh's attempts. The process was not unlike undressing a large doll.

When the unfortunate victim was naked, Sera stood back and sucked in a breath of surprise. Black stitched lines criss-crossed the man's right arm and torso.

Hugh heaved a sigh and laid both hands flat on the table. "Emmery stitched him up and made him presentable, but it is easy to see the extent of his injuries."

Even with her limited medical knowledge, Sera could guess that the man had been mauled. There was an odd *hollowness* about the sewn wounds that her brain couldn't understand. There were also several deep lacerations on the right arm.

"These look defensive. As though he held up his arm." Hugh demonstrated and then used his other hand to mimic clawing the limb out of the way. Then he tapped the man's chest. "Once they had him on the ground, the creature, or creatures, did this."

Sera closed her mind to the horrific scene Hugh's words conjured and had to wave a hand before her face to banish the image. Whatever had attacked the man, it was no serene lapdog. Unless there was a roving pack of rabid King Charles spaniels. "Can you tell if there was more than one?"

He huffed and rolled the man slightly to inspect his left side. "No, but if there were a pack, I would expect the damage to be in other places about his body. Dogs tend to tear from different sides, but this is all centred on the right."

Chunks of flesh had been torn from the man's arm and torso. The skin stretched taut where the doctor had attempted to cover the holes. This was what had resulted in the uncomfortable emptiness of a hollow drum, even though she couldn't see beneath the skin. Her brain had unconsciously made the connection. A morbid part of Sera wanted to tap the skin to see what sound the chest cavity made.

Hugh leaned closer and inspected the damage. "This was no human assailant, or at least not one with any blade I am familiar with. This was done by teeth or claws. Even though Doctor Emmery did an admirable job of cleaning the wounds, you can see how irregular and jagged the edges are."

Sera stared at the victim. "I will proceed as though the reports are correct, and I am looking for an inhuman assailant. Now the question is, what did this to him and will it strike again?"

"I cannot narrow it down any further than something with claws. It must be larger than any dog I have seen roaming the streets, to make wounds of this size. Unless there was a pack feasting on his innards, missing flesh, and muscles." The surgeon continued his thorough inspection from the top of the victim's head to the soles of his feet.

"Before we finish here, there is one more possibility." Sera held her palms out over the body and closed her eyes. She let a trickle of magic rain down on the corpse, then called it back to her. It whispered over her skin with a faint, yet oddly familiar, tingle.

"Anything?" Hugh asked.

"Possibly. There is a very faint trace of magic about him, and the only word I can use to describe it is *old*. I cannot place what it might mean." She stared down at the one person who could give them answers if he could speak.

That sparked another idea. She would visit Ethel out in Bunhill Fields to see if she could assist.

"Old magic? Could it be an old item he touched or an old spell used on him?" Hugh ventured.

Sera hung onto the tingle that burrowed through her, and created a memory of it to examine later. "I will have to puzzle over that one. It might not be connected to his death at all."

With no more to be done, they dressed the corpse and placed him in the simple coffin. They closed the door to the cool storehouse and crossed the yard back to the house. Within, they found the doctor had experienced an influx with the rain, and people waited in the hall. Hugh, unable to stop himself, tended to a man leaning heavily on a friend.

Sera fell into the role of nurse, and asked Mrs Emmery to point out where bowls and bandages might be found. She procured whatever Hugh deemed necessary for each person who sat on the step to be attended to.

After an hour or so, Doctor Emmery emerged and cast around for his next patient. He stared at Hugh, stitching a gash while the man sat on the step. "Why, many thanks, Mr Miles. With your assistance, I might actually be finished with this lot early tonight."

With the last patient seen to, at least for now, they sat on the worn settee in the doctor's office to discuss the murdered man. "What did you make of him, Mr Miles?"

Hugh rolled up his field kit on his knee before stowing it away in his satchel. "The wounds do not appear to have been inflicted by a human assailant. Unless they used some weapon shaped like teeth or claws."

Doctor Emmery scratched at his scalp. "Poor chap lost large chunks of flesh and muscle. I had a terrible time making the remaining skin cover the wounds. Had to use sawdust to pack out the cavities."

"Do you have his personal details?" Sera asked. "I would like to talk to his family to see if this is a random attack, or one with an underlying motivation."

"I don't believe he has any family—at least, none have come forward so far to claim him. His name is Harvey Perdith and he lives not far from here. That's all I know, unfortunately." He shuffled papers on his desk until he found one with the few details shared by those who had found the deceased.

Sera took the sheet and glanced at the address.

"Thank you. Have there been any other attacks of a similar nature? Not just recently, but at any time in the past few months?"

Doctor Emmery rubbed his jaw. "Not that I am aware of. But it depends where such attacks happen. Not all the bodies cross my threshold. There are other doctors who might have attended if there had been such a death."

That would complicate matters, although Sera assumed that if such deaths had occurred previously, the Mage Council would have been alerted. Or there would have been chatter in the streets, due to their grisly nature.

With the scant details of the man's life and death tucked into her pocket, Sera and Hugh left the premises. She stood on the road and gazed at the threatening sky above. Why couldn't the man have died in a warm library right next door to a combined coffeehouse and bakery?

"What do you wish to do now?" Hugh asked as he pulled the collar of his coat tighter around his neck.

"What would Captain Powers do? He would probably start by seeing where the victim met his untimely end, and talk to any witnesses. I shall do the same. Then I will search Mr Perdith's home for any clues that he might have been targeted over a dispute with someone. And I need to ask the council for any record of similar deaths in recent months. I wouldn't put it past Lord Ormsby to forget to pass on such information. How I wish for the advice of the captain! Have you heard when he will be returned to us?" Apparently, the two men were in regular correspondence with each other.

Lightning lit the sky, and thunder rumbled in response. Hugh pulled Sera closer as they headed for a building with a sheltering overhang. "No. In fact, we have lost him for some time. He has been posted to India. It will do wonders for his career, but nothing for our Kestrel investigations."

"Blast." She had lost access to the keen investigative mind who asked the probing questions. But there was a more than suitable substitute within the membership of the Kestrels. All she lacked was field experience. "Well then, I have another idea. I shall ask Kitty to accompany me."

Hugh missed a step and turned to her, jaw slack. "Miss Napier? Are you sure that is wise? I will admit to great unease at the idea of two young women peering into dark alleys in such an area. Even if one is England's most powerful mage and the other is able to argue herself out of any tight spot."

A smile crept over her lips at his concern. She had pondered the need for eyes in the back of her head in such situations and now had a solution. "We will be sensible, and I shall bring my man to accompany us. But what do you think of my idea? Will we not make a formidable team?"

The surgeon shook his head and huffed a quiet laugh. "With you two combining your abilities, I think the crime rate in London is about to drop substantially."

"This storm is about to get worse, and I know you must return to your patient. Let us leave this matter for now. I shall return tomorrow with my new investigative partner." They left their shelter and hurried along the road, searching for a hackney for the journey home to the north side of the Thames.

AFTER RETURNING to her home in Soho, and changing into dry clothes, Sera sipped a hot cup of tea while she penned a note to Kitty.

> *Are you up for an adventure? I require your help to investigate a death in Southwark if you are game and available tomorrow?*

It took an hour for the reply to appear on the ensorcelled paper.

> *Finally! I will collect you at ten and will be appropriately prepared.*

Sera wondered what her friend would consider *appropriately prepared*. For some reason, the image of Kitty dressed like a pirate appeared in her mind—complete with cutlass and pistols shoved into the sash knotted about her waist.

"Whatever it is, it must be sensible for the occasion," Sera muttered to herself as she placed the page in the desk drawer.

A knock at the front door interrupted her quiet contemplation. After a brief conversation, Elliot appeared in the doorway of her study holding a large, flat box. "Parcel for you."

She rose and untied the string before peeking under the lid. "Perfect. Could you take it to my room, please?"

The footman huffed as though greatly inconvenienced by the request, but he did it anyway.

Sera had given much thought to the words spoken to her by Noemi at Mistwood. What if her path was to embrace the darkness in life, and to embody Nyx? With that in her mind, a week ago she had commissioned a new outfit—the one just delivered.

The next morning, Sera dressed in her new clothing. The box contained a long coat made in a dark grey wool. Sera had taken inspiration from a military-styled riding habit. The piece in her hands combined a jacket and skirt. The front was double-breasted, with smart silver buttons surrounded by black frogging. A deep hood with black trim would offer protection from the rain. The skirts of the garment flared out from her waist and grazed her ankles, giving the appearance of a woman's apparel. But the clever bit was the open front, which allowed for easier movement. Underneath, she wore a soft linen shirt, black breeches, and knee-high boots.

She grabbed her leather satchel containing a glow lamp and the paper from Doctor Emmery, and slipped the strap over her head. Feeling rather pleased with her appearance, Sera bounced down the stairs.

"What do you think?" she asked, twirling around to make her skirts flare out.

Elliot waited in the foyer, his assistance also required for the day. The footman stared at her and rubbed the back of his neck. "Well, at least life isn't dull in your service."

Out in the street, Kitty waited in a hackney. Elliot climbed up next to the driver. Sera found her friend attired in a plain russet-coloured riding habit with a long cloak. Kitty gestured to Sera's open skirts as she settled herself. "I thought to copy what you normally wear, but you have gone and adopted a different fashion. It is rather rude of you not to have told me."

"This is part of my new persona. Some of the mages adopt long robes covered in magical runes. I thought this was a melding of riding habit and highwayman, with a dose of night goddess." Sera pulled the split skirt over her breeches to add extra warmth against the invading chill.

"What is it we are investigating?" Kitty asked as the vehicle set off through the busy London streets.

"A most gruesome murder, possibly by a lycan-thrope. Today, I want to find any who witnessed the event and see if we can locate anyone who knew him." As they travelled through the city and across the bridge, Sera told Kitty all she had learned.

As they alighted from the hack, Sera caught a glint of silver under her friend's cloak. "Are you carrying a pistol?" she whispered.

Kitty pulled the cloak across her body, obscuring the weapon hanging from a leather belt. "Of course. Did you think I would accompany you without some means of protecting myself? I'm quite a good shot."

"It's not loaded, is it?" Sera tried to moderate her tone, not very successfully.

Kitty arched one finely shaped brow. "Of course it is. If we get into trouble, do you think any ruffian is going to wait while I faff about with powder and ball?"

Elliot stared at them, opened his mouth, then shut it again. Sera could just imagine what he was going to say—probably a request for his own pistol. They could have that conversation later. Mr Napier would have ensured Kitty was well trained in the firearm's use. But she didn't want the thing accidentally going off if Kitty were bumped or knocked down.

"At least let me add a concealing and safety spell to it." Sera considered what she wanted done, formed the spell in her mind, and then rubbed her hands together. When they tingled with the enchantment, she lightly brushed them over the weapon. "It is now concealed from view of anyone except us three, and will not fire unless your hand is on the grip."

"Where do you want to start?" Elliot asked.

Sera put herself in Captain Powers' highly polished boots. She knew where the cavalryman would begin. "Where Mr Perdith ended."

SIX

Sera pulled out the sheet of paper from Doctor Emmery containing directions to the alley where Mr Perdith had been discovered. It took only one enquiry of a passer-by to put her on the right track. While the seedier neighbourhoods were used to assaults at night, such things were normally committed with fists or knives. Being eaten alive by dogs or a lycanthrope stuck in everyone's minds, and people wanted to avoid the spot in case the canine responsible returned. After a ten-minute walk, they stood in the road and stared at the narrow gap between two buildings.

After some thirty feet, the dim strip formed a T-junction where another building had been constructed close to the others. The shortcut made a dog leg around that building before coming out on a road on the far side. Sera paced the length of the alley and then returned to the opening. She studied the grimy brick, but whatever events the buildings had seen that night, they held their silence. Nor could she find any magical residue in the dampened earth.

The day was chill with the threat of rain and no one lingered long on the streets. How to find the people who might have witnessed the attack that night, or who would know if Mr Perdith had difficulties in his life?

Her gaze was drawn to a building not far away that squatted on the corner of a crossroads.

"What do we do now?" the footman asked.

She gestured to the sign giving the name of the establishment: the Loaded Hog. "We go to the pub. I want to talk to whoever the victim spent the evening with."

Elliot rubbed his hands together. "Marvellous. I knew there was a reason I liked this job."

The interior of the tavern was obscured by mullioned windows made of thick glass that contained swirls and bubbles. The walls were lime washed and had the uneven timber supports popular two hundred years ago.

Elliot hauled on the brass door handle and held it open for Sera and Kitty. Silence fell as they walked into the tavern and suspicious eyes watched their progress. The Loaded Hog had a warm atmosphere due to the enormous fire at one end of the room. The lanterns cast a yellow glow over the patrons. The floor and tables appeared clean and conversations were murmured.

They approached the bar, where a black cat lay curled up at one end. A man wiped down the wood with a damp cloth, carefully going around the slumbering cat, who didn't seem to care that its odd choice of a place to sleep inconvenienced anyone.

"You lot lost?" the barman asked, eliciting laughter around him.

"Oh, I think I'm exactly where I'm supposed to be. Three ales, please," Sera said.

The owner stared at her and sniffed. "I don't serve your sort here."

A smile spread over her face as she wondered what exactly was her *sort*—a woman, a mage, or someone who washed regularly? Which of the three was more offensive to the assembled patrons? She leaned against the counter and rubbed her hands together. A dark mist formed between her outstretched palms and grew into a crow that hopped along her arm.

The presence of a bird, no matter that it wasn't real, drew an instant reaction from the cat.

"You wouldn't want Nyx to send her crows to pull loose the souls of your customers, now, would you? That might be rather bad for business." Sera winked.

The feline stretched, then crouched over its front paws with haunches high as it stalked closer to the corvid. Sera sent a trickle of magic to the crow and it hopped along the bar as though unaware of the predator at its back. If the cat leapt, the bird would dissolve into mist.

Silence dropped so heavily over the room that for a moment, Sera thought she had gone deaf.

Then someone gasped. "Bloody hell! It's the night mage with her crows! Where's the dragon?"

Apparently, her black panther hadn't inspired suffi-cient terror to be carved into their memories, but at least they remembered her other apparitions. And herself. No one ever pondered what had happened to the golden boy and his Pegasus.

The barkeep's eyes widened. "Of course, milady. So sorry I didn't recognise you." He grabbed three tankards and filled them from a keg behind the bar. He placed them on the counter and then used his cloth to wipe a spilled drop down the side of one. "Is there anything else you'll be wanting?"

The cat leapt, then skidded along the bar when its prey burst apart in a puff of black mist.

"I'm on the hunt for whatever killed Harvey Perdith. Is there anyone here who knows what happened that night?" Sera called, turning to survey the crowd. Only two types of men were in a pub before noon—those who worked at night, and those without employment.

"We knew him and heard his screams. Poor sod," a man called from a long table in the centre.

Five men were clustered at a table capable of seating twenty. Their only similarity was the pewter tankard clutched in each man's hands. One was excep-tionally tall, one diminutive, the other three of the same height when seated but of different widths. Even in hair colour they ranged from black, two browns, one redhead, and a dirty blond.

"Did you know him well?" What Sera wanted was

the circle of friends who might know of any troubles Mr Perdith had with others.

"We numbered him as one of us." The shortest of the group had a deep voice, barrel chest, and the ingrained grime that reminded her of miners and coal men. Sera wondered if he had a hint of dwarf running in his veins.

"Then you are just the group of fellows I need to talk to." Sera grabbed her tankard and approached, climbing over the bench to sit next to the tall man with a gaunt appearance, as though he could not eat enough to fill his frame.

"What if we don't want to talk, Nyx? Will you break our bones and suck our secrets from the marrow?" the redhead asked with a narrowed gaze.

Now there was an evocative image. She tucked the idea away for the next time she wanted to terrify an audience. She could have her obsidian dragon snap open bones for the tasty morsels inside. Kitty sat next to the short, stout man. She seemed oblivious to any danger to her person, assuming a sharp word was as good as any blade. Or comforted by the invisible pistol tucked at her side.

Elliot took a spot across from Sera and next to Kitty, where he could keep an eye on both of them at the same time.

"Will you answer our questions if we win a wager?" Kitty nudged the man with her elbow and a dark smudge of coal soot transferred to her tawny wool coat.

"What sort of wager?" He eyed her.

Kitty tapped the tankard before him. "If I can drink more ale than you, you'll tell us what we want to know."

"You have chosen poorly there, miss. Bart might be short, but look at him. He holds more ale than any keg!" the man with dirty blond hair said.

Laughter broke out around the table. Sera glared at her friend. What on earth did Kitty think she was doing? She pushed her concerns at her friend, who smiled sweetly across the table.

You have your magic, and I have mine. Trust me in this. Kitty's words were murmured directly in Sera's ear with no one overhearing.

"Keep the ale flowing, my good barkeep!" Kitty held high a gold coin.

A barmaid swooped down like a kestrel spotting a mouse in the dried grass, and snatched the coin from Kitty's fingers.

"A ha'penny on the lady!" one chap cried out, and a coin was tossed to the middle of the worn table. Soon, a cluster formed around them, bets were called out, coins tossed down on the wood.

Elliot, being in his element, immediately took over running the book. Using a pencil and a notebook he pulled from his jacket, he wrote down names and bets. Most of those present bet against Kitty, except for an adventurous few. The table was cleared and two fresh tankards were placed in front of Kitty and Bart.

"Ladies first." Bart bowed his head to Kitty.

She picked up her mug and tapped it against the

one in Bart's hands. Then she lifted it to her lips, before lowering it a moment later. "If I fall off this bench drunk, I assume one of you gentlemen will help me to my feet? And no one would be so loathsome as to take advantage of an intoxicated woman or peer up my skirts, would they?"

Once she had their assurances they would look after her and she was perfectly safe, and a few muttered she'd be on the floor in under five minutes, Kitty guzzled the entire container dry.

"Blimey," one man gasped as she slammed the empty tankard on the table.

Bart chuckled and soon his empty one hit the worn wood also.

Over the course of the next hour, Sera learned one amazing fact about her friend. She could drink a prodigious amount of ale. The competitors were now on number six each, although they were both taking a lot longer to finish.

"I think I'm in love. Will you marry me, miss?" someone called out to bursts of laughter.

Kitty stared at the fresh ale placed in front of her and met Sera's gaze. "I'm starting to wish I had brought along a *bourdaloue*."

Sera snorted. She did wonder how her friend's bladder was coping with all the liquor sloshing around inside.

Kitty drew a deep breath, but seemed reluctant to pick up the drink.

Worry rippled through Sera. Perhaps now was the

time to intervene. Before she could call a halt to the proceedings, Kitty held up one hand and, with a slow and consistent motion, drained her ale. The empty added to the tally on her side of the table.

Bart huffed and pulled his drink closer. He swayed slightly on his seat as he began to drink, but he had difficulty finding his mouth. Ale spilled down his chin. He paused, and the pewter tankard tumbled from his hand mere seconds before he slumped forward and his forehead hit the table.

A roar went up around them. "Miss Napier wins!" Elliot yelled, jumping to his feet.

The happy men who had backed Kitty cheered. A few set Bart the right way up and gave him a shake to check he still breathed.

Kitty held up her hands. "Well, gentlemen, that is settled. If you'll excuse me for a moment, when I return we shall discuss events which led to Harvey Perdith meeting his unfortunate demise."

"Elliot, order some food for Kitty to soak up all that ale. We'll be back shortly." Sera hustled her friend out a side door and around to an alley, where she cast a cloaking spell while Kitty crouched over a drain.

"Oh, good lord, but I thought I was going to burst." Kitty adjusted her skirts and washed her hands in a barrel full of water, conveniently filled by an angled piece of broken gutter.

"Are you going to tell me how you did that?" Sera gestured with her head towards the pub. She was determined to puzzle out how Kitty could outdrink a man who probably considered it a full-time occupation.

Kitty burped and rubbed her stomach. "Can I eat first? I have such a craving for something meaty."

Sera narrowed her gaze at her friend. She didn't know how Kitty had done it, but the faint tingle from the other woman implied a certain unfair advantage in the recent match.

"It can wait until the road home. So long as you assure me you aren't too terribly affected." Only now did she wonder if she should have asked Hugh to accompany them, in case her friend became ill from all the ale.

"I rather think my bladder is unhappy with me," Kitty muttered as they headed back.

When they re-entered the tavern to another round of cheers from the men, they found platters of food waiting. A feast had been laid out before them of steaming pies, warm bread, slices of cheese, and cold meat. A pottle contained an onion relish, and pats of butter sat in another. Sera pushed the platter towards her friend, concerned about Kitty's wellbeing and what her father would say if she returned to their home drunk and reeking of ale.

For herself, Sera placed a thick slice of cheese between two slabs of bread, dotted on some relish, and took a bite. "Since my friend has defeated your companion, tell me, who is your storyteller to narrate Harvey Perdith's last night?"

"I am Isaac and shall tell his tale. I considered him a

fine friend." Isaac, the tall cadaverous looking man, spoke with a slow, soft tone. "We sat at this very table that night. Harvey was in a fine mood. He believed his fortunes were about to change."

Kitty demolished a pie and then piled meat and cheese on a slab of bread. "Why? Was he to come into money, or change employment?"

"He kept quiet on that. Would just tap the side of his nose and say he was on the way up and we'd soon know everything." Isaac made the same action against his narrow nose.

Kitty huffed. *Could have been gambling with the wrong crowd,* she mouthed to Sera, and magic whispered the words inside her head.

"What about his family? Did he have any troubles at home?" Tomorrow they would search his home. She wanted to know if they would find anyone there. The doctor said no family had claimed his body, but that didn't mean he had none. It could be that their grief hadn't yet allowed them to take the next step.

The men shook their heads, and Isaac continued. "He didn't have any family. Harvey was a foundling and never knew his mother. Nor did he ever marry. Always said he was saving himself for a wealthy noblewoman."

That elicited sad laughter, and the men murmured into their drinks.

Kitty swallowed a mouthful of bread and cheese. "Let us return to the events of that night. After spending time in your company, and dropping hints of some reversal of fortune, Mr Perdith decided it was time to return home. What happened next? Did he leave alone?"

"I accompanied him to the door, along with Bart and Simon," Isaac said in his measured way.

"Show me where you went. Elliot, stay here with Kitty and make sure she eats more of that." Sera pointed to the platter.

Another man stayed with Bart as the man snored, his cheek pressed to the table. The other three followed Sera out the door. They stood in the light drizzle and she waited for the story to continue.

"We walked in this direction. Bart and Simon went that way, towards their homes." Isaac gestured first one way and then the other with a long, skinny arm.

"Then we shall proceed in the direction Mr Perdith took." From their earlier explorations, Sera knew it had been only a short stroll to the alley where the man had met his end.

When they reached a point across the road from the narrow passageway, Isaac stopped. "We parted company here. That way is a shortcut to Harvey's lodgings, while mine lies at the end of this road."

A moment of silence fell as they remembered the deceased man. In a gentle tone, Sera asked, "Did you see him enter the alley?"

Isaac's shoulders heaved, and he stared at the broody sky. "No. I kept walking, as rain had begun to fall. Then I heard him shout."

Simon joined the conversation. "We were farther

along the road and didn't pay much mind to the noise at first. You get used to hearing fights around here. But then Harvey screamed and it sent a chill right through me." He pulled a face and a shudder ran through his frame.

Sera could imagine the terror and pain in such a sound, to alert his friends to something seriously amiss. "What did you do, when you heard him scream?"

The brick buildings on either side of the alley leaned fractionally towards one another, filtering the rain and leaving dry spots at their base. One structure had windows and had most likely been built first, before the other rose up and blocked out light and sun.

"We ran to help," Simon rasped.

"What did you see?" In Sera's mind, the happy patron of the tavern strolled the alley, thinking of his warm bed, but never reached the other end.

"Very little. The rain and clouds obscured the moon and this stretch was like spilled ink. Only snatches of light seeped in at the edges." Isaac had a poetic turn of phrase for such a horrific event. "Harvey was on the ground. His scream turned to groans. Something larger than a man was hunched over him."

"There were noises. As it... ate him." Simon spun away and leaned his forehead against the brick.

"We yelled and waved our arms. Bart drew his knife. The creature looked at us and its eyes glowed yellow in the night. Then it leapt up there." Isaac pointed to a window on the first floor. "We rushed to help Harvey and lost sight of it after that."

"What do you think it was? A man, a dog, something else?" Sera wondered if there was some magical process that she could sprinkle over the corpse and have it reveal whether the murderer was man or beast.

Simon and Isaac exchanged a long look. "Whatever it was, it was no man. It possessed a tail."

SEVEN

A tail? That rather narrowed down her suspects. Next she needed to determine whether it had been a random attack, or if Mr Perdith had been targeted. "Do you think it was waiting for him in the alley, or had it followed him in from the street?"

Isaac glanced up and down the street as though it might be waiting yet. "We didn't see anyone else, but our eyes were on home and not what lurked behind us. It could have hidden in the shadows, waiting for someone to venture down the alley."

It could have been an opportunistic slaying if the creature had pressed itself to the brick, waiting for a victim to pass. If Mr Perdith had been targeted, Sera would have expected someone, or something, to have followed him from the tavern. "Has there ever been an attack like it around here before?"

Simon scratched his head. "Wasn't there some

man, years ago, who died in a field but someone saw a beast with a tail?"

That perked up Sera's interest.

"He was drunk and had an altercation with a cow, is what I heard," Isaac said.

Sera didn't know of any man-eating cows. Nor did they have claws. If the attack had been entirely random and the creature had already moved on to another area, it would be near impossible to find. Or had it chosen its victim deliberately and watched from a distance, where men could not see it?

"Can you think of anyone who might have wanted to harm Mr Perdith? Any arguments, or bad blood with anyone?"

The men exchanged long looks. Clearly no one wanted to admit their deceased friend had a dark side. Gambling debts, mistreatment of someone with a protective family, a falling-out over an illicit enterprise. There were any number of ways a man could end up getting stabbed in the dark.

"Harvey was a good bloke, worked hard, kept his nose clean," Simon said.

Sera sucked on her bottom lip. She would have preferred a handful of potential suspects over an unknown killer choosing victims at random. Panic would spread if she did nothing. "You said he had been in a good mood that night, because he believed his fortune was about to change. Do you think that might have had any role to play in his death?"

"That was the only thing he refused to disclose.

Said he wanted to wait until he knew for sure, but that he would always look after his friends." Isaac walked farther into the alley and stopped where a dark stain marred the packed earth.

There was little more she could learn here. "Thank you, gentlemen. If you think of anything at all that might help us find who did this, please send word to me in Soho."

"What if it comes back?" Simon asked, deep worry lines across his forehead.

"I am counting on it. I shall be here, prowling the streets. Tell everyone that Southwark is now under the protection of Nyx. All monsters, whether they be man or beast, will answer to me." Sera held out her arm, and the phantom crow from the tavern flew down to perch on her wrist.

Sera returned to the tavern and collected Kitty and Elliot. Then she found a hackney to take them back to Mayfair. As they crossed the bridge, she regarded her friend with a worried eye. "I still can't believe you drank all that ale."

"It was fortunate you pushed a very large platter of food at me that soaked it up." She patted her stomach.

Sera didn't believe that for a moment and had already guessed at some underhand tactic. "You're not even slightly affected. You either tell me what you did, Miss Napier, or I shall not include you on any future adventures."

"You wouldn't dare spoil my fun." Kitty's eyes widened.

Sera crossed her arms and stared out the window.

Kitty huffed. "Oh, very well. I won because I cheated."

"I knew it!" They had all seen Kitty drink the ale. It wasn't like she'd tipped it out into a nearby potted plant. In the alley, Sera had felt the faint tingle of a spell and had to know what manner of ensorcellment her friend possessed. "How?"

Kitty held up her right hand and wriggled her fingers. Next to the magical feather ring on her little finger, she wore a rather plain black band.

Sera pulled her hand closer and examined the item. Tiny runes were etched in the onyx and emitted the faint tingle. "What spell is embedded in this ring?"

"It removes the alcohol from your drink and deposits it into the drink of another. Father uses it when he needs to keep a clear head while entertaining clients or opponents. I slipped it on before I left today. Something told me it might come in handy. I rubbed it against my tankard before drinking and then tapped mine against Bart's so it knew where to funnel all the alcohol."

Sera burst into laughter and hugged her friend. "I knew I couldn't do this without you."

"So much for my brilliant plan, though. It sounds like you learned very little." Kitty turned pensive as she watched people scurry along the roads.

"Perhaps not, but we are only at the beginning of this investigation. More important, we gave them a tale that will be told over and over. Of the mage and her crow made of mist. Of the noblewoman who outdrank a keg-shaped dwarf. Tomorrow, we will search Mr Perdith's lodgings for any clues as to what he might have been involved in that was going to change his fortune."

The man's comment might have been mere puffery, but at the moment it was the only tiny clue Sera had that other events might have been in play.

After dark, Sera would return and roam the streets. The dead man's friends might not have remembered any arguments or a reason that someone, or something, might want to do him harm, but the possibility remained. Whatever killed the man had either acted of its own volition or been commanded by someone else.

Once she saw Kitty safely to her door, the hackney conveyed them to Soho, where Elliot alighted. Sera headed on to mage tower. On the way, her ring tingled with the unmistakable touch of Lady Abigail Crawley. Sera closed her eyes and let her mind find her friend. She sat at her writing desk in her Mayfair home. Once permitted to borrow the mind of a nearby sparrow, Sera hopped to the ledge and tapped on the glass.

Abigail rose and opened the latch. "You had better be a messenger for Seraphina."

"It is I, Sera," the bird chirped as it clung to the stone.

"Grandfather is most displeased with both of us." Abigail sat on the windowsill and gazed down at the little bird.

"I do not mean to cause trouble with your family," the sparrow chirped, and fluttered its wings.

"The bracelets, Sera. You must deliver them to Grandfather. He has instructed me to fetch them from you with dire warnings if they are not entrusted to him." Abigail's full disappointment settled over the bird.

The bird ruffled its feathers. "They are safe where they are. Let us discuss this later, in person."

"If you burn too many bridges, Seraphina, you might find yourself stranded with no way across the water," Abigail murmured. Before Sera could ponder what that meant, her friend continued, "Very well. We shall discuss it shortly. Along with the more agreeable subject of Lord Thornton. He is most keen to see you again."

"As you please. I must go now, Abigail." Sera broke her link with the bird as the hackney trotted through the gate of mage tower.

Blast. She had known Lord Rowan would pressure her to hand over the Fae objects, but it seemed unfair of him to use her friendship with Abigail against her. She might have to comply.

She paid the driver and waved him off, not knowing how long her task would take. Passing the oak, she brushed the last brown leaf clinging to a slender branch. Inside the tower, Sera stood in the circular chamber and pondered where to start. Perhaps it might have been more useful to ask the Bow Street Runners. As she berated herself for hurrying to the one place she thought would know everything, Lord Pendlebury's head, and then his body, emerged from the stairwell.

"Lady Winyard, you look a little lost today. Is everything well?" he asked as he approached.

"I rushed here for information, but now I think I have come to the wrong source." She managed a smile for him.

He tucked a large tome under his arm. His rank allowed him to remove books from the hidden library to study in his office within the tower. "That does sound intriguing. Is this regarding your corpse?"

"Yes. I want to know if there have ever been similar deaths. But I confess I don't even know where to start to find that information. It's not as if anyone keeps a record of every crime committed in London." There would be a handy ledger to peruse in such cases. While there were records kept in the courts of criminals and sentences, each district did something different and there was no central repository of such knowledge.

"Even if there were such a record, you would disappear under a tidal wave of paper trying to find any similarities within it. It would need a spell to only return results that met certain parameters." He rubbed his chin with his free hand as he considered the idea. "I do have a suggestion that might work, but you will still be inundated with information."

"I am open to any possible methods to find similar crimes." Not that she considered it likely, but who knew what creatures lurked in the shadows? Simon had certainly thought there had been one, even if Isaac had dismissed it as a tangle with a cow.

Lord Pendlebury repositioned the book under his arm. "Since it is in the newspapers at the moment and much discussed, we could cast a reminder enchantment over the city. Anyone who remembers something similar would be prompted to come forward and share their memory."

"Oh, that would be brilliant. Perhaps, if Lord Ormsby agrees, we could have a secretary compile any such reports so I could comb through them later?" Or if he were feeling petulant, the Speaker might insist she sit in the middle of Charing Cross Road for a few days to receive such information.

"I do have a small amount of authority as second to the Speaker. I think we can organise something without bothering Lord Ormsby," Lord Pendlebury murmured, mischief glinting in his eyes.

"Thank you." A grateful sigh worked its way through Sera. How she wished the older mage had been successful in his attempt to win her guardianship all those years ago. Young Sera might have been raised by someone more akin to a kindly uncle than the resentful master Lord Branvale had proved to be.

"Let us go to my study. We can cast the spell together now." He gestured for her to follow him up the stairs.

Sera watched her foot placement on the steep spiral, although part of her thought it would make a faster slide down than the ride she'd had from the church belfry not long ago. "While I have the opportunity, I wanted to say I appreciate your efforts thirteen years ago to try to secure my guardianship."

He paused on the step and half-turned, his lips tight. "Lord Rowan thought an unmarried man of twenty-eight unsuitable to raise a young girl. And yet Lord Branvale..." his voice trailed off, and he tightened one hand into a fist. "Well, since we cannot alter time or change the course of events, I did what little I could. It is difficult enough to be wrenched from our families at a young age, without being placed in a cold home with no comfort."

What if mages could be left with their families and receive their instruction with a tutor? Her heart tightened for the little girl who could have grown up making daisy chains with a loving father under the watchful gaze of a gargoyle guardian. Then she breathed through the moment. "Your kindness did not go unnoticed. And some would say that the pain of losing our parents is the price we pay for the power we wield."

Lord Pendlebury nodded and continued on up the stairs. As Lord Ormsby's second, Lord Pendlebury occupied an inviting space that overlooked the growing oak. "Do have a seat. I shall summon a tea tray for us."

The study had a round window some three feet in diameter. The top half of the window could be opened to let a spell free or admit a winged visitor or even fresh air on a warm day. A settee in a bold green and gold stripe was placed at an angle to the window, so a person could contemplate both the sky above and the tree below. Sera seated herself and let her curious gaze roam the room.

The desk faced the window, with a wall of shelves behind it. Stacks of papers occupied one side of the desk, a rosewood correspondence box the opposite side. The books on the shelves were interspersed with random objects that seemed to be personal mementoes. A smooth, pale stone on one. An azure blue vase no bigger than her hand on another. A figurine carved from wood shook a spear from a top shelf.

Lord Pendlebury placed the book he carried in the middle of his desk, then turned to regard those behind him. He ran a finger along their spines before selecting a particular volume. He gestured to a padded chair, which moved itself to stand next to the settee.

"I believe this will assist. We have cast such a spell before—when King George hosts public outings and we want to ensure a good turnout by reminding everyone." He opened the book on his lap and flipped the pages.

Once he found the correct page, he slid the book towards Sera. The casting seemed simple enough and required that she focus on whatever she wanted to act as the memory aid. In this case, the mauling death by a lycanthrope or something similar.

A knock sounded at the door. With a wave, Lord Pendlebury opened it and gestured for the retainer to enter. The man in purple and gold livery entered on silent feet and placed the tray on the low table beside the settee. Then he tucked his hands into his wide sleeves and asked, "Will there be anything else, my lord?"

"No, thank you." When the retainer departed, Lord Pendlebury poured tea and offered Sera a slice of cake that looked like the delicious raisin-laden one Rosie made. "Have you cast with another mage before?"

She had battled against Lord Tomlin, not alongside him. Even when she had worked with Lord Pendlebury to entertain the king, they had worked on separate spells that created a whole, rather than one spell drawing on both their magic.

"Lord Branvale did not see any need to teach me how to work with another mage. I admit I cannot fathom how we will not interfere with each other." Should she add *does not work well with others* to her list of faults? No. She had amply demonstrated how she relied on her friends, and they all pulled together to find solutions to problems.

He huffed a noise. "It is no different that if I laid down one sheet of paper and we both began to draw. We don't have to consciously avoid where the other person is drawing, and we might even embellish what the other person is doing as we cover the page. Working together is the same. Once we start, your magical instincts will know how to join and augment the casting."

She sipped her tea and nibbled cake while they discussed aspects of the spell they would each concentrate on. They decided to have people report to the Guildhall, where a council employee would gather their recollections. Then she set aside her cup and plate and brushed crumbs from her hands. Sera fixed the gruesome crime in her mind and used the image as the seed for her part of the spell. Lord Pendlebury worked on the part that would disseminate it across London and prompt people to report similar incidents.

A glowing ball of orange mist took form between them as they worked. Just as Lord Pendlebury had said, Sera found her magic conducted a dance with the energy coming from him. She instinctively tailored her part to fit with his and then added and strengthened where needed. After an hour, the mist pulsed with the changing red and russet tones of an autumn leaf and had grown to more than a foot in diameter.

"I believe we are done. What do you think of our creation?" Lord Pendlebury gave it a push, and the orb spun between them.

Sera brushed her magic over it one more time. "I cannot find any fault in it."

"Excellent." Lord Pendlebury rose and lowered the top arc of his window. "Brilliant timing, too. There is a fog descending on the city. They are helpful in sending a spell like this to seep into every home and sprinkle a reminder over everyone."

With gentle bursts of magic, they manoeuvred the orb to the edge of the open window. Outside, an early twilight fell over the city. With a nod from her companion, they both gave the spell a push. It was like releasing a harvest moon into the sky as the bright ball rose and drifted closer to London. When it reached a distance high overhead, it pulsed a fiery red and then popped like a dandelion clock. Millions of tiny sparks seeded themselves into the mist.

"Nothing will happen tonight, but I will ensure a man is ready at the Guildhall tomorrow morning. I will have him gather any stories and we will dispatch them to you at the end of each day. The spell will be most effective tomorrow, but the effects fade rather quickly, I'm afraid. No one will remember it within five days. Do not set your hopes too high, Lady Winyard. You may be inundated with tales of every dog bite from the last ten years." He huffed a quiet laugh.

"Let us hope not. I emphasised that I sought tales of fatal attacks or terrible maiming from something larger than a man." She would rather have a thousand sheets of paper to comb through to find anything that helped, than be met with silence. Besides, her fellow Kestrels could help with the reading if she asked them.

"It was a pleasure to work with you. You have quite a unique touch, Lady Winyard." The older mage inclined his head to her. "Always happy to assist."

Sera took her leave, her thoughts muddled as she summoned a hackney to take her home. On the ride back to Soho, twilight had an orange tinge as their spell did its work and touched all beneath it.

EIGHT

The next day, with Elliot in tow, Sera collected Kitty and they once more travelled to Southwark. This time, they sought the residence of Mr Perdith on a narrow street not far from the tavern. Once they alighted from the vehicle, they stood on the footpath and surveyed a tired row of cottages. The grey stone was stained by coal smoke that blew back over them when the wind turned north to south and pushed it across the Thames. They were modest homes, often rented by working-class men with regular employment, and offered better conditions than the cramped tenements.

Not far away, a fine row of golden terraces was under construction. Parts of Southwark were being transformed into wealthier suburbs, as the new bridges made the south side of the Thames more accessible. How long, she wondered, before the cottages were demolished to make way for fancier homes for the middle classes?

She gestured for Kitty and Elliot to follow. "Apparently Mr Perdith has no family, but I don't know if he lived alone or not." When she found the correct rusty metal number, she rapped on the peeling green paint of the front door and waited.

Kitty stood one step below. Elliot leaned on the post at the end of the path, the short length of railing that had once separated the cottages now long gone. Most likely the strip of fence had been stolen to sell as scrap. Kitty glanced up and down the street. Curious locals with grubby faces stared at the two women, but the casual way Elliot cleaned under his nails with a shiny blade deterred them from approaching.

A woman emerged from the neighbouring cottage and glanced at them as she pulled her door shut. "You won't be getting any answer there, lovey. He's dead, God rest his soul."

"Did Mr Perdith live alone?" Sera asked.

"Yes. Poor sod. Horrid way to go." The woman clucked her tongue under her breath as though she had warned Mr Perdith about such a possibility.

"Thank you." Sera stepped back, as though they were going to leave, and considered the facade of the cottage. Once the neighbour set off down the road, Sera approached the door and laid her palms against the wood. She was getting rather good at breaking into places. Magic tickled the lock and played with the simple tumbler until with a satisfying click, it gave way and the door swung open.

Inside, the cottage was modest in size, with the front door set to one side and facing a set of steep stairs. Downstairs was one large room. What served as a kitchen lay at the rear. A bench with cupboards underneath ran under a rectangular window that offered a glimpse of a small overgrown yard beyond. It seemed Mr Perdith had no interest in gardening or growing vegetables. A fireplace to one side for cooking had hooks above for a kettle or pots, and a cast iron plate that could be swung over the embers. The kitchen area had a worn table with four mismatched chairs around it and a hand-knotted rug underneath. The front of the space facing the street was being used as a parlour. A worn sofa and a lone armchair were positioned close to a second, smaller fire. The narrow stairs clung to one wall and climbed upward, where Sera assumed they would find a bedroom, or possibly two smaller ones, tucked under the eaves.

Given that a bachelor lived alone in the house, it was tidier than Sera expected. Nor did it smell mouldy or like old socks. Although to be fair, Hugh lived alone and his room was also tidy. Perhaps she needed to re-evaluate her opinion of the ability of men to care for themselves.

"Where do we start?" Kitty walked to the stairs and rested one hand on the worn timber rail while she surveyed the room.

"Let's look for letters or overdue invoices that might indicate financial problems in his life. Or anything that hints at the reversal of fortune he told his friends about." Sera eyed a desk. It sat against the wall, the window to its left so the light would fall over the shoulder of anyone seated there.

"I'll search his bedroom," Elliot offered, and trotted up the stairs, leaving Sera and Kitty the kitchen and parlour.

"I'll search the kitchen, in case secret correspondence is hiding among those dirty dishes." Kitty strode with purpose towards the row of cabinets and open shelves.

"I'll see if anything magical lingers here first." Sera anchored herself in the middle of the room, letting her power flow through the soles of her boots and the floor to connect herself to the earth, her source of magic. With her eyes closed, she let her senses roam through the house. Tendrils peered under floorboards, behind walls, and up in the attic space. But not a single twinge hinted at anything magical hidden in the house, nor did she find any residue of magic having been used.

She called forth the memory of the odd tingle emanating from Mr Perdith's corpse. What had caused it? She had eliminated anything magical residing in the cottage, but that still left a number of possibilities. He might have been an aftermage. Perhaps Sera's magic recognised the trace in his blood, although when questioned, his friends said he had not displayed any gift that they noticed. Or he might have come into contact with a spell, or a magical assailant. There were a number of possibilities she mulled over.

Oh! He might have discovered a magical item that would bring wealth and change his fortune. If so, could he have been murdered for it? She added the idea to her list of theories.

With one task done, Sera turned her attention to the desk covered in papers. The first thing that grabbed her attention was the worn red cover and faded gold lettering of *Debrett's Peerage and Baronetage*. Not the sort of reading material one expected to find in the cottage of a commoner. She thumbed through the pages. Some entries were scribbled on, others crossed through. Had Mr Perdith made the notes, or had they already been in the book when he acquired it?

Putting the thick book down, she next picked up a pamphlet entitled *A Master Key to the Rich Ladies Treasury, or The Widower and Batchelor's Directory*. Dated 1752, the booklet detailed the single ladies of England and the size and composition of their fortunes. Like Debrett's, there were notations and crossed-out entries, as though a bachelor had been working his way through the list.

At first, she thought the items might have belonged to Mr Perdith's father. Then she recalled his friends saying he was a foundling. Had these books been why Mr Perdith had told his friends he was waiting for a change in his fortunes? He might have sought to prey on a vulnerable daughter or widow and run afoul of her family.

"No, these are too old," Sera muttered. The *Directory* and Debrett's were both nearly thirty-five years old. If Harvey sought a rich wife, he would want a recent version of the salacious gazette, not to court a wife old enough to be his mother. Might he have thought an old, childless widow, all alone with her fortune, would have her head easily turned by a young and robust man? Putting aside the horrific injuries she had observed on his body when Hugh examined him, he had possessed a pleasing countenance. It would have been more so when animated by life.

Pushing those questions aside for later, she sorted through the other papers. From what she found, Mr Perdith appeared to have been a budding artist. A stack of papers were all painted with the same patterns, as though he practiced brush strokes and colouring. It made her think of a child's effort, where an adult might draw an outline for a youngster to finish to their own tastes.

She picked up one sheet and compared it to another, then selected a third. Mr Perdith's attempts all seemed to be exactly the same. At the bottom, he had written the same name over and over. The only variation in the pages was found in the name, where some had a different swoop or size of the letters used to form *Horatio Valentine*.

"Most odd," she murmured. Perhaps this was the

reversal of fortune Mr Perdith had mentioned to his friends. He might have sought work as an illustrator, and these were samples he sent to potential employers. But that didn't explain the gazette and Debrett's. Or, like many enterprising men, had Mr Perdith had his thumb in more than one pie?

Deciding order would be necessary for her part of the search, Sera made a pile of the drawings on the floor by the chair while she sorted through the other papers. There was little else on the desk, apart from a box of paints. Next to it, three brushes of different thicknesses stood in a jar, all carefully cleaned.

The three of them worked in near silence apart from the shuffle of papers from Sera, the tread of Elliot's boots in the rooms above, and the odd clang of a pot from Kitty.

After over an hour, the steps rattled as Elliot came down. "Nothing much up there apart from what you'd expect. Clothing, shoes, a book, but no love letters by the bed. I couldn't find a single naughty sketch under his mattress or hidden under the floorboards."

"Nor is there anything interesting hidden in a tin in the kitchen, apart from a few mouldy potatoes. And before you ask, no root vegetables were hollowed out and used to hide treasure." Kitty joined them near the window overlooking the street.

"Blast." Sera tossed the last paper back in the lone drawer. While it had been a slim hope that they would uncover a threatening note or one luring him to the fatal spot in the alley, such a discovery would have sped along her investigation. She picked up the stack of drawings and placed them in the centre of the desk. "There was nothing of interest in the desk, apart from his efforts in drawing and an old copy of the *Rich Ladies Treasury.*" Sera waved to the stack of papers, jar of brushes, and the pamphlet sitting atop Debrett's.

Kitty picked up the gazette and held it at arm's length. "I'm glad the mysterious *Younger Brother* no longer compiles his list of eligible ladies, or we might both have found ourselves within its pages and targeted by fortune hunters." Dropping it back to the dull red copy of Debrett's, she reached for one of the painted strips on the pile of papers on the floor. "He seemed rather intent on learning to paint."

"I shall enquire with his friends if he mentioned anything about an art tutor or dreams of being an illustrator. Although there is no variation here. He only practiced the same design over and over." Sera gestured to the other pages, all with the same pattern. Some were outlined in pencil and waited to be filled in, others were completed in muted blues, greens, and bronze with the same dash of bright red at one corner.

"Hang on." Elliot took the sheet from Kitty. "I've seen something like this. It's hanging up in the bedroom."

"Another drawing?" Sera rose and tucked the chair back under the desk.

"No, this one is fabric," he said.

Curious, the two women followed the footman up

the narrow stairs. The upper floor was split into two modest bedrooms. One room was almost empty, containing only a bed frame with a bare mattress pushed up against the wall. The other room showed signs of occupation. A set of clothes hung over the back of a chair placed under the dormer window. The woollen blankets were thrown back, the bed unmade.

"Here." Elliot strode to the bedside.

Pinned to the wall next to the bed like a small banner was a strip of fabric bearing the pattern replicated in paint downstairs. Two inches wide, it was about eight inches long. On seeing the original, the randomness of the design made sense. The strip was patchwork. Someone had cut out squares of fabric and neatly stitched them together. Parts were now faded where, over time, sunlight had sapped its vibrancy.

Sera unpinned the fabric and turned it over. The back was lined with navy silk and the tiny stitches made in bronze thread. "This seems old, but it must have been significant, given he'd placed it by his bed and was drawing it repeatedly."

The squares were an odd mix of silk, brocade, and thick cotton.

"Maybe his mother gave it to him?" Elliot soon lost interest in the worked piece and walked to the window to gaze out on the street below.

"That might explain its significance, since he had no family. The scraps could be cut from clothing they wore." Sera could imagine a distraught son taking the

97

last thing from his mother's workbox when she passed away.

Kitty took the length of fabric from Sera's hand. "This reminds me of something I have heard about. It's itching at the back of my brain, but I cannot make it reveal itself."

"We shall take it with us, along with the more unusual papers on his desk. They're the only clues we have about his last few days on this earth." Sera couldn't imagine anyone being murdered over a bit of patchwork. That left her with a random act of violence.

Already she could hear Lord Ormsby in her head, crowing about her failure. Why couldn't they have assigned Tomlin to this case, and given her the troublesome pixies?

Downstairs, they packed up the handful of papers, the book, and the *Directory*. With nothing more to learn from the cottage, Sera locked the door behind them and they headed back across the Thames.

* * *

ONCE HOME, Sera placed the satchel of papers by her desk in the little workroom. Then she headed upstairs to change her gown. Her feet were leaden as she contemplated the afternoon visit. No longer could she put off seeing Abigail. Her friend might appear the perfect English rose, but she possessed sharp thorns.

While she wanted to see her friend and share in her excitement over her grand match and forthcoming wedding, there would be a rebuke over the Fae bracelets.

Braced for whatever the old mage's granddaughter would throw at her, Sera summoned a vehicle to take her to Mayfair. With perfect timing, the butler swung open the door as she reached the top step.

"Lady Crawley is expecting you, Lady Winyard. She is waiting in the blue parlour." He narrowed his gaze slightly, as though her friend's disappointment had infected the staff.

The butler led her to one of the smaller parlours at the side of the house. The walls were covered in a blue and white patterned wallpaper above the chair rail. The panelling was painted a pale sky blue. Abigail sat at a circular rosewood table, papers and a large book that seemed to contain fabric samples, open before her. Wearing a gown of bright green brocade, she harmoniously complemented the decor.

"Lady Winyard," Abigail murmured as she rose.

The butler bowed and exited on silent feet. Sera kissed the air beside her friend's cheek. Abigail remained strangely silent once their greetings were out of the way. She gestured to two settees covered in a wide blue and white stripe. Sera took one, Abigail the other, as though they were opponents staring across the chessboard.

Sera laced her hands on her lap and sat with a ramrod straight spine. Better to get one issue over and sorted so they could move onto happier topics. "I know you are disappointed, and I never meant to cause any ill feeling between you and your grandfather. The runes on those bracelets are tiny and it is a time intensive labour to transcribe them. All I asked of Lord Rowan was time to complete my examination of them."

A delicate sigh escaped Abigail. "My grandfather and I only want what is best for you, Seraphina. These are dangerous items and Grandfather worries they will make you a target for those who would seize them for themselves."

Sera stared at her hands. Given only a few people knew of their existence, how would those with dark intent know about them? "They are safe for the time being. And I have reassured Lord Rowan that I will entrust them to him." But not until she was ready to hand them over. "I simply want the opportunity to try to decipher them myself before your grandfather does it. He has been helping me work on my transliteration and translation of the Fae language. I freely admit part of me wants to have his approval at my efforts. I don't think Lord Branvale ever told me I had done well or that he...that he was proud of me."

There was her sad admission. The child inside her cried out for affection and approval from a paternal figure. To have her labours recognised and to be encouraged towards greater achievements. While she delighted in finding her father and becoming acquainted, she did so as an adult.

There was that annoying time issue again. Sera

soaked up the love given by her father, but how she wished she could direct some of its light into the gloomy days of a much younger Sera. Not for the first time she imagined a different course of events where, after having stolen her as an infant, her father raised her under the watchful eye of gargoyle protectors.

NINE

Silk rustled and the settee next to Sera dipped as Abigail moved to her side. Her friend took her hand, the blue fire of her engagement ring flashing atop their laced fingers. "I understand the desire to have the approval of our elders. My grandfather is a formidable man, and has done much, most of it unseen, to shape this country. It is a shame he did not raise you and teach you how to use your magic. You must remember that we love you, and because of that love, we worry for you. This is why you need a steady male influence at your side. Someone to love you, support you, and advise you."

Sera already had such a person—Hugh Miles.

She hid her feelings for Hugh deep inside. At the thought of him, the silver disc tucked inside her chemise warmed against her skin. There were some things she wasn't ready to share with her friend, no matter how much she leaned upon Abigail. If there was any hope for a mage duchess to one day wed a poor surgeon, that was a topic for another day. Today she tackled more immediate concerns.

"Once I have proven my worth as a pupil to your grandfather, I will hand the bracelets over. I promise." Such a promise gave Sera some wriggle room. The old mage had exacting standards and it might be years before he deemed her translations sufficient. That was also assuming she found time to work on them. Her energies were constantly being pulled in different directions.

A frown remained on Abigail's porcelain brow. "Grandfather will not be pleased. Why can you not study them while they are in his care?"

Sera sucked in her bottom lip before she pouted and said, *Because they are mine and he cannot have them!*

In this game with Lord Rowan, she needed to make a more strategic move. "But Abigail, I *am* receiving the wisdom and instruction of your grandfather. It will take me some months to master the Fae runes, and I fear he will have to put up with me as a regular student at his side." She drew the conversation away from the physical items and focused on her need to learn from the old mage. Hopefully Abigail's concern that Sera should have some sort of *steadying influence* in her life would override her desire to see the dangerous jewellery in her family's hands.

Abigail made an approving noise in the back of her throat. Then squeezed her hand. "I shall make it plain to him that you need his guidance. His secretary can set up a regular weekly lesson for you."

Sera smiled. That was progress. Of a sort. Hopefully Abigail could sweet talk her relative by letting him think Sera was an eager disciple for the wisdom dripping from the end of his long beard.

Abigail waved a bowl of marzipan fruit under Sera's nose. "Let us move on to more pleasant topics. Lord Thornton is most keen to see you again. With the drop in temperature, Grandfather is going to freeze the round pond in Hyde Park to allow for ice skating. He does it every other year, and it is quite a feat, due to the pond's size. There is always a grand gala that lasts all week while it remains solid enough to walk on. There will be a festival in two nights' time, when Grandfather will work his enchantment over the pond and turn it to ice. Do say you will join our party?"

Sera selected a miniature apple and bit into the icing treat. Night-time skating did sound like fun. But it would mean that for one evening, she wouldn't be able to patrol the south bank. She had promised the people they would be safe from whatever had attacked Mr Perdith. She met her friend's eager gaze and couldn't find it within herself to disappoint Abigail again. Tonight, when she did her rounds, she would set enchantments to trap the creature if it prowled the neighbourhood. She could always summon a hackney if they were triggered, and make her way across the river at speed.

"I'd be delighted to join you. What does one wear

for ice skating?" While she had played in the snow with Kitty as a child and tossed balls of the stuff over their shared wall, she had never been skating. Would it prove more or less difficult than riding a horse?

Abigail squealed. "Wool and fur. Skating can be dreadfully cold. I am given to understand you can't enchant warm air around yourself, as it simply melts the ice faster. You could drop through a hole."

Sera mulled over her limited wardrobe. She had an idea of what might suit, with a few magical enhancements. "I promise I will be suitably attired for the evening."

"Excellent." Abigail rose and rang for tea. "Speaking of attire, what is this I hear about you striding about Southwark wearing breeches? Please tell me it is not true?"

How had she found *that* out?

"The council has me investigating a gruesome crime. Breeches and boots are more practical for navigating darkened alleys," Sera said. "Filled with who knows what."

Abigail screwed up her face. "I have more than one thing to speak to Grandfather about. It simply isn't appropriate for Lord Ormsby to dispense such tasks to you. Your gifts would be far better suited to horticultural magic."

Sera rolled her eyes and snorted like a disgruntled horse. "I have tried pointing that out to the Speaker. At this moment, Lord Tomlin is traipsing around a grand garden relocating pixies, while I was told to hunt a rogue lycanthrope. At this rate, I will begin to think the Speaker doesn't like me."

For once, Sera wouldn't object if Abigail used her influence with her grandfather to quietly lean on Lord Ormsby. Not that she particularly minded her current task. She believed she threw herself wholeheartedly into any assigned endeavour, whereas Lord Tomlin would have baulked at dirtying his shoes in a dark alley. But how she longed for a marvellous horticultural challenge!

"I will take matters in hand. You need have no worry over that," Abigail said as a footman delivered the tea tray. She poured tea into a delicate cup with a blush pink rosebud on the side, and passed it to Sera. "The skating gala will be such fun. I forget you have never had the chance to see Grandfather's display. It is rather early in the season, as he normally does it with the descent of winter. But he wants to retreat to his estate in Devon before it becomes much colder." A moment of worry flashed across Abigail's face.

"Do you worry he might overexert himself?" As far as Sera knew, magic did not diminish with age. But the body's ability to recover from its use was affected. Just as the elderly might take longer to recover from an injury or sickness.

Abigail sighed. "Yes. It is a topic I often discuss with Mother. But he is stubborn and convinced he is as young as ever."

Here was a concern of her friend's that Sera could help to alleviate. "If he does not object, perhaps I could assist with the spell and take some of the load from his shoulders?"

"Oh, yes!" Abigail's eyes lit up. "And of course there are the wedding enchantments to plan for spring. I thought my carriage could be pulled to church by unicorns with blush pink manes, like this rosebud." She tapped one finger against the side of the cup.

Pink unicorns? How on earth would Sera achieve that? If they found a matched pair of greys, that would make the illusion easier to maintain. Then all she'd need to do would be to add the mythical horn, a touch of colour, and some sparkles. Sera winked. "I think I can manage that."

Conversation moved to the grand event and Sera's head spun with all the minutiae that had to be thought of in advance. The wedding trousseau would take months to complete. Although it merely sounded like an excuse for an entirely new wardrobe.

"We are to go to Europe for our honeymoon. I cannot wait to see Rome." Abigail let out a sigh.

A twinge of jealousy cut through Sera. How she longed to travel and see the world!

After a pleasant visit, the two women parted on much better terms. While it weighed heavily on Sera that she would need to hand over the Fae bracelets—eventually—perhaps it was for the best. She hadn't asked Hugh where he'd hidden them, satisfied with his assurance they would remain undisturbed until she required them. But there would always be a risk that someone might discover them.

Sera returned home to discover her first influx of stories prompted by the remembrance spell. A large crate sat on the floor by the settee. A wooden box that had a vague yeasty aroma, as though it was normally used to transport fresh bread, sat on the low table in her parlour. Within both were stacks of paper, weighed down by a spell to stop them from flying away while being transported.

A quick glance told her that some had only a few lines of text. Others were densely covered on both sides.

She pulled out a more fulsome sheet from the box and began to read. *It was a bitterly cold night in January, four years ago, as I trudged home for my supper...* Apparently some of the memories were more like novels. Others brief poems. On digging deeper into her first delivery, Sera decided that the secretaries stationed at the Guildhall must have been chosen for their attention to detail, and the patience of saints.

Sadly, Lord Pendlebury's prediction had proved correct. It seemed nearly everyone in London had rushed to report every single dog bite they had ever heard of in the last ten years. Thankfully, the men recording the memories were efficient filters and such tales were easily discounted. While their tales were still recorded (it would be rude to turn anyone away after they had been called forth by magic) those pages were marked with a blue *D*. For either *dog* or *discard*, Sera wasn't sure which. These had been placed in the separate crate, where they could be ignored. However, those memories that were of a more serious nature still filled her current box, and more would continue to arrive each day before the spell wore off in five days' time.

The well-trained scribes had endeavoured to answer three basic questions with each report—who, where, and when. Sera requested a pot of tea and settled in the armchair. Scooping a handful of reports from the box, she made a start. Hugh had written up notes of his observations of Harvey Perdith to augment what Doctor Emmery reported. With that handy for comparison, she began to read.

On a newly acquired sideboard, she intended to make two piles. One pile of stories would be discussed with Hugh. The second pile was for those memories that contained horrific wounds to the deceased. Discarded accounts would be added to the dog bites in the large crate.

After some hours of labour, Sera had only a handful of memories in the first pile. The space for the second category remained empty.

By the time the teapot was drained and she scraped the last papers from the box, twilight had fallen outside and it was nearly time for her night-time patrol. As Sera contemplated the darkening clouds, a man bounced up the steps and rapped on the door.

Elliot stomped up from the kitchen to answer it. A muffled conversation took place, then he appeared in the doorway.

"Parcel for you." Elliot entered the parlour holding a rectangular package. In size it was somewhat like a book, but much thicker. He set it on her desk, then leaned against the wall, curiosity simmering in his dark eyes.

Sera removed the string and brown paper to find a polished wood tea caddy. A note sat atop it. *"A token of friendship,"* she read aloud. The signature was that of the Earl of Thornton.

As she lifted the lid of the box, a delicious aroma wafted into the parlour. He had sent her the special tea he mixed only for close friends and family.

"That smells expensive." Elliot leaned closer to sniff the tea, which had dried flowers and citrus peel nestled among its leaves.

"I imagine it would be, if it were for sale. Take it down to Rosie, please." A smile warmed her heart, then a little sadness washed over it. Why couldn't the earl set her pulse racing the way Hugh did? As though summoned by her thoughts, the large shape of the surgeon appeared out of the descending shadows and crossed the street to her door.

Sera leapt from her chair and opened the front door herself. "Hugh." She breathed his name, took his chilled hands in hers, and tilted her head for a kiss.

Elliot took his overcoat, and Hugh followed her into the parlour, where he settled into his armchair. He regarded her with a worried frown and his fingers tapped his knee as though something pressed on his mind. "I have been kept awake at night, worrying over your intention to prowl the streets of the south bank after dark."

A retort flared up in her mouth. It was bad enough that Abigail protested her behaviour, but she'd thought Hugh would understand.

He held up a hand to hush her words before she gave them voice. "Before you say you can protect yourself... yes, I know. And I appreciate your abilities. All I ask is that you allow me to accompany you. My concern is the possibility of numerous attackers, or someone wielding magic among their number. There are so many scenarios and in a few of them, you might be injured."

Sera gathered her thoughts, sifting through them to try and explain why she'd taken on such a risk. Part of it was to understand the common people better and to use her gifts to ease their lives where she could. But there was another, deeper reason.

"Some months ago, when that pistol was fired at Lord Zedlitz, I acted instinctively to throw out my parasol as a shield. But my reaction gnaws at me. Despite Captain Powers' reassurance that I'd done the right thing. I have read books detailing the brave accounts of mages as they faced enemies and cast spells to save soldiers. But how do you train for that? How can I know what my mind and magic will do in such a moment?"

He leaned back and rubbed his jaw with one hand. "I studied anatomy books, but drawings are quite different from having a man with a wrecked leg screaming for mercy as someone hands you a saw."

She let out a breath. "You understand, then, that I

must test myself. You know I would rather encounter a thief with you or Elliot to watch my back as a challenge to my instincts. But what if I had to face a hundred soldiers waving swords, all intent on taking my head off, only to discover my brain freezes at such danger?"

"Will you go out tonight?" Worry simmered in his gaze, but he never told her no or tried to control her actions. He simply asked to stand at her side.

"Of course. The creature must be found. Tonight, I thought to wander Vauxhall Gardens. If you have no other calls upon your time, I would value your company." Twilight turned the sky dusky grey outside the window and Sera's stomach grumbled. Now that her body reminded her, she couldn't remember if she'd had luncheon or not, so intent had she been on poring through the sheets of memories. "Rosie will feed us supper before we venture out," Sera murmured from behind lowered lashes.

"How can I refuse such an offer when it is garnished with a meal?" He winked and held out his hand.

After supper, they took a hackney across the Thames and alighted near the pleasure gardens. While the temperature dropped, Vauxhall was enveloped in warm air that enabled men and women to strip off their bulky overcoats. The area was as busy at night as London streets were in the day. Lights were strung across the paths, held aloft on high poles, casting their golden glow on those below. Laughter rang out as people rushed to see the entertainments.

Sera summoned a raven from the Tower to accompany her and the bird flapped down to a nearby tree for its greeting. She approached the huge bird and stroked its glossy feathers.

"Hello, my friend. Might I ask your assistance to be alert to any trouble?" she asked.

The raven made a noise deep in its throat and rubbed its beak against Sera's hand.

With her sentry in place, they continued through the gardens. Some people waved in greeting as they recognised her, others hurried faster along the path. Overall, it pleased her that more people stopped to watch with open expressions than to scowl and disapprove. One man crossed himself and then spat on the ground in her direction.

"Have a pleasant evening!" she called to him. She would meet prejudice with kindness. The man might have been raised by narrow-minded individuals who had never learned how to accept other people for who they were.

The raven hopped from tree to tree as Sera and Hugh strolled the walkways and took in the sights. Stalls sold food and drink, so they chewed hot chestnuts and sipped mulled wine as they walked.

"I hear there is a tightrope walker." She suspected the person used a touch of magic to hold their position on the rope, but she still wanted to see the spectacle for herself.

Hugh gestured to where a large crowd assembled.

"She performs above, while a brightly painted elephant does tricks below."

What would happen if it rained? Would all the paint dribble off the creature's grey hide? "How sad to make an elephant do tricks far away from others of its kind."

Hugh offered her the last chestnut before tossing the paper in a brazier. "There are rumours it is a type of shifter, enslaved to its fair owner. After the performance, he turns back into a man, to be locked in a caravan until the next night."

Sera stared at him. She had seen Erin somehow fit her human form into a crow's body, and then expand from that creature to a human. But an elephant? That seemed like an awful lot of shifter to hide inside oneself.

TEN

fter an uneventful evening wandering the
Gardens with Hugh, then a few solid hours
of sleep, Sera arose the next morning and
descended to her parlour. She ate a late breakfast while
attending to her correspondence. When her left hand
was halfway between plate and mouth with a piece of
toast, the ring on her little finger vibrated. An image of
Kitty flashed into her mind.

Taking a quick bite of jam-slathered toast, she
opened the drawer in her desk where she kept the
ensorcelled paper she shared with her friend. As she
drew it out, words scrawled themselves across the sheet
in a rush.

*I remembered! The strip of fabric we
found in Mr Perdith's house is like those
left with foundlings. My maid Berne told*

*me the tale. Her mother had to give her up
as a babe. She cut a strip of fabric from
a blanket. Half is given to the mother, half
kept by the hospital. Berne still had the
strip as a touching reminder to keep hope
alive. She was nearly ten when her mother
reclaimed her by presenting her matching
piece of material. —K.*

Sera sat back and let the revelation sink into her mind. If a mother were forced by circumstances to leave her child with the Foundling Hospital, why was Harvey Perdith scouring Debrett's and the *Rich Ladies Treasury*? Noble families sent *indisposed* young women off to the country, or to the Continent, to give birth far away from prying eyes. Later, they could deny it ever happened and keep their reputations, and virtue, intact. The resulting children were placed with rural families and either grew up ignorant of their noble parents, or were claimed later and passed off as the offspring of distant relatives.

What clue had made Mr Perdith think his mother was a noble? Now it made sense why he had been searching in books thirty-five years old. He wasn't looking for a rich widow to court. They were sources from the year he was born.

Dipping her quill into the ink, Sera wiped the page clear with one hand and wrote a reply.

He thought his mother was a noble and sought to find her in the Treasury!

That would explain his careful copying of the length of patchwork. The woman who had so lovingly stitched the piece would have recognised it in an instant. That made another thought cross her mind, and she added another line for Kitty.

I wonder if Horatio Valentine was the name given to him by his mother?

It was a somewhat pretentious name. Certainly not one an overwhelmed working-class mother would bestow on a child she'd birthed in a crowded, dirty tenement. Or perhaps she might have, if she had hoped her child would rise to his name and seek his fortune elsewhere.

Kitty's reply marched across the page.

The Foundling Hospital keeps records. We know the year and have only to find his entry to confirm.

"No time like the present," Sera said to the empty room. To Kitty, she wrote:

Are you free this morning?

She had sorted all the written memories she had received so far. Her only other task for the day was to sit in the library at mage tower and pick through their history from around the time Morag would have reached her majority. Sera had a vague theory that the entire council would have been needed to erase the birth of the Crows from the genealogy. She hoped to find a reference to some mysterious illness that had rendered them all unconscious for a few days that might prove her right.

The reply came while she finished her piece of toast.

Will collect you in one hour.

Excellent. That gave her sufficient time to finish her breakfast and dispatch the waiting correspondence.

Exactly on time, a smart curricle with two matched bays in harness pulled up at the pavement in front of Sera's house. Kitty held the reins, the vehicle only large enough for the driver and their passenger.

"A bold choice, given it is likely to rain," Sera said as Elliot helped her up to the seat. The waxed top was folded back, and they could put it up if the weather turned, but the little vehicle wasn't as dry and warm as an enclosed carriage.

"I understand you have some sway with Mother

Nature. Tell her we do not want any rain to ruin a lovely autumn day." Kitty slapped the reins against the horses' rumps and the equines walked on.

"I shall try my best," Sera murmured. It was a glorious day, with nary a cloud in the sky and a crisp edge in the air that would have been chill if she hadn't been warmly dressed.

They journeyed out to the Foundling Hospital, situated in Bloomsbury and surrounded by fields. A stone wall encircled it, and Kitty slowed the horses to a walk as they passed through the gate. Before them stood a plain red brick building with two wings built around an open courtyard. Trees were planted in the open areas and there some children played, chasing one another around the obstacles.

A child of about twelve rushed forward to take charge of the horses while an older gent approached at a slower pace.

"Where might we find someone in charge?" Sera asked, as the man helped them down.

"You'd be wanting Matron, milady. You'll find her in there." He gestured towards the cream arches that created a colonnade across the centre stretch of the U-shaped building.

As they walked under the arches and into the hospital, the temperature dropped and a chill ran over Sera. Already she missed the autumn sunlight and its illusion of warmth. An open door bore a brass plaque reading MATRON. From within, a booming voice was delivering a scolding for laziness.

"Perhaps we should wait until she has finished with the unfortunate currently before her," Kitty said, pulling Sera to one side.

Like naughty children, the two of them leaned against the wall and listened. Sympathy for whoever faced the angry matron washed over Sera. It sounded as though the malcontent was a vile offender who needed to be transported to far-off Australia for their transgressions. After a few more minutes, blessed silence fell and a boy of no more than ten, with stooped shoulders and a lowered head, scurried from the office.

"Poor mite," Kitty murmured.

Sera rubbed her fingers together and then pointed to the boy's pocket. A rounded shape took form as she gifted the lad with one of her incredibly bouncy balls.

Grumbling came from within the office, but neither of them moved. "You're the mage. You go first." Kitty prodded Sera in the side.

As Sera approached the doorway, she felt less protective mage and more sacrificial offering. Behind a dark wood desk stood a formidable woman who would have been near Natalie Delacour's size. Sera wondered for a moment if the matron were from the Londinium clan, but so far in her acquaintance, gargoyles had been rather taciturn and not prone to shouting.

Another creature came to mind as she took in the matron's gnarled face and thin lips—ogre. They did have a reputation for being both large and loud.

The older woman scowled, which made her small eyes almost disappear into her weathered face. Before she could launch a verbal assault, Sera introduced herself. "Good day, Matron. I am Lady Seraphina Winyard and this is my friend, Miss Napier. I am here on business from the Mage Council and wish to discuss certain records you may hold here."

Matron huffed and dropped back into her chair without a single protest from the wood. The chunky limbs of the chair appeared to have been carved to support the weight of more substantial creatures. "What business do mages have with my foundlings?"

"This is old business. I am investigating the background of a man who might have been a foundling at this hospital some years ago." Sera waved two fine-legged chairs over from behind the door, so that she and Kitty could sit. The wooden feet of the chairs made faint noises of protest as they crossed the floorboards, then positioned themselves exactly behind the women, so all they had to do was sink elegantly to the seats.

It was probably deliberate that no chairs were arranged before the desk. Children would be forced to stand as they were held to account for any breaches of the rules.

"What year?" Matron barked the question.

Definitely a dollop of ogre blood, Sera thought. "We believe 1752 or possibly 1753. I'm not entirely sure when he might have been left here."

The matron heaved herself to her feet and turned to the wall of books behind her desk. A fat fingertip walked along a shelf until she found a particular volume. Having tugged the book free, she placed it on the desk with a thump, then turned it around to face Sera and Kitty. The pages bulged in odd places and when she opened it, Sera discovered pieces of fabric and even buttons pasted or stitched to the paper.

"Do you know whom you are looking for, milady?" She raised curious eyes to them and her tone evened, as though she had needed time to shake off her anger.

Sera moved her chair closer, then extracted the sketch from her reticule and laid it on the desktop. "The child was left with a strip of fabric in this pattern, and we believe his given name may have been Horatio Valentine."

Each page recorded pertinent details about the children. Gender, date of birth, any distinguishing features, given name, and the new name allocated by the hospital. Sadness seeped through Sera's fingertips as she searched the register. Page after page repre- sented a baby separated from their mother. Given up in the hope they would have a better life than a struggling woman could provide. Each with the hope that one day, things would improve and they could hold their child in their arms once more.

"What happens to the babies?" Kitty asked as she leaned over Sera's shoulder.

"We send them to wet nurses in the countryside. Then, when they are three years old or thereabouts, they come back to us and are educated and trained. If their mothers don't claim them, girls go into service at sixteen. Boys are either apprenticed or go into the military at fourteen." As she spoke, the matron's shoulders relaxed and a sense of pride crept into her voice.

"Do many mothers return for their children when circumstances allow?" Sera couldn't imagine what the mothers endured, leaving their child to be raised by others and never knowing if they would see them again.

The matron let out a sigh. "Not many. It's a rare case when a mother returns clutching their token to find their child."

Kitty perked up, having a happy tale to tell. "My maid was reclaimed. She was nearly ten when her mother remarried and was able to offer her a home."

A brief smile pulled the matron's lips back and revealed a snaggle tooth. "She'd be a lucky one."

Sera kept turning pages, scanning the tokens left and the names of the children. None of the items matched. Then a thought occurred to her. Why did Mr Perdith still have his token when they were attached to the book? "When children leave here, do you give their tokens to them?"

"Oh, no. They stay with the register." Matron crossed brawny arms.

"So if a foundling has their token, what does that mean?" Sera suspected she already knew the answer, but wanted it confirmed.

Matron frowned, and it caused deep lines to rupture across her forehead like a boulder cracked by a chisel blow. "It means somebody took something they weren't supposed to touch. I cannot be everywhere all the time, and some of the children think they can circumvent our rules."

When they reached the end of the register without finding Harvey Perdith, the matron pulled down another one. After half an hour of scanning every page in it, excitement caught inside Sera.

"Here he is! Horatio Valentine, renamed Harvey Perdith." The date his mother had surrendered him was recorded, along with a description of the baby. Where the strip of fabric had once been pasted was now a roughened area with a tear.

"Looks like Harvey took his token when he left." Kitty smoothed down a piece of the thick paper that had been torn when the glued token had been ripped free.

"Now we know he was a foundling and have his date of birth." She tapped the notation: December 13, 1753.

"He would have been conceived sometime in February or March of that year," Kitty said.

"Do noblewomen leave their babies born out of wedlock here?" Sera murmured the question, not sure how to tackle the sensitive topic.

The matron grunted. "Can't say I've ever seen a noble cross this threshold. Even with her face disguised, you could tell by the cut of her cloak, the boots she wears, and the cleanliness of her fingernails. Such a woman would run a risk of discovery. Back then, we had ballots to draw which children we took. A noblewoman would run the risk of losing the ballot, and she and her child would be turned away."

That caught Sera's attention. "A ballot? Like a game of chance?" As if the mothers weren't under enough stress, had they then to gamble to see whether their child would find a place or not?

The matron became quite animated as she delved into the history of the hospital. "This place was established to hide the shame of women and give illegitimate children a decent path in life. But there were so many children being left here that rules had to be introduced. At first, on admission days, we might have one hundred children and only twenty spaces, for ten boys and ten girls at a time. Sometimes there were fights among the mothers."

"A hundred children at a time? Good lord, what hardships so many women must endure." Kitty leaned on the desk, clearly taking a keen interest in the running of the hospital. "How did this ballot operate?"

"There was a bag containing three different coloured balls. White, orange, and black. Each woman would put her hand in and draw out a ball. A white one meant we would take the child so long as they were healthy. Orange meant the child would be inspected if a white ball child failed the medical examination. A mother who drew a black ball was turned away immediately." The ogre shuffled to another shelf and drew down a worn leather bag with a string gathering the top. Sticking her hand in, she drew out a dull white ball and handed it to Kitty.

After examining the bag and the worn balls that determined a child's fate, Sera thanked the matron for her time and they walked back to the curricle. As they rattled down the drive, Sera mulled over what they had learned. "I can only conclude Mr Perdith was mistaken. Why would a noblewoman run the risk of discovery this close to London, and the added risk of having a one in three chance of drawing a white ball from the bag?"

Kitty hummed as she guided the horses through the gate and back along the road. "Assuming that he was correct, which we admit is a slim chance, then there must be some advantage the hospital offers that made the risk worth it. One thing springs to mind —anonymity."

"But so does giving the child to a family in the country. Isn't that why it is done, to protect delicate reputations in London?" Sera tried to follow her friend's line of thought. No, more likely Mr Perdith's mother was a working-class woman who had poured her love into stitching a special token. She might have taken in sewing, which was why she had access to finer fabrics.

"But does it really offer anonymity? Either the mother must give money directly to the family to support the child, or trust an intermediary to do so. What happens if any of the parties involved want more to hold onto her secret? Or if the family's circumstances change or they give the child to someone else? Whereas she can leave her child at the hospital and they place the babe with a family and ensure its welfare. She would always know where the boy was, until she thought it safe to claim him once more."

Sera blew out a sigh and leaned back in the seat. "I cannot fathom what might have motivated his mother all those years ago. If she cared so much she made the patchwork strip, why not ensure he grew up with a good family?"

"Not all women have the choices available to us. Imagine, if you will, if Abigail were in such a situation —unwed, with child, carrying the weight of expectation and desperate to save her reputation."

"Abigail has a mage for a grandfather. He would ensure no one ever revealed her secret." Having said the words, insight like a crack of lightning exploded in Sera's mind. "Oh! What if magic *was* involved? When Hugh and I examined the body, I found the faintest magical trace." She had given up on the idea of there being any significance in the victim's being a foundling —until now.

When Kitty turned to Sera, a sad smile touched her lips. Her opinion had tumbled in the opposite direction. "We're struggling with theories. Most of the time, the most obvious and simplest explanation is the true one. Mr Perdith was obsessed with the idea his mother was noble, when perhaps she was a woman who could only gift her child a fancy name and lovingly craft a bit of patchwork. Your assailant might simply be an Unnatural creature passing through Southwark who has now moved on to another area."

Sera screwed up her face. If Kitty's analysis were the correct one—and it did seem the most obvious—she would hand Lord Ormsby another failure. "But none of this explains the magical trace rising off his body."

"Again, what would be the simplest explanation? What if he ate something crafted by an aftermage cook or with a magical ingredient, and died with it still in his stomach?"

How unfair of Kitty to pick apart the more fanciful story Sera wanted to craft around the circumstances. Sera wanted the truth to be extraordinary, when it might be entirely ordinary.

She blew out a resigned sigh. "I am seeing conspiracies everywhere. I shall wait and see if anything comes from the remembrance spell Lord Pendlebury and I cast. If there are no other similar deaths, then I will admit you are right, it was a passing assailant, and we may hope they have gone far, far away and don't return. All this is merely a flight of my imagination, to think that the circumstances of the man's birth had anything to do with how he died."

Eleven

Later that day, as twilight fell, Sera walked through the settlement nestled next to Bunhill Fields and towards the rickety cottage of Ethel. The old aftermage sat on her porch, smoking a pipe and drinking tea from a mug. Like the first time they had met, an empty mug sat beside her, ready to be filled for Sera. Or whatever visitor the spirits had told the old woman to expect.

"Hello, Ethel. I hope you are keeping well. Is there anything I can do for you before winter arrives?" Sera worried the cottages weren't warm enough, and she surveyed the exterior to see if she had missed any worn areas in roof or walls.

"Good evening, milady of the night. You've taken care of the draughts and leaks. Now all I need is my pipe and my tea." Ethel gestured to the teapot.

Sera poured herself a steaming mugful before taking the chair next to the old woman. She settled back and watched as the sunset painted the cottages in deep pink, with a blush of orange. Without their knowing it, she had adopted the odd little village and considered herself guardian of their needs. Over successive visits to Ethel, she had repaired their homes and dispensed her glow lamps to provide reliable and safe lighting.

Her next idea was to create shingle pathways before the winter rains turned everything into mud. That took more magic and the co-operation of Mother Nature. Concentrating on the sweep from Ethel's steps to the next cluster of cottages, Sera imagined a network of threads connecting them all. She whispered words of magic over the teacup rim, asking the earth goddess to send small pebbles and lime chips up through the dirt to create a durable pathway. It would take time, like nurturing the oak sapling at mage tower. But over the coming days and weeks, the more solid surface would emerge from the soil.

"I took your advice and mentioned tea to Lord Thornton. He kindly sent me a small container of it." Sera sipped the tea and savoured the floral notes.

Ethel cackled. "You could do far worse than a lord with his own tea plantations."

Sera shrugged. She liked the earl, but a marriage needed more than an appreciation of tea. "There are so many lords and I have a pantry to fill. If only they were all so generous with their gifts."

The aftermage chortled so loudly Sera worried she might choke on her drink. Ethel drew a wheezing breath and her eyes glistened with humour. "Being given things is grand. Once, many a pretty bauble was draped around old Ethel's neck. But a woman's soul needs more than sweet presents."

Sera took another quiet sip of tea. The old woman's words echoed a realisation that took up residence inside her.

Ethel turned a milky gaze on her. "I don't think you sought old Ethel to discuss what your gifts are worth. But I'm happy for the company. Too many of those who want to talk to me are dead."

"I sought you out to talk to the dead, if it's at all possible. I need your help with a man who died recently after a most vicious attack. Is there any way you could reach him to ask what happened?" With no family, Mr Perdith's body would go into an unmarked pauper's grave unless his friends organised something. That would make things more difficult if Ethel needed to stand near his physical remains to contact him and they only had a vague location.

At the moment, at least they knew where he was.

Ethel made a noise, half-cough and half-snort, as though something were trapped between her nose and throat. "I can try. It'll be like standing at the door of a busy pub and hollering."

Sera had tried that tactic, too. "I will take whatever assistance you might be able to provide. I admit to struggling in the dark with this one, and cannot discern why he met such an end."

She wanted to believe there was more involved

than a random strike. Partly so she could reassure the residents of Southwark that they weren't in danger, and partly so she could catch the culprit and dangle the beast in front of Lord Ormsby.

Ethel slurped her tea and then placed the empty cup on the ground. "I refuse to believe our Nyx is lost in the dark. Perhaps you shouldn't rely on your eyes, when you need to feel your way instead."

Ethel and her forthright manner had a way of making Sera see a problem from another angle. Perhaps the aftermage was right. In the dead of night, one needed to rely on other senses than one's eyes.

"What do you need from me for the best chance of reaching Mr Perdith?" Unsure how such a process might work, Sera had tucked something into her reticule.

"Do you have something personal to him that I can hold?" Ethel rose and tapped her pipe out against the edge of the step before setting it next to the teapot.

Sera dug out the strip of fabric that had hung by the man's bed. "I believe this was significant to him. It's a foundling token."

Ethel took the material and dropped back to her chair. She laid the strip across her left palm. Then she held out her right hand towards Sera. "If you could lend an old lady a little assistance."

Wondering how, exactly, but willing to try, Sera took Ethel's hand. The aftermage rubbed a patch on the fabric with her thumb. She closed her eyes and breathed deep through her nose, which made a slight whine like a mosquito.

A tingle ran across Sera's clasped hand and up her arm. Closing her eyes, she concentrated on the feeling and let the old woman's magic wash over her, the way she did when casting with another mage. Once she had the taste of the working, Sera pushed a tendril of magic into Ethel.

The aftermage gasped as Sera's power augmented her gift. Then she murmured, "Come on, lad, help us find what attacked you."

Something tugged at the air around Sera and, cracking one eye open, she peered into the darkness that had dropped swiftly with the setting of the sun. A shape shimmered and took form just a few feet from where they sat. Was it Mr Perdith, or another soul drawn by the aftermage's reaching into the other realm?

Ethel sucked in a breath. "You'll not get anything of use from this one, milady. He's too... shredded," Ethel muttered, her head swaying from side to side.

"Shredded?" The body had been horribly clawed, but Sera would have described him as *eaten* rather than *shredded*.

Ethel let out a choked cry and let go of Sera's hand. She thrust the length of fabric back at Sera, then picked up the teapot and poured the cooling contents into her cup. Leaning back in the chair, she took a long drink.

The glistening shape dissolved, like mist on water.

After a silent minute, Ethel met Sera's gaze. "The suddenness and violence of what happened to him shredded his soul. Poor lad is in pieces in the afterlife. It'll take him a long time to stitch himself together so he can move on."

Blast. While she had learned nothing of Mr Perdith, Sera never regretted any time spent in Ethel's company. "Well, at least we tried. I wonder if the suddenness you feel means he had no inkling of the impending attack."

There could still be a clue in their attempt. His soul's surprise might indicate it was random, as opposed to his doing something objectionable and waiting for an assailant to take issue with it.

"There were two things the scraps left of his soul screamed at me over and over—*betrayed* and *cursed*." Ethel tapped a sharp fingernail against the pewter mug.

"Cursed?" Now, that was interesting. "If his soul clung to those words, I wonder if someone betrayed him or put a curse on him?" That would explain the faint magical tingle. It might have been the residue of a curse.

"Best way I can explain it is, betrayed by someone close and cursed to meet such an end. Poor sod." She slurped more tea.

Ideas spun in Sera's head. She pushed aside the idea of a random killing once and for all. She would pursue the direction that made her senses tingle.

"Thank you, Ethel. It seems there was far more to Mr Perdith's death than meets the eye." She would need to talk to his friends again. Betrayal implied someone close. Someone he trusted. Perhaps someone who had accompanied him from the Loaded Hog that night.

Returning to her home, Sera had little time to prepare for her evening. Tonight she wanted to prowl in circles around where Mr Perdith died. As she smoothed the lines of her coat and tucked an emergency spell into a pocket, movement outside the window caught her eye.

Hugh hopped down from a hackney and stood on the footpath. On spotting Sera at the window, he waved, and a grin lit his face. Sera found an answering smile came unbidden to her own lips.

"Don't wait up," she murmured to Elliot as she headed out the door.

"I doubt you'll want breakfast before noon tomorrow." The footman chuffed in laughter as he held the door and winked at her.

Sera took Hugh's hand and climbed into the small hackney, which took them across the bridge. They alighted close to the Loaded Hog tavern.

"Where would you like to begin?" Hugh asked as they surveyed the area. Darkness cast long shadows in the poorer areas, where there were no lights to banish them.

"I want another look at where Mr Perdith died before making a few circuits around here. Then I need to talk to his friends again, but I think I'd rather find them in daylight, and without the others around. Particularly Isaac, who was last to part company with him that night."

Could the tall, thin man have attached a curse to his friend as they said their good-nights, and summoned a beast to the alley? It was a remote chance, but someone had betrayed the deceased man. Or so his soul said.

Now doubts assailed her. "Do you think souls are reliable witnesses as to what happened in their final moments? Ethel said Mr Perdith could only scream of being betrayed and cursed. But to die in such a fashion, you *would* think you were cursed. That doesn't mean there actually *was* a curse placed on him."

"I am no expert in such matters, but I imagine such a violent death would scar a soul." Hugh fell into step alongside her, his fingers brushing hers as they walked.

Sera created three phantom crows to circle above them. She wanted people to know that Nyx walked the streets at night to protect them. It should also stop any thieves from leaping upon them.

"Kitty says the simplest explanation is usually the most likely. But I cannot forget the whisper of magic rising from his body, and the idea of a curse rings true inside me. The thing bothering me is that the creation of a curse to set such a creature upon someone would be beyond the ability of an aftermage. Only a mage could craft such a hex." *Dark magic.* The words shivered through her veins. To do such a thing to another person would not have been sanctioned by the council.

Then again, neither would the curse she had embedded in Lord Hillborne at Mistwood Manor.

That set loose more ideas in her mind. "We only

have the word of Mr Perdith's friends that he was a good, honest man. What if he showed a different face to others, and the unknown person turned to a mage?"

"Would anyone around here approach a mage for help?" Hugh asked. "That seems to be the purview of nobles, who have the wealth and connections to seek magical solutions to earthly problems."

That stopped her in her tracks and destroyed her emerging theory. "You are right. I am the first mage in a very long time to make myself available to these people and at no cost. Few could afford what the others charge for potions and spell work."

Her next words were cut off by a startled scream from a side street. Sera glanced at Hugh, then increased her pace, following the sound.

A woman cried, "Get off!"

Then came a throaty masculine laugh.

Rounding a corner, they found a woman up against a wall. A man loomed over her, both hands planted on the brick by her head. He used his larger size to pin her in place.

"I told you to sod off. You're drunk." The woman shoved with both hands, but the man remained in place and laughed off her efforts.

Anger swirled through Sera's veins as she remembered how Lord Hillborne had likewise used his size to hold her against a panelled wall.

"Let me try first," Sera murmured. She approached them, as the woman struggled to free herself. "Let her go. The lady has made it quite clear your attentions are unwanted."

The man swung his head to her, his eyes laced with red. His beard was unkempt, and sooty grime marred his face below the hairline. In the dark, the two almost merged as though his entire face was furred.

"She ain't no lady and this is no business of yours. Shove off," he growled.

Sera stopped a mere yard from the couple.

The woman turned wide, pleading eyes in Sera's direction. "Get help. Please."

"Help is here," Sera reassured the woman. Then she spoke to the man. "I'll only say this once more. Let her go."

"Or what?" He spat on the ground at her feet.

That took her aback. "Did you seriously just say *or what* to a mage?"

Before he could answer, Sera brought her hands together and murmured a spell over them. Then she flung it at the assailant. A dark ball hit him in the shoulder and knocked him sideways, freeing the young woman. She ran and hid behind Sera.

As the man staggered and swatted at the ball, it ruptured and spiderwebs shot into the air. The strands covered him and the more he struggled, the more they pulled tight around him.

"Get it off!" he screamed.

Sera tilted her head and regarded him. "Did you get off when this woman asked you to? I think not."

With a wave of her hand, she added the sting of a nettle to her dark web.

The man cried out. "It hurts! Get me out of this or you'll be sorry!"

"He seems to be a slow learner." Hugh stood at Sera's side. "First he challenged you with his *or what*, now it's *you'll be sorry*."

Sera yanked her trap and the man's feet were swept out from under him. He hit the cobbles with an *oomph*.

"How, exactly, will I be sorry?" She stalked to the fallen man and peered down at the fly caught in her web. His struggles grew fewer and fewer, until the strands cocooned him. Sera held out her arm and one of her phantom crows swooped down and alighted on her wrist. "Especially once my crow pulls out your soul. Or do you not possess one?"

The man's mouth made an O, and he stared in horror at the bird. He heaved back and forth as though attempting to roll his body away. "I'm sorry, Nyx— I didn't realise it was you."

"It shouldn't matter if you knew it was me or not. You don't treat women like that." Anger surged through Sera and her hands curled into fists. Startled, the crow hopped to the ground and began to peck at the web around the man's head.

"I don't want to lose my soul," he wailed. All his bravado of a few moments ago was gone.

"I think he has learned his lesson," Hugh said.

Sera wasn't so sure. Bullies were all alike. They cried for mercy when caught, but were back to their old ways as soon as they were freed. As the man thrashed on the ground, in her mind's eye his features melted into those of a viscount who abused those under his power, and then back again.

"I'm not so certain that he has learned anything... yet."

The crow caught an object between the strands of her web and worried at it, pulling a gossamer shadow free from the man's side. He sobbed as the crow walked backward, dragging an elongated image of him.

"I'll do anything! Please! Tell it to stop! Oh, God. I'm sorry." Sobs wracked his body and tears made pale streaks down his dirty cheeks.

"Enough, Sera." Hugh took her hand and wrapped her curled fingers inside his cupped hands.

She drew a shuddering breath. A crowd had gathered, drawn by the man's strangled cries. They probably thought the rogue lycanthrope, or whatever it was, had caught another victim.

"Very well. I shall release him. But know I will be watching." She waved the crow away. The bird let go of the imaginary soul and it retracted into the man with a snap. Then she swiped her hand to sever the strands of her web and freed the assailant's arms and legs.

He scrambled free and leapt to his feet, frantically wiping the black web from his clothes.

"You are marked by my crow. If I ever hear of you making untoward advances to women, or using your size to intimidate again, I will personally pull your soul free, feed it to my crows, and let them feast on your flesh." The bird returned to Sera's shoulder.

The man's eyes widened like those of a panicked horse, and the whites glowed in the low light. Then he pulled his forelock and took off at a run down the street, his form vanishing in the dark.

"Thank you, milady," came a voice from behind. "He's a nasty one. Thinks any woman wants to offer his ship free harbour."

Sera released her anger and turned to the woman who had been his victim. "That is one less predator on the streets, but I fear there are many more. I hope the story of tonight will spread."

She surveyed the crowd, a mix of men, women, and children. The women nodded and smiled at her. Some of the men had narrowed eyes, and she hoped her words were dripping through their minds.

The image of the crow trying to steal the man's soul would certainly stain their memories for some time to come.

TWELVE

The rest of her night passed uneventfully. After a few hours' sleep, the next morning Sera sat at her desk and pondered what little information she had about Mr Perdith's unknown killer. On one corner sat the worn copy of Debrett's, the pamphlet, and a drawing. On the very top of the pile, the strip of patchwork. She picked up the fabric and held it to the light. Sera imagined the man's mother selecting with care the scraps to use, and stitching at night by the light of a guttering candle to have something unique to leave with her child. The only thing he would be able to touch as a reminder of her. How many tears had been stitched into the fabric?

Questions swirled inside her. Having started down the path of Mr Perdith's origins being significant in his death, Sera couldn't stop herself. If the unknown mother had indeed been a noble, why run the risk of placing him in the Foundling Hospital?

She imagined herself in such a situation. A young woman who had made an unwise decision, perhaps carried away by the passion of a moment. Something she could well relate to, remembering the heated encounter with Hugh after they had raced to the bottom of the belfry. What thoughts had flown through the woman's mind when she'd realised a new life quickened inside her? Did she delight in conceiving a child, or mourn the loss of her reputation and the inevitable scandal that would follow? If she had siblings, they would likewise have been ruined alongside her and barred from society.

In such cases most men failed to step up, take responsibility, and offer marriage. Or the woman might have had a liaison with a man who wasn't a suitable husband. Such circumstances would leave her with few options. If she stood determined to bear and raise her child, she would be cut out of the family and cast adrift with nothing. Or a trip to an apothecary or midwife might relieve her condition before anyone noticed. That left a third option—having the child and giving him up for another to raise.

Sera's thumb brushed over a grey and blue square with what seemed to be a clawed foot in the top corner. "What drove you to your chosen course of action?" she asked the phantom mother.

Assuming the woman had been of sufficient means to acquire a spell that would ensure she pulled a white ball from the bag at the hospital, she would have had the resources to purchase a potion to loosen the life inside her. If that were an option she'd wished to pursue.

As Sera slid the fabric through her fingers, she pondered the forks in life's path, where each created its own branch of outcomes. She stroked the bright red piece of embossed velvet that had a curved corner and pattern of criss-crosses. A navy square had a silver tail that reminded her of the strong appendage with a tufted end like a lion.

Then she let out a low gasp. Of course! How could she have missed the clues?

"Mr Perdith's friends said he always believed he had a noble mother, and that she'd given him a clue to her identity! Noble families have heraldic arms. The colours and shapes on the patchwork must echo those used in her family crest." The fabric still in one hand, Sera grabbed the gazette of eligible women.

Flicking through the pages again, she stopped at one underlined name. Then she pulled Debrett's towards her and thumbed to the page of the family possessing the underlined name. Their coat of arms had a lion rampant, its front paws on the crest. Its tufted tail curved to one side, just like in the navy patch.

She leaned back in her chair and let out a sigh of understanding. "Harvey was looking up families in Debrett's and crossing off any names that were too dissimilar to his token, but sending a drawing to those that might match."

Dropping everything, she rubbed the mage silver

ring on her finger and thought of Kitty. Next, she snatched up the paper from the desk drawer. She had to tell Kitty that her theory, no matter how remote, was correct!

Mr Perdith's mother was a noble. Clue is the token. Patches are elements of a family crest.

Having sent off her message, Sera could do nothing except wait. The woman had been remarkably clever. The trail she'd left with her infant son was so subtle that almost no one would notice and expose her. Except for Sera, and a man most determined to find the mother who had given him up.

Sera found a clean sheet of paper and turned to the gazette. She would list out the women's names who had been underlined but not stricken through. Those would be the ones Mr Perdith thought most likely. As she scanned the pages and noted the young and eligible women, another thought occurred to her. Had the passage of time changed the woman's mind? Once, she had left a clue as to her origins. But what if she no longer wanted to be found and had sent the beast to silence her child?

Her ring vibrated with a response from Kitty. Closing her eyes, Sera let her magic soar across London to find her friend. Tendrils pulled her towards a dark stone building surrounded by skeletal trees. Reaching for a co-operative thrush scratching in a garden bed nearby, Sera sent it to tap at a window.

After a few moments, Kitty appeared dressed in a padded cream jacket that buckled down one side. With one hand, she flung open the window. In the other, she clutched a fine mesh mask. Since Sera disapproved of her friend carrying a pistol when conducting their enquiries, Kitty had redoubled her efforts with fencing lessons. Sera didn't have the heart to tell her that most assailants in a dark alley would carry knives, not epées or foils. Although Kitty did favour a sabre.

"Well done, Sera," Kitty said to the thrush, her cheeks flushed pink from her recent exertions. The building must have been some sort of gentleman's sporting club that allowed the wealthy Miss Napier to train.

"Sending out the paintings was a subtle message, was it not? The mother would instantly recognise her work, and know her son sought her out," Sera chirped, curling the bird's claws into the edge of the windowsill, seeking purchase.

"That must have been the reversal of fortune he mentioned to his friends—finding his noble mother and being elevated in rank." Kitty set down the fencing mask and held out her hand to the dark brown bird.

"Thank you." One thing bothered Sera, and she peered up at her friend through avian eyes. "Trying to find one's mother is no motive for murder, though. Particularly to end him in such a gruesome fashion. Even if she had changed her mind and did not want him to intrude on her life, she could have ignored his message and he would never have known."

Kitty leaned against the wall and curled her hand towards her, bringing the thrush inside, away from the descending chill. "If she mentioned it to anyone, the most obvious answer would be a jealous sibling. One who did not want an older brother reappearing in their noble home and sharing in their fortune. Of course an illegitimate child can't inherit, but a mother could still make a bequest from her personal property."

Sera turned that idea over. Even that didn't make much sense. But then a tiny idea whispered through her. "What if he *was* legitimate? Is it possible his parents were married, but the young mother was forced to give him up for some reason or to keep her marriage secret? She might have thought it a temporary measure until their marriage could be recognised and she could claim him."

Kitty brought the bird closer until they were eye to eye. "I like that idea. She might have made a hasty match without her parents' approval. Or the man might have been told to go off and improve his fortune before he would be accepted. There are many possibilities. That might explain why she left him with the Foundling Hospital—so he would be close to her in London and easy to retrieve."

A ripple of anxiety coursed along Sera's connection with the bird, its mind distracted by the dim interior of the room. "We will discuss this in person when you are free. I must let the thrush go before he darts away and flies into a wall."

"I will send word when I am home." Kitty lowered her hand and let the bird hop back to the windowsill. Then she plucked up the mask. "I have an opponent I intend to soundly thrash before I leave here."

With a goodbye chirp, Sera released the bird from her magical thrall and it flitted away into the autumn sky. Scrubbing her hands over her face, she let her mind reacquaint itself with her human form.

How she loved to fly with the birds and how she envied the Crows that they could shift from avian to woman whenever they wanted. Could she find a spell to allow her to do the same?

But first, she intended to reach back through time and find Horatio Valentine's mother.

With renewed enthusiasm, she continued to make her list of names. In all, it contained twenty women marked as being possible candidates. Then another thought dashed cold water all over her plan.

The women in the gazette were all of eligible status —meaning single or widowed. Thirty-five years had passed since then. It was a truth universally acknowledged that an eligible woman in possession of a fortune, must be in want of a husband to manage it for her. Most, if not all, of the underlined women had probably married and changed names. Possibly even more than once. And that assumed they hadn't died in childbirth, which snatched so many young lives.

What she needed was a way to determine their

married names and current whereabouts. That required a particular set of skills and knowledge that neither Sera nor Kitty possessed. But there was a specialist in such an area who could be consulted—Abigail, with her in-depth understanding of society, its unspoken rules, and its many players.

After she had drawn on Abigail's specialist knowledge to find her twenty women, that would raise another delicate problem. How was she to approach the women who had been in the old gazette and ask if they had left a child at the Foundling Hospital thirty-five years before?

Sera was confident her friend would know the etiquette of such a scenario. It would probably require two cups of tea and one slice of cake, before seamlessly moving from a discussion of the landscape painting on the wall to the subject of long-ago illegitimate children.

Sera wrote a note to Abigail and asked if she would be at home for a visit about a delicate matter. It was a little unfair of Sera to word it in such a way; Lady Abigail might think Sera needed advice about the earl. But she wasn't above a tiny bit of misdirection if it made her friend clear some time in her busy schedule for her. While the wedding was still a few months away, it dominated Abigail's every waking moment.

A reply came within the hour, saying that she could spare a few minutes for Sera before dashing off to an appointment with her modiste to discuss the extensive trousseau needed.

"Excellent. If Abigail is pressed for time, we will be

all business and she will not have an opportunity to corner me about Lord Thornton." On the verge of calling for Elliot to go find a hackney, Sera remembered their previous discussion.

Instead of yelling, she let loose a tendril of magic to curl around the streets, finding the driver she had used before snoozing on a corner. Her magic gently tapped on his hat to wake him, and whispered in his ear that he was needed. With her ride on the way, she quickly made herself presentable and shoved the list of names, the worn copy of Debrett's, and the pamphlet into her satchel.

The footman appeared as she rushed down the stairs, and held the front door open. "I appreciate you're not screaming for me down the hall."

"Occasionally you have rather brilliant ideas, Elliot. It's why I hired you." She grinned at him and skipped down the steps to the waiting vehicle.

She fidgeted during the ride, the traffic slow around London despite the cold weather. When the hackney stopped outside the Crawley mansion, Sera burst out, paid the driver, and hurried up the footpath. A chill wind whistled across the square and she hurried along the path, grateful for the efficient butler who perfectly timed opening the door so that only a minimal amount of blustery cold entered the house.

"Lady Abigail is in the blue drawing room today, Lady Winyard," he intoned, and gestured for her to follow.

It seemed silly to have to follow someone when she

was perfectly capable of striding along the hall on her own, nor would she get lost. But she reined in her impulse to charge past him and waited to be announced.

Abigail curtseyed, and Sera kissed her friend's cheek.

"Thank you for seeing me. I know you are busy with the planning." Sera glanced at the desk, where a second large book of fabric samples lay open. The image was a poignant reminder of the scraps pasted into the register at the Foundling Hospital.

Abigail gestured to the laden table. "My life is an absolute whirl! I wonder how Mother and I will have everything done before spring. The seating arrangements alone will take at least a month, and the skill and patience of a diplomat."

Secretly, Sera suspected her friend was loving every moment. Marrying the future duke would be a society event to rival a royal wedding.

"I have a further imposition upon your time. I am sorry. I need your expertise on a matter related to my investigation. There is a slim chance the poor fellow who was killed in Southwark was trying to find his mother, whom he believed to be a noble. I wonder if that somehow resulted in his demise."

"Well, I am intrigued as to how he came to be separated from his mother." Abigail took Sera's arm and led her to a round card table that had a tiny area of clear space.

From her satchel, Sera removed the pamphlet, the

worn copy of Debrett's, and one of the sketches. "He made notes in this pamphlet. I believe he sought out women whose family arms have the same colours or features as this sketch."

Abigail pulled the pamphlet towards her and tapped the cover. "Oh, I recall Mother mentioning this. I believe she is within its pages." She flicked the pages to find the *R* section and ran a finger down the names. "Ah, here she is. Elizabeth Rowan, with a modest fortune compared to her contemporaries. Luckily, my father appreciated that while her dowry was not large, there were certain other benefits to having a mage as a father-in-law."

Sera had already searched for her friend's mother and seen her name struck through. It would have been rather awkward if they'd discovered a half-sibling that Abigail knew nothing about. "There are twenty names he underlined but had not yet struck through. I want to visit each of them and ask if they left a child at the Foundling Hospital."

Abigail sucked in a breath, and when Sera looked up, her friend's eyes were wide with horror. "No, no, no. You do not walk into a noblewoman's parlour and ask if she gave up a child years ago. Particularly when the implication is that the child was born... out of wedlock. Think of the scandal, Sera."

"I'm sure no one is bothered by it now. It has been thirty-five years. These women have most likely been married for many years and borne other children. Why, they are probably grandmothers," Sera said.

Abigail pursed her lips. "There is no time limit on ruination. They could be ostracised and turned out of their homes by their husbands. You would leave them bereft of any comfort in their old age."

"Then how do I ask the question without asking the question?" Sera suspected that Kitty would have approved of the direct approach. All these matters of etiquette and propriety made it difficult to talk about certain topics and hampered her investigation. How much simpler life would be if subjects such as having a child when unmarried weren't considered taboo. Sera's parents hadn't been married, and it didn't bother her.

Pages rustled as Abigail found the other names. "You ask by inferring it was someone else, like a servant. In such situations as you are implying, the child is usually placed with a family. It is decidedly odd for them to be left with the Foundling Hospital. Are you certain the man's mother is within these pages, and it wasn't simply a lonely man's fancy?"

Sera picked up the sketch. "I admit it is a very slim possibility, but I have no other reasons for why he died. See this patch here, with the tail? It is similar to that of the rampant lion on one of the crests. Mr Perdith had told his friends that his fortunes were about to change."

"Perhaps he meant to blackmail the poor woman." Abigail took the drawing between two fingers and studied it.

"Unless we find her, we can't know." There had been no hint of blackmail amongst the papers Sera had found in his cottage. No letter from a noble vowing never to give in to his financial demands, or asking where to leave payment.

Abigail drew Sera's list of names closer and scanned them. "The issue is discovering who, if anyone, these women married. I will consult with Mother, since they are her contemporaries. She might even know if there were whispers about the *delicate condition* of any of them. Then I shall accompany you to pay calls upon them."

Having been reassured that Sera wouldn't charge into people's parlours with accusations of illegitimate children, Abigail seemed to hum with good humour by the end of the visit.

THIRTEEN

By the end of the week, the remembrance spell had waned and washed away with the autumn rains. The number of people trudging through fallen leaves to have their memories written down had dwindled to only one or two. The Mage Council recalled the scribes, and the remaining notes were bundled up and delivered to Sera's doorstep. Each afternoon, she spent an hour or two reading the tightly written pages. Each one was an entry from someone's life as they recalled an event that, to them at least, seemed eerily familiar to the gruesome murder.

Sera refused to give up hope that she might stumble upon the assailant in this way. Every night she roamed the south bank of the Thames, on the alert for a shifter on the prowl. Either Elliot or Hugh accompanied her, and Sera used her gifts where needed. So far she had encountered nothing except the usual criminality that occurred under cover of darkness. Among the lower classes, the stories spread of Nyx wandering the streets at night to protect the vulnerable. Sera considered that alone worth giving up her evenings.

That afternoon, she took the last box of papers and set it down beside what she considered Hugh's armchair. She had learned one lesson from her afternoon reading: at times London was plagued by roaming packs of hungry dogs. As gruesome as the reports were, they were easily discarded due to either the person's seeing the *mangy mutts* responsible, or the injuries were either too superficial or inconsistent with those of her victim.

She dipped into the box and pulled out the topmost sheet, being the account of someone who had what sounded like an encounter with a pitchfork. Holding the page on her outstretched palm, with a puff of magic, she made it fly to the sideboard and settle on the discard pile. Another wave summoned the next page into her hand.

The upper right corner gave the date of five years earlier, and a location not far from Vauxhall Gardens. As she read, a shiver ran down her spine. Sera clutched the paper more tightly and sat up in the armchair. In the fatal attack, the unfortunate victim suffered long gashes to his right arm and body and lost a large amount of flesh from the right side of his torso. She pressed the page to her chest while she digested the contents.

Then she scanned the account narrated to the

scribe and re-read the details to ensure she hadn't made a mistake.

> *My father encountered a fearsome beast that tore at his body, ate his flesh, and stole his life. I saw it with my own eyes. I was with him that night. Pa shoved me out of the way as the demon dropped on him from above with a piercing cry.*

Here were eerie similarities to the death of Mr Perdith, but they were five years apart. The *piercing cry* was another odd detail. Sera had expected more of a howl or snarl from a lycanthrope. Two deaths separated by time created a problem with her theory that Mr Perdith's actions in seeking his mother had resulted in the attack. If she set aside the motive that had consumed so much of her time, what did that leave to identify the responsible beast?

A creature that might only rarely venture into the city to take in the entertainments and dine on a Londoner. Or something else might have kept it away for the intervening years. Or somebody might have had it under control, but it escaped. More thoughts bloomed in her mind like a meadow in spring. What if whoever was responsible for the beast had been occupied elsewhere for a few years? The puppet master might have been in jail for some petty crime. Or it might be a travelling aftermage, peddling his wares—and death.

"Blast." Sera cast an accusatory glare at the sheet. It had ruined her previous theory, and now she didn't know where to place her focus.

She needed to consult with Kitty, who had cautioned her all along against constructing too elaborate a scenario from scant facts. The older death lent weight to a random Unnatural killer.

Not wanting to lose the remaining afternoon light, she sent out a ripple of magic to summon a hackney driver in the area. Shoving the paper into her satchel, she grabbed a cloak and ran out the door before Elliot could climb the kitchen stairs.

In Mayfair, she found Kitty at home, reading a book in the parlour. The volume was so fat and large, it rested upon a wooden stand.

Sera paused, the chunky book tugging on her curiosity. Then she remembered her purpose. "Someone reported a death from five years ago that sounds very similar to that of Mr Perdith. I was hoping to call on the family this afternoon, before nightfall. Do you have time to accompany me?" She frowned at the book, which seemed to absorb her friend's attention in the same way fabric samples did Abigail.

"Of course. I always have time for a Kestrel investigation." Kitty closed the book, but left one hand resting on the cover. "To satisfy the question written across your face, this is a legal tome of case histories from Father's study. I am researching an argument for equal rights for all sexes and classes of citizens in England—including Unnaturals. It is monstrous that they are treated like flea-ridden dogs hunkering at the side of a road."

Since their experiences at Mistwood Manor with the elegant vampyre Contessa Ricci and the Crows, both Sera and Kitty had become determined to ensure that such creatures were allowed the same rights and protections as all people. But in a world controlled by a few powerful and wealthy men who had no interest in equality for all, they were aware of the battle before them.

Nervous energy to keep moving fizzled through Sera's veins. "I have a hackney waiting outside. Or do you wish to take your family carriage?"

Kitty rose and took Sera's arm. "Certainly we must take the more discreet method of transport. No point in borrowing trouble, as Father says, by drawing attention to ourselves with a larger carriage."

Her friend was already dressed in a simple, warm gown for staying at home, and it took no time at all for her to don a hat and cloak. While they travelled over the bridge to Southwark, Sera showed Kitty the written recollection and they discussed possible connections between the two men.

Mischief sparkled in Sera's eyes. "I shall ask if he was a foundling or suspected he had a noble mother."

Kitty snorted and batted Sera's arm. "You mock my more careful approach."

"Not at all. I simply refuse to give up on an idea

that I have invested so much time in." Sera stuck out her tongue. Her theory had been rather grand until the older death had found its way to her reading pile.

As the light faded, they alighted from the hackney and wandered along the street to find the correct address. The row of identical terraces were two storeys tall, with dormers in the roof to allow light into an attic, and stairs spiralling downward to a basement kitchen level. These were larger and more respectable homes than the modest cottage Mr Perdith had inhabited. That reduced the possibility that both gentlemen had moved in the same circles.

Sera knocked on the door and the barking of a dog and the shouts of children came from within. A maid answered it with a harried look on her face and a child of about eight pressed to her side. In her arms, the young girl held a small, wiry terrier that growled in warning.

"Yes?" the maid asked, trying to hush the protective dog.

"I am Lady Winyard. I have come to talk to Mr Daniel Grove, if he is at home?" Sera peered around the maid at the modest interior. Two more children appeared, older but equally curious.

"Come in, milady. I shall fetch him for you. Mrs Grove is in the parlour." She showed Sera and Kitty through to a parlour that overlooked the street.

Mrs Grove sat before the fire. A young girl sat on a stool at her feet and read from a book, but both stopped to stare at them.

"Lady Winyard, ma'am. She wants to talk to Master Daniel," the maid whispered, then retreated to find the person in question.

"He's not in trouble, is he? I am sorry, my lady, but I do my best." The woman half-rose from her seat.

Master, not Mr Daniel Grove. So he was only a boy? Sera waved for her to sit. Mrs Grove looked like she seldom had time to sit and relax. Her hair was streaked with grey, and lines were etched across her forehead as though life constantly vexed her.

"No, he is in no trouble. I wish to hear his account of the memory he passed on to the Mage Council scribes." Sera and Kitty sat on a settee opposite the mother and the cheerful fire took away the chill from their time outside.

A deep sigh heaved through the woman's shoulders. "I told Dan to let it be. Yes, we lost my husband five years ago now, and he left me with six children to raise alone. Lucky he left me this house, but I have struggled to keep this lot fed and clothed." She reached out and stroked the girl's hair.

Sera turned to Kitty with wide eyes and mouthed, *Six children?* No wonder the mother appeared exhausted.

A clatter at the door heralded the arrival of Master Daniel. A tall, lanky lad of some fifteen years, he possessed light brown hair that was too long to be tied in a queue but not short enough to be tidy. Wary hazel eyes darted from Sera to Kitty as he approached and stood at his mother's side, one protective hand curled around the back of her chair. He had a defiant set to his jaw that quietly impressed Sera. Like her, he was a youth who had seen how cruel life could be and was determined to not let it bend him.

"I'm Daniel Grove. What business do you have with me?" he said in a clear tone with only a tiny waver of uncertainty.

Sera pulled out the sheet of paper and held it out to him. "I need you to tell me about the night your father died. I think his death might be related to that of another man recently."

The lad sucked in a breath and turned to his mother. "I told you, Ma! Soon as I heard about that recent one, I said it was the same beast that killed Pa. I spoke the truth back then and now. But no one ever believed me. Said a lad of ten wasn't *reliable.*" He spat out the words.

Sera schooled her face into a serious expression. She liked him. He would give no quarter, even to a mage.

"Neither my friend nor I doubt your account," she began. "In fact, we sought out such recollections so that I could learn the truth behind these attacks."

Mrs Grove reached up and patted her son's hand. "Mind your manners, Dan. Lady Winyard and her friend are here to help. Perhaps they might even give your Pa the justice he deserves."

"If it's not too difficult for you, could you take me through the events of that night?" Sera hoped the memory wasn't too painful for the lad. "There may be details you have recollected since you spoke to the council scribe."

Mrs Grove shooed her younger daughter from the room, and Daniel perched on the rolled arm of the chair. "Pa had taken me to the Gardens. It was a special treat—I wanted to see the performers and the fireworks. He took me to see all those lights strung across the paths. Then we watched a man and woman walking along a rope suspended high above us. We bought roasted nuts and pies from the carts. It was a grand evening."

Sera steeled herself for the oncoming horror, even as Dan described the wonders he'd seen in Vauxhall Gardens. "It was getting close to midnight and Pa said it was time to head home. We cut across the field to Angel Street. I could see the houses, and lights burning in a few windows..." He swallowed and his gaze darted to his mother. She took his hand and gave him an encouraging nod.

"We were at the edge of the field, just before the row of houses across the street from us." He gestured off in an easterly direction. "There was this piercing cry, like a hawk makes as it stoops. I never saw it coming. The thing moved that fast. Pa must have. He picked me up and tossed me in the long grass. Before I could get to my feet, he cried out to stay away. Then, there was a thud..." He clenched his jaw and curled his hands into fists.

Sera could imagine what ran through his head— that he should have fought alongside his father. "You were ten and unarmed. Your father threw you to one side to save your life. Did you see what attacked him?"

"I couldn't see much in the dark, but there was a bit of light from the houses that showed their outlines. Pa screamed and fought. But it was bigger and stronger." He stopped and drew a deep breath, his shoulders tense as his mind relived the scene.

Kitty leaned forward and focused on the youth. "Not all fights require swords or pistols. Words have their own power. What you tell us here will, we hope, lead us to the culprit and bring justice for your father."

He met Kitty's gaze with one moistened by unshed tears. "I was scared, miss, I'll tell you that. I peeked over the top of the long grass. Pa was on the ground, that thing on top of him. Ripping, tearing..." Mrs Grove gave a shuddering gasp, and he gripped her shoulder. "His screams turned to whimpered pleas, and then he fell silent. The noise brought men out to investigate. They yelled and waved lanterns." The lad's voice tapered to a rasped syllable and he bowed his head.

"How long do you think the attack lasted?" Kitty asked in a gentle tone.

Daniel shook his head. "Years, but only seconds. Perhaps a minute or two at most."

"When we experience something horrible, time expands, and it seems to go on forever." Sera remembered those seconds on a rooftop, just before her friend had leapt and she had been sure she could still reach him. A few seconds had felt like hours.

Kitty leaned forward, an open expression on her face. "What did it look like?"

"You'll not believe me." He crossed his arms and stiffened his spine. A lad used to being told he'd imagined it, or worse, made it up.

Sera smiled. "I'm a mage, and while I'm not much older than you, I have already seen many things that other men wouldn't believe possible. If anyone will believe you, it's us."

He huffed and used his hands when he spoke, drawing a shape in the air. "I saw a tail, and it had long claws on its paws. Whatever it was, it was no dog."

"You're sure?" Sera desperately wanted to believe him.

He met her gaze with certainty. "As sure as I am that two fine ladies are sitting in our parlour and not two alley cats."

Briefly Sera toyed with turning them both into cats, as you never really knew what form someone harboured deep inside them. But the lad was adamant, and she would never tease him about his father's untimely death.

"It sounds more feline than canine," Sera murmured. What if, instead of a lycanthrope, they pursued some sort of large cat shifter? A tiger or panther might attack in a similar fashion, dropping from a roof or tree, and resemble what the lad described.

"Is there anything else you can tell us that might help?" Kitty prompted.

Daniel glanced at his mother and wet his lips. "Wings. I swear it had wings. That's the only way it could appear and disappear so fast."

Sera let out a surprised, "Oh." A cat with wings? She would need to consult the mage library.

"That would explain how it appeared to ascend the building after attacking Mr Perdith. It could have flown. We need a more fulsome description, Master Grove. Size, colour, wingspan?" Kitty's brain swung into action, teasing out the details from her witness. She scribbled notes and details on the back of the council scribe's paper she'd taken from Sera's satchel.

Once they had exhausted Daniel's memory and the lad had begun to sag, Sera moved to a different topic. "Mrs Grove, was your husband by chance raised at the Foundling Hospital?"

She shook her head. "Oh, no."

Blast. There went that idea.

"He was a foundling, but his mother left him with a family in Winton. That's a town just north of London," she said as she stood to show them out.

Disappointment trickled through Sera that her time in pursuing tokens from the Foundling Hospital had been wasted. "Did he know his mother?"

They gathered in the entranceway. "No, he never knew her. The family she left him with reckoned she was a noble, from the way she dressed, and from the carriage that stopped outside their house that day. But he never saw her again. Mr Grove never got on with his foster family. He said they were cruel and treated him like a servant. At fifteen, he simply left one day, and walked to London to make his own way in life."

"Did Mr Grove ever try to find his mother?" Excitement welled up inside Sera. Here was the thread that might connect the two men in death and perhaps in life.

"No. He said if she didn't want anything to do with him, he wanted nothing to do with her. He did just fine on his own. He found a job in a printing press and worked his way up until he owned his own business." Mrs Grove touched a hand to the wall, as though acknowledging him.

"He did a fine job, to provide such a life for you and your children. Was the name Grove given to him by his mother, or did he adopt it for himself?" Sera needed some link from baby to mother. Mr Perdith had his strip of patchwork. What clue had Mr Grove's mother left behind?

FOURTEEN

"Oh, that I cannot answer, milady. I never thought to ask, as it's always been our name. And now it's too late." Mrs Grove's smile dropped away.

There might still be some way to trace his origins, however remote the possibility. "Do you know the year he was born?" Sera grasped for any link between one man and another.

"Oh, that I do know. November 1752," Mrs Grove said.

Before they could continue digging into Mr Grove's origins, Daniel narrowed his gaze at Sera and issued his challenge. "Will you find what did it?"

"Yes. I intend to make the night safe for all Londoners." She certainly hoped she would find the beast. Two such horrific deaths were two too many. Not to mention that two failures in a row would be a cause of jubilation for Lord Ormsby, and she was not about to permit that.

No, she fully intended to disappoint the Speaker greatly with this assignment and find the creature responsible. "After all, who better to seek a creature that attacks in the dark than the goddess of night?"

Mrs Grove paused, about to reach for the door latch. "Good. That will bring us a small measure of peace. Might I ask, milady, where did that dragon go? Caused a right scare, it did, when it climbed out of the Thames."

"I'm sorry for the fright he caused. He only attacks in defence of me. He is slumbering now and only emerges when I need him most."

As Kitty swung her cloak around her shoulders, she turned to Daniel, a speculative glint in her eyes. "Where do you go to school, Master Grove?"

"I'm done with that. I'm a working man. I have Ma and my siblings to support." He flashed a grin as the young girl carrying the dog returned to stand next to him.

"Do you like your current employment?" Kitty tugged her hat onto her head.

He screwed up his nose. "I'm a butcher's assistant. It smells awful in the summer and it doesn't make much use of this." He tapped the side of his head with a fingertip.

"The printing business had to be sold. Dan was too young to take it over and the money from its sale has been enough to tide us over, until recently." Mrs Grove sounded disappointed that her son couldn't follow in her husband's footsteps.

Kitty huffed. "Would you consider a change in career, if you could earn as much as a printer with the potential to derive a comfortable living in the future?"

Sera wondered what Kitty was getting at. The turn in conversation made no sense to her, and she wanted to pursue the fact that Mr Grove had been left by his noble mother to be raised by a foster family. Those circumstances couldn't be a coincidence. Two men, both born around the same time, both given up by noble mothers, both meeting an identical gruesome death.

The lad's eyebrows rose in interest. "Earn more, you say? I'd be right tempted, miss, if you tell me this job is cleaner than the butcher's, too."

Kitty nodded, as though she had made some decision. "My name is Katherine Napier. My father is a solicitor, and he's always looking for bright young lads who might consider a career in the law."

Daniel stared at Kitty, while his mother gasped. Now Sera understood Kitty's questions.

"But how would that be possible, Miss Napier? Dan dropped out of his schooling two years ago, even though I told him we would manage." A frown furrowed Mrs Grove's forehead.

"He could work as a clerk in my father's offices and continue his education. I believe Daniel has enormous potential, if there were someone to give him the right opportunity. Once he catches up with his schooling, we could then sponsor him to university. It would mean a lot of hard work, but you could maintain the life for yourself and your family that your father established with this home." Kitty fished in her reticule and pulled out a creamy calling card.

"Me, a solicitor?" He stared at her like she had gone daft.

"Yes. You have a fine mind and determination. As I said earlier, not all battles are fought with swords. Some of us wield words to make changes in the world. Would you be part of it?" She held the card between two fingers. "If so, call at my father's offices. I will ensure they know to expect you."

"I don't have anything good enough to wear. We're ordinary folk," he muttered, staring at the hole in the toe of one boot.

Kitty threaded her arm through Sera's. "Do you see my friend here, the mighty mage who is now a duchess? Lady Winyard used to be a kitchen maid, and her parents were unwed. She had to escape a magical trap and seize what she wanted. Sometimes life will open a door for you, but you need to be brave enough to walk through it. Besides, we will provide some appropriate clothing for you to wear."

The lad grinned and stood taller. "Thank you, Miss Napier. I'll not let you down."

Kitty stuck out her hand and shook Daniel's. "No, I don't believe you will."

Outside, the two women climbed into the waiting hackney and headed back across the Thames. Sera decided to tackle the events of the afternoon in reverse order and raised the last issue first. "Hiring for your father, now, are you?"

"A smart lad like Daniel is worth a dozen lazy nobles who are half-baked by Eton. Besides, now that we are quietly taking on Unnatural clients, Father needs to consider the long-term future of the firm. I see a future partner in that young man. And after losing his father in such a horrific fashion, I think he deserves a leg up in life." Kitty pulled her cloak tighter about her.

Sera whispered a warmth spell to keep the autumn chill at bay. Then she tried to contain her excitement as she broached the subject that made her heart race. "Mr Grove had a noble mother who gave him up."

Kitty let out a sigh. "I am surprised you didn't leap on that fact with great excitement in their hallway."

"I did. Inside my head. I don't think his family would have appreciated my throwing up handfuls of coloured sparks to celebrate the discovery. It cannot be a coincidence, Kitty. Two noble mothers who gave up their babies in the same year, only for those children to meet the same gruesome fate years later?" Sera drew two lists in the air, using her magic to form the letters from blue glowing mist.

"I will admit you may have uncovered enough to establish a tenuous connection. But do not run too far ahead of yourself, Sera, lest you trip." Kitty reached out and erased the more fanciful of Sera's ideas, that the two men had been twins separated and raised by different people.

"But you agree there might be a connection,

however slight at this point." Sera wiped away the list and instead created a panther that hovered before them. Then she gave it wings. Such a creature had a terrifying advantage, being able to drop on its prey from the sky and equipped with sharp teeth and claws. Would it prove to be a shifter, wandering the streets like any other man or woman, or some sort of creature pulled from the mists of legend and story?

"Two does seem rather coincidental. But five years is a long time between attacks. Nor do lycanthropes have wings," Kitty murmured.

"Or cats. If both men were attacked by the same assailant, it looks somewhat like a wolf or panther, with wings and a tail, that leaves bite and scratch marks." There were innumerable creatures it could have been. Sera would study the books in the hidden library to find something that seemed likely. "There is one other thing I want to ascertain, but it will be a rather unpleasant task. I shall ask Hugh to accompany me."

"Oh? More midnight escapades?" Kitty's eyebrows shot up in interest.

Sera called to mind the tingle that she'd sensed in the first victim. "Yes. Mr Perdith had a faint magical trace when we examined his body. While it has been some years, I want to see if anything lingers around Mr Grove."

Kitty screwed up her face. "I will leave you two to your evening of digging up long-dead corpses. Turning to less magical matters, I cannot see how their lives were intertwined. Perhaps we can shed some light on events long ago once we have the married names of the women Mr Perdith identified as possibly being his mother." Kitty settled back against the seat.

"That is going to prove rather awkward to pursue. Abigail has informed me I cannot simply *ask* the women if they gave away a child born out of wedlock thirty-five years ago." Sera huffed and crossed her arms.

Kitty chuckled. "Of course not. You must broach the subject indirectly."

"Abigail suggested I imply it was a servant in the household at the time." Sera held in her frustration. She would play by Abigail's rules, since it meant so much to her friend. But that didn't stop her from trying to find ways to circumvent those rules she considered too restrictive.

"Hmm. That might work. But you probably need a barb in there somewhere, to ensure the woman knows you really mean her. I shall think on that." Kitty turned her mental resources to the sorts of questions Sera could ask, to ensure they flushed out the quarry they sought.

That evening, Sera again prowled the streets with Elliot at her side. Stories of her grew. She only had to appear at the end of an alley with a phantom crow on her arm for a ruffian to let his mark go with a cry, and flee.

She awoke the next morning early, with too much to do to sleep late. Her body would simply have to cope on a reduced number of hours in bed. As a mage, she had the means to brew a potent coffee that would keep her mind functioning while she patrolled the south bank. She could even sell the formula to a coffee shop. Men such as Hugh, who worked all hours, would probably queue up for a cup of something to revive their senses.

Dressing in her favourite dark green habit, she walked to the mews to hire a horse. At mage tower, she left the equine munching hay in the small stables nestled beside the wall. Down the spiral stairs she went to the hidden library. Consulting the map, she struck off for the section on mythological creatures, but when she rounded the corner, her good mood deflated. The relevant shelves stretched for over twenty feet and were nine feet tall. On both sides of the aisle! Apparently, writing about such beasts had been a popular pastime throughout the ages.

"Where to start?" she murmured to the tomes. They did not reply.

She could probably safely ignore books on sea creatures. No one had mentioned a salty odour or webbed feet when describing the assailant. Choosing the first book from the closest shelf, she flicked through the dense text. Her plan had been to scan the books, looking for pictures that matched the details she had of the beast. Then she frowned at the book. "Where are the pictures?"

Deciding to ignore that one, Sera moved on to the next. She worked as the clock hanging above the door quietly marked the passage of time. A gentle waft of magic made pages fall open as her gaze assessed the images. Anything that had a tail, wings, and claws was set to one side. When the clock chimed ten o'clock, she had a pile of books beside her that was nearly waist high and she had only made her way down half of one shelf.

Hands on hips, Sera reconsidered her approach. "There has to be another way."

She paced up and down the stacks as she muttered out loud. "Do I need to know *exactly* what killed the men?" Forewarned would be forearmed. Especially if the creature had certain attributes that made it harder to capture. But was identification a pivotal step in discovering the beast? Stopping, she rapped her fingernails against the wood of a shelf.

There were two ways to find the killer. Start with the two men and work towards it. Or try to guess what it was from the brief details provided by Daniel Grove. One method meant doing something active, the other would see her chained to a desk for weeks.

Sera narrowed her gaze at the books. "Away you go. I shall return when I have more of a description." With a wave of her hand, the books all rose and flew back to their places.

There was one other thing she would research while in the library. Finding the area that covered the history of mages and their feats, she plucked out a volume for around the time of Morag. "Let's see if anything untoward happened."

Taking the book to the long reading table, she took a seat and began scanning the pages. Much of it was about acts of war the mages cast in various skirmishes about England and abroad. Then entertainments performed for the king. These sounded very similar to the fish she conjured that had so delighted King George.

Excitement bubbled through her when her eye caught mention of an illness that had affected all the mages at the same time. "In the winter of 1473, a most terrible malady struck this council. Every adult member suffered, unable to rise from their sick bed for seven days. King Edward grew most anxious, fearing another country had cast an evil spell over his mages to rob England of their magnificence. There was much rejoicing at court when the nine men recovered."

A snort escaped her. The entire council struck down at the same time for a similar number of days could have been a dark curse, cast by another country. Assuming they could all have been infected at the same instance. It was far more likely the men had worked together to erase Morag's children from the genealogy, and drained themselves to exhaustion in the process.

Armed with that knowledge, which lent credence to the tale of the Crows and her theory that female mages could have gifted children, Sera replaced the book. On the ride back to Soho, she considered how to use the information. She would certainly sprinkle it into conversation with Lord Rowan the next time she called upon the old mage.

Then other ideas spiralled through her. Knowing that she could have gifted children by taking another mage or Unnatural as a lover, would she do it? A face hovered before her, one with kind eyes. A man with a gentle nature and no magic. Who, while he contained a trace of long-ago gargoyle blood, was no shifter or mythical being.

No. She would take no man without love, no matter how powerful he might be.

And love would make any offspring of such an ordinary man magical in their own way.

FIFTEEN

That afternoon, as the sky turned to muted orange and deep cream with the advent of twilight, Sera donned her grey coat. A touch of magic added an illusionary front panel to complete the skirt. But she still wore breeches and boots underneath for the extra warmth. Another brush of her power added a thick hem of black fur with tiny silver sparkles that would catch the light. Matching trim encircled her deep hood.

"Perfect," she murmured as she twirled in the parlour.

The Crawley family carriage collected her, and she nodded to Lady Crawley, then touched Lady Abigail's hands in greeting. As the carriage got under way, the women conducted their covert business.

"Mother and I have discussed your list and added the married names of the ladies in question. Three remain unwed to this day, but there is no hint of impropriety around any of them." Abigail extracted the sheet from her reticule and handed it to Sera.

Beside each name was a neat notation with the lady's new name and rank. Three had small circles next to the name, denoting no change in name or status. Knowing her friend, even if there were rumours surrounding any of the women, nothing would ever be committed to paper. That might ruin a woman's reputation if the pages fell into other hands.

Lady Crawley met Sera's gaze. "Normally, when a young unmarried woman goes off to *visit a sick relative* in the country for some months, or unexpectedly takes a grand tour, there is a flurry of rumours speculating as to which gentleman might have been responsible for the young lady's removing herself from society for such a period of time. These instances are most odd. I cannot recollect even the vaguest rumours concerning the names underlined. The only one that sparks any memory is Miss Pearson. From what I remember, she simply stopped attending social events, though she was never in the inner circle or much sought after. I assumed she had merely embraced her spinsterhood rather than suffer the humiliation of being a wallflower at every ball."

"Thank you, Lady Crawley, for your assistance." Sera tucked the list into her reticule. In the coming days, she would call upon each one and gently probe events from the woman's youth.

If Kitty's simplest explanation theory held, the women were not in any way connected with her deceased men. As such, there was no rush to quiz the women about any inappropriate behaviour years ago. Except for the niggle at the base of her skull that refused to go away.

Something bound Mr Perdith and Mr Grove in both life and death—and she would dig it up.

Oh! That sparked a reminder. Would Mr Grove's remains have the same faint magical emission as those of Mr Perdith? She needed Hugh's assistance to pursue that notion, but the surgeon had been busy with his patients lately and didn't have the time for nocturnal adventures.

"Seraphina, are you listening at all?" Abigail tapped her on the knee and drew her attention away from mauled corpses and grave robbing.

"I'm so sorry, Abigail. I was miles away." She offered her friend an apologetic smile. "I also have to admit I cannot ice skate. Is it terribly difficult?"

Abigail and her mother exchanged a look. "I am sure Lord Thornton will ensure you don't fall. Just keep hold of his arm."

Twilight had deepened to early evening by the time they alighted at Hyde Park. A large crowd had gathered and a festive air permeated the park. Lights on poles were placed every three yards around the entirety of the pond. The teardrop shades emitted an icy blue-white light. More lights shimmered above the pond, as though Lord Rowan had cast a spider web covered in glow worms. Musicians were tuning their instruments under a striped gazebo next to what appeared to be a small stage. Food and drink sellers with hand carts were dotted around the pond's edge and delicious aromas made Sera close her eyes and inhale. Children ran squealing around the trees and then darted back to where their parents stood.

Sera stared at the silvery expanse of water; the pond so large it was difficult to see the other side in the deepening light. "Does your grandfather freeze the entire thing?"

Such a feat would take a great amount of power, and she wondered if it were safe for the elderly mage. The shine would disappear from the evening if the effort stole his life, and he keeled over.

"Goodness, no. But he will transform a large portion of it. What he does is leave the very middle unfrozen, but he creates a fence around it so skaters do not fall in." Abigail looped her arm through Sera's and they headed towards the largest crowd gathered near the musicians. Other tents were set up with settees, cushions, blankets, and tables for people to sit and watch the skaters.

Lord Rowan stood by the water's edge on a wooden platform. He wore a cloak of deep purple, the silver runes around the hem morphing and changing shape as he muttered under his breath. His white eyebrows shot up as they approached and he smiled at his grand-daughter.

"Abigail. And Lady Winyard. Would you care to assist an old man so we can entertain the masses?" He held out a gnarled hand to her.

Abigail gave her an encouraging nudge, like a proud mother propelling her offspring onto a stage.

"Of course, my lord. I shall follow your lead." Sera took the offered hand and stepped to his side.

Excited chatter rose from the people clustered on either side of them. Lord Rowan cast a silence bubble around them so they could converse unheard. "You continue to defy me, Lady Winyard, and I allow no one to do that. My affection for my granddaughter has granted you some leeway, but you *will* comply with my instructions."

Sera met his steady gaze with one of her own. She had anticipated this confrontation. Abigail might have been satisfied with her claim to be a willing student of the old mage, but she assumed the canny wizard would see through her ruse. She had given much thought to what would make her finally hand over the Fae bracelets. "Of course, Lord Rowan. I shall willingly hand over the items concerned in return for all you know of pairings between mages and Unnaturals."

He huffed, and one side of his mouth pulled up in a brief smile. "Is that all?"

If that demand didn't elicit a response, perhaps her next one would. "No. Continuing along that line of enquiry, I also need to know everything about Nereus, or the offspring of two mages."

He froze, then drew a slow breath through his nose. "You *have* been busy with your studies. I see we have much to discuss. But this is neither the time nor the place for a history lesson. Shall we say next week?"

She inclined her head. The gauntlet was thrown down, and it appeared Lord Rowan would pick it up. A tingle of anticipation swooped through her. Finally, she would have the answers she sought.

"Abigail said you do not freeze the entire pond, but leave a circle in the middle clear." Sera returned to the topic at hand as the bubble of silence dissolved.

"Yes. It conserves my energy and leaves a spot for the fish to surface. Wouldn't do to distress the children by having all the fish float dead to the top when the ice melts. I shall start, if you could augment the spell with your ability." He rolled up his sleeves and started to chant. His words turned into snowy owls that circled the pond, flapping luminescent wings.

Sera took a moment to appreciate the showmanship, somewhat like her ravens, but less terrifying. The words he uttered were nonsensical to her ears, and purely for the amusement of the crowd, so that they could *see* something magical happening. The actual casting that would freeze the water spun like an insubstantial thing made of mist before the mage.

Thankful for her previous experience with Lord Pendlebury, she trusted her magic to work alongside another. With a gentle touch, she let her gift entwine with the growing spell. For a few breaths, she did nothing but let the casting wash over her so she could understand it. Then Sera let her instinct guide her. Following the path laid down by the other mage, she added her unique touch along the way. Shafts of light and dark played over each other where their magic touched.

Unlike the ensorcellment she'd worked with Lord Pendlebury, they did not create a glowing orb this evening. Instead, they crafted a gossamer-soft blanket that seemed knitted with strands of the night sky. Sera poured her magic into the net until her obsidian threads vibrated with the spell.

When the threads were so densely packed that the orb appeared to be a solid black ball, Lord Rowan made a satisfied noise in the back of his throat. "It is ready."

Sera stepped back, letting him have his moment now that her bit was done. Lord Rowan tossed the ball into the air, where the strands began to wriggle and unfold. Then, like a fisherman with a net, he threw the magical blanket towards the pond. The owls swooped down and grabbed the edges with their outstretched claws. They flew to the edges of the pond, stretching the net out between them until it grew impossibly large and encompassed the entire pond.

Once the water was covered, the owls let go. The net drifted to the surface and solidified as it dropped. When it touched the water, a loud *crack!* rang out, and the water froze in an instant. Ice glittered before them, leaving only a dark shadow at the very centre. The tinkling of icicles rubbing against one another added a light refrain as a waist-high silver railing rose from the pond to keep skaters from venturing near the middle.

Gasps were followed by applause. Excited conversation broke out and people moved to the edges of the pond to tie skates over their footwear. Some children were already prepared, and they dashed out onto the surface like minnows.

Lord Rowan bowed to Sera. "Thank you, Lady Winyard. A most interesting collaboration. I sense, however, that Dewlap's shadow has settled over you and taints your magic. We thought you might have avoided that."

Taint? Shadow? That took her aback.

Before she could voice the question, he continued. "Right. That's my bit done. I'm off home for a hot chocolate and to read my book. I shall see you on Friday in my study."

Sera stared after the old mage. A host of new questions crammed her brain and jumped up and down for attention. Lord Dewlap was the mage who had died and passed his magic to her newborn self. But Lord Branvale had never mentioned any shadow or taint. Apart from her being a girl. Or had he also sensed something else, like Lord Rowan had?

"Lady Winyard?" A soft masculine voice interrupted her thoughts.

She glanced up to find Lord Thornton at her side, a shy smile on his lips and a pair of skates slung over his shoulder. Light from the lanterns glinted on the golden rims of his spectacles.

"Lord Thornton. How lovely to see you." He was a nice chap. Why couldn't she keep him as a friend? It was ridiculous that a woman could have only marriage or nothing with a man. Surely friendship could cross gender lines.

His smile increased in size. "I am hoping you will rescue me from tripping over eligible debutantes. With you on my arm, none will dare fall in our path. Or if they do, perhaps I could impose on you to use your magic to sweep them towards someone else?"

At least they had that in common. He also chafed under the expectation of marriage. Sera considered how much more annoying it was to have potential matches clinging to you every time you stepped out in public. At least her suitors were exceedingly few in number, and disinclined to public displays. "I shall endeavour to save you from the incoming wave of hopeful mothers and the daughters bobbing in their wake."

"You have no skates, Lady Winyard. Shall I fetch a pair for you?" He gestured to a tent where they could be hired.

She grinned at him and tapped the side of her nose. "Do not worry about me."

With a confused chuckle, he led her to a bench, where Lord Thornton buckled on his skates.

Having never skated before, Sera had no intention of falling on her bottom repeatedly and getting cold and sore while she learned. There were a number of benefits to being a mage. She lifted the hem of her coat, raised her boot, and grazed the middle of the sole with a finger. A black blade appeared. Then she repeated the process on her other boot.

"I suspect that is cheating," the earl murmured as he finished attaching his blades and held out his hand to her.

She took his warm hand. "Of course it's cheating. What is the point in being a mage if I can't give myself an unfair advantage every now and then?"

He laughed and tucked her hand into the crook of his elbow. Out on the ice, bolder skaters zoomed in and out of couples and groups. Other skaters took a leisurely pace somewhere in the middle, and beginners stayed close to the grassy banks. Sera put one skate to the icy surface and immediately her foot shot out from under her. The earl steadied her, although his lean form had none of the solid security of Hugh's.

"This is much trickier than it appears." Even with magical blades and using bursts of magic to keep herself upright, Sera's feet wanted to go in two different directions.

Lord Thornton proved to be a confident skater, and he lent her balance and forward momentum. That meant her depleted magical reserves didn't have to work too hard to keep her upright and her feet under her. Abigail sailed past on the arm of her fiancé, the two of them a striking couple as they displayed their prowess by performing a number of spins and even skating backwards.

Sera's confidence grew as her body became accustomed to the smooth way of travelling, and she found the right amount of magic to ensure her feet stayed where they should and her body didn't topple over.

They made a slow circle around the enormous pond that encompassed some seven acres, and talked of gardens and much smaller water features.

"My estate has a rill, which I have always found more peaceful than a showy fountain," the earl said.

"I am creating one in my garden in Soho." Then she wished she could recall the words. Hers was barely twenty feet long. His was probably well over three hundred feet.

"I would love to see it one day. How do you plan to landscape around it?" He angled his body as a lad skating backwards nearly collided with them.

Sera released a puff of air to spin the boy in another direction. "I am planning the planting very carefully. Simple greenery, I think, rather than any distracting display of flowers. I wish to create a restful area where I can escape the bustle of the city."

"I think we are much alike in that, Lady Winyard. I admit I only venture into London when I must and to take my seat in the Lords." He pulled her a little closer as they neared the far side of the pond. Here, the lights on poles were farther apart, and it created a shadowy and intimate setting. With the musicians and food stalls all at the opposite end, there were no people lingering on the grass here.

"Have you been listening to the arguments about the Regency?" The decline of the king's mental state had worked in her favour to clear outstanding matters in Parliament. She wondered if the earl supported Queen Charlotte or the Prince of Wales.

"I am sure that will all be settled by Christmas in a satisfactory manner. Now, it is too lovely an evening to spoil with talk of politics." He pushed off more strongly and sped them along.

Sera needed a trickle of magic to maintain her balance as Lord Thornton set a faster pace through the more experienced skaters. If she let go, she would fall. Would he stop and help her to her feet, or skate on alone?

She inhaled the chill wafting off the ice. It was a lovely, fantastical evening. And yet... it stirred up stormy emotions she could no longer ignore.

Sixteen

Despite not returning home until well after midnight, Sera had too much to do to sleep for long. She roused at eight, and asked Vicky the maid to fetch her a breakfast tray to have in bed while she considered what to tackle first during daylight hours. Visits would have to be paid, but they didn't occur until the afternoon. No one would be at home to her if she knocked on their door before noon.

She still mulled over what sort of winged beast had claws and a tail like a cat, but couldn't face more hours poring over dusty old books in the mage library. She also wanted to dig up a body, and that required a certain companion. As she finished breakfast, Sera decided to find Hugh first and, if possible, satisfy her curiosity about the remains of Mr Grove.

She had sent a note to Mr Grove's widow and asked where he might be found, under the pretence of wishing to pay her respects. No need to alarm the family by advising she intended to dig up the unfortunate man. Once dressed, Sera used her mage silver ring and the help of a nearby raven to track down Hugh. After travelling there by hackney, she paced outside the door of a tenement in the East End as feeble screams of pain came from within. When silence fell, she stared at the door, her heart climbing up her throat.

Then a reedy cry came from within, followed by a cheer. She let out a breath and smiled. A long and difficult delivery had ended with a live birth. It was another half hour before the surgeon emerged, his beefy forearms and hands scrubbed clean, though red stained his rolled-up cuffs.

"How fares the mother?" Sera peered around him and was relieved to find the woman sitting up in bed, nursing her newborn with her family clustered around her.

"She's exhausted, and I told her no more. Another birth like that might be the end of her. Besides, they already have five to feed. If you could brew something to help her in that particular department, she'd be more than grateful." He fell into step beside her as they took the stairs down to street level.

Sera fixed the address in her mind. There was a dark brew on a dim shelf in her study that would bring the mother permanent relief from bearing any more babes. "I have been working on a number of potions that stop a woman from conceiving. So far I have brewed one that has an irreversible effect. I can offer it to the new mother. Another I am working on is designed to be temporary and taken on a regular basis, however, I have not yet perfected it. Once I am satisfied with the potion and I know how often it needs to be taken, I shall make it available to my noble clients and those who frequent our friend the apothecary. How goes the apprentice?"

Hugh and the apothecary had searched to find a woman to train up in feminine physiology who could advise customers of the shop about delicate issues they could not discuss with a man.

He took her hand and entwined his fingers with hers. The touch reminded her of the intimacy of the previous night when she'd skated arm-in-arm with Lord Thornton. Unease churned inside her. She didn't have it in her to play the coquette and enjoy the company of both men. She needed to make a decision before she hurt anyone and wounded her heart. Or Hugh's.

"I have found a very capable young woman who agreed to give up her quiet life in the countryside to work in London. She is a fourth generation aftermage with a gift for herbs. Her rural upbringing means she has some skill with animal husbandry, and her mother is a gifted midwife." Hugh rubbed his thumb over her skin, which did nothing to dispel the emotions battling inside her.

"I look forward to meeting her. Between the two of us, we will soon have numerous remedies available for the particular issues that plague women. Imagine if we were able to give women the ability to control when they wished to conceive." Ideas bloomed in Sera's head that would create a better life for women. To give them the power to decide when they had birthed enough children, or to have the freedom to decide they did not want any at all. Then they could concoct potions to ease monthly symptoms, to assist the mother during pregnancy... or some way to detect and treat cancers in the breast before they advanced and stole lives.

That made her wonder how Vilma progressed with her gothic novel about Mistwood.

"What adventure are we embarking on this morning? The hour is still early, so I assume we are not stalking the Southwark beast." He flashed her a wide smile.

"No. We are seeking someone who might be one of its earlier victims, a Mr Grove. Do you remember how I detected a faint magical tingle from Mr Perdith?" At his nod, she continued, "I believe I have found another victim, killed five years ago. I wish to see if the same tingle lingers in his remains."

Hugh flexed his arm. "Ah, you called upon me because of my ability with a shovel."

Sera laughed and wrapped her hand around the impressive bicep. "And because I enjoy your company." The moment of levity passed as she recalled Master Daniel's narration of events that night. "The attack on Mr Grove resulted in wounds similar to what we saw on Mr Perdith. He had long scratches on his right arm and right side. And there were chunks of flesh missing. His son said the beast... feasted upon his father."

"Poor lad. Did he say what did it?" Hugh hailed a hackney to take them to the other side of the Thames.

"From his description, it is not a lycanthrope, but some sort of large, winged cat. Like a flying panther." After she had examined what remained of Mr Grove, Sera would prepare for her afternoon interviews with possible mothers for Mr Perdith.

"A flying panther? That doesn't give the birds much of a chance." Hugh angled his body in the small conveyance, his knees pressing against Sera's.

"I've not read of such a thing, but Daniel was most insistent about what he saw. His father is buried in the churchyard of St George's. He shouldn't be too difficult to find, as his family regularly visits his grave." Sera peered out the window as they crossed the river. Hardy fishermen braved the cold temperature to catch what they needed for the day.

Pedestrians thinned as autumn took a firm hold of the city. Sera's task of finding the women underlined in the gazette became harder, as many nobles had left London once the season ended and would not be back until Easter. She might have to ask Lord Ormsby for leave to wander the countryside, visiting each noble estate to ask awkward questions as they prepared for Christmas festivities.

They hopped to the ground not far from the row of terraces where the Grove family lived, in a place where a church had stood since medieval times. Fifty years ago, when the old one had deteriorated beyond the point it could be repaired, the parish had raised the funds for a complete rebuild. Made of red brick with white details, the squat white base of the spire dominated the front portion. Sera didn't have much time for churches. Briefly she wondered if her father or any gargoyles had had a hand in the church's construction, but familial pride said if they had, it would have possessed better proportions.

They walked around the church to the graveyard at the rear to find the sexton. They found the man trimming a hedge with a pair of worn shears. When Sera advised him of the purpose of her visit, he shook his head and muttered about having enough work to do burying them, let alone digging them up again.

"Should you not wait until dark?" His entire face wrinkled in concern.

"I do not wish to alarm anyone, and will cloak the area in a spell to shield us from the public view. Nor do we require assistance. Mr Miles and I will complete the task as quickly, and discreetly, as possible."

Her assurances that she wouldn't create a public spectacle seemed to mollify him. "Very well, milady. You'll find him over there. Help yourself to a shovel from the shed." He waved towards a stand of old trees before returning to the yew hedge.

Sera slowed her pace as they walked among the gravestones and markers. Mr Grove had a modest headstone, slightly raised from the ground. *Beloved husband and father*, it read below the dates *1752 to 1783*. She asked his forgiveness for what they were about to do, then whispered a spell to encase them in a reflective sphere. Anyone who glanced in their direction would see only the trees, graves, and the shadow of the church.

"Let us make a start, then." Hugh took up the shovel and thrust it into the soil.

Mr Grove had been buried for five years and the ground had settled.

"I should have asked Nat to help. Her gargoyle form can dig a hole faster than my magic." Sera ignored the shovel and instead worked with Mother Nature. She loosened the earth and broke it up, to make it easier for Hugh to dig out.

Not that Sera exerted too much magic, as Hugh stripped off his overcoat, jacket, and then rolled up his shirtsleeves. She rather enjoyed watching the play of muscles in his broad back as he wielded the spade. Soon they had quite a pile beside the grave and Hugh's shovel made a thud as it hit the coffin.

He scraped off the dirt, exposing the timber. Then he climbed out and sat on the edge. Taking a moment to wipe his face with the tail of his shirt, he said, "Do you want me to crack it open?"

"No. I will do it." Sera used puffs of wind to blow excess earth from around the lid of the coffin. When the full length was revealed, she sent tendrils of magic to worm between lid and coffin and worked it upward until the nails popped free. Before she could contemplate how best to levitate the lid away from the bottom, Hugh jumped back down into the hole.

Easing his fingers under the head end, he walked

the lid upright and left it jutting up at the foot of the coffin. Sera covered her nose with a handkerchief at the pungent aroma that broke free of the ground. After five years, Mr Grove had lost the meat from his bones, but dried lengths of tendon were visible under his clothing and hair still clung to his scalp.

She reassessed her magical shield as a family wandered along the path. She didn't want a child to see the gruesome sight. Once certain they remained invisible to those visiting the interred, she took Hugh's hand and climbed into the hole beside him.

He shot her a worried look. "Will this work? I would have thought any magical trace would be long gone, even assuming it has the same cause as Mr Perdith's."

"I'm not expecting a result, but I have to be sure." The odd tingle from the recent victim still haunted her senses. Familiar, yet not. More frustrating still, she had no idea what caused it.

She knelt and, her gaze averted from the grinning skull, held out her hands over the torso. Closing her eyes, Sera let magic ripple downward over the corpse like a gentle spring rain. When she called it back to her, once again, a faint familiar tingle brushed over her palms.

Opening her eyes, she studied Mr Grove. "The residue is much fainter than what I sensed rising from Mr Perdith, but there is still a magical emission from Mr Grove. It is infuriating not to be able to identify the source of it."

What did it mean? A theory formed in her mind, one that linked the two men by magic. Or by a curse.

Hugh lifted a decomposing jacket and peered beneath. "His chest cavity is packed with sawdust, probably to mask the missing flesh. Surely what you sense cannot be in his blood or stomach contents, as both have long since dissolved. Could it be something lodged in his bones? Bone will endure far longer than tissue."

An idea flashed through her mind. "Do you think there is a small bone that Mr Grove would not miss? As a sort of contribution to finding his killer?"

Hugh arched one eyebrow, but said no more. He picked up the left hand that had turned skeletal and prised free the end segment of the little finger. "Would a distal phalange suffice?"

Sera held out her hand and Hugh placed a bone nearly an inch long on her palm. Closing her eyes, she concentrated on the item, and the familiar emission tickled her skin. "Yes. While only a trace, I can still feel it."

Once out of the hole, Sera extracted a cloth from her satchel and wrapped the bone with care. Mr Grove's donation to the solution of his murder would be given the respect it deserved.

Working together, they replaced the lid. While Hugh brushed dirt from his clothing and put on his waistcoat and jacket, Sera used waves of magic to rake the piles of dirt back into the grave. With each layer, she exerted magical pressure to solidify the covering.

Soon, they were left with bare earth with only a slight rise. To mask their recent activity, Sera murmured to nature and sprouted grass over the disturbed soil. While it didn't exactly match the surrounding lawn, it would pass all but the most careful inspection.

Only one piece of turf remained stubbornly out of place and ruined Sera's careful work. Thinking it needed a manual solution, and not a magical one, she jumped on it.

A man strode along the path and stopped to stare at them, his gaze taking in Hugh leaning on a shovel. Then he pointed a finger at Sera, stomping on the raised dirt. "You there! What do you think you are doing?"

Before Sera could respond, Hugh grabbed her hand and tugged her off the grave. "Quick. This way!"

They took off at a run across the lawn, the man yelling for them to stop. Laughter bubbled up in her chest. It was silly to run. They could have invented a tale for the stranger and they had the sexton's permission. But instead, they disappeared like a couple of fleeing resurrectionists who had been caught in the act in broad daylight. Hugh kept a tight grip on her hand as they raced along the paths and through the trees. Away from the churchyard, they sprinted down the road, only slowing their pace when pedestrians blocked their way.

They turned down a dim alleyway, and Hugh spun her towards him. They both breathed a little hard from the exertion and humour raced through Sera's veins. A part of her mind registered that she was having more fun running from a churchyard with the surgeon than she did skating under magical lanterns with an earl.

"I love you," Hugh murmured. He hardly needed to say the words—they shone in his eyes and embodied every action he took.

Sera rested her hands on his shoulders. "I know." Then she kissed him, pulling him into the shadows until her back hit the cool, solid brick. Another, but much warmer, solid surface pressed on her chest.

This was where she longed to be. Having adventures, defying expectations, and kissing a man who loved her with all he had, and who would support her without question. Yet, at the same time, he challenged her to become a better person. Not to mention the trace of gargoyle blood in his veins that gave him a slight immunity from the worst of her temper.

When Sera gazed five, ten, or twenty years into the future, she saw only Hugh at her side. Not a nice noble with a tea plantation. But how to make it happen when king and council would oppose any such match?

She let out a sigh. How to make the impossible possible?

Hugh pulled back and framed her face with his large hands. "Is anything amiss? I didn't realise my declaration would so distract you."

She traced his bottom lip with her thumb. "Why can't we run away and leave London far behind? To cross the hot plains of Africa, or explore the lush jungles of India without Lord Ormsby *tsk*ing under his breath and scrutinising my every action."

He placed a kiss on the side of her neck. "Because Nature gave you a great gift, and with that comes a certain responsibility. As much as I love you, I'm not sure I could walk away from my duties as a surgeon. Although I suppose even in Africa and India they need doctors."

Now there was a way of thinking about her gift that hadn't occurred to her before. Nature had made her a mage to serve the people, but who said she could serve only in England? What would happen if she boarded a ship and sailed for France... or America?

SEVENTEEN

With a few hours to fill before Abigail would let them make their calls on those women who remained in London, Sera decided to journey out to mage tower. As she rounded a stack in the hidden library, she came upon Lord Pendlebury peering at a shelf.

"Lord Pendlebury! I thought you had left us for Scotland?" From what she recollected, he had been tasked to investigate some aquatic creature inhabiting a loch.

"Good day, Lady Winyard. I have had to postpone my departure. I am still trying to research what exactly might be plaguing the locals. It would greatly help if they could at least agree on what the thing looked like. Some say it is long and sinuous, others that it has a squat body." He straightened and pushed a book back into place.

"I have a similar issue trying to find what stalks

Southwark. The eyewitness descriptions I have gathered do not seem to indicate a lycanthrope is responsible. I have spent some time here, trying to match what details I have to some other beast." As they spoke, the title on a spine caught her eye and she tugged free a book about the role of large cats in myth and legend.

"Did our remembrance spell assist with finding other witnesses?" Lord Pendlebury plucked a volume for himself, scanned the first page, and then thrust it back into its spot.

She clasped the book on large cats to her chest. "The spell worked remarkably well. Thank you for the suggestion. It brought to light a similar case from five years ago. I am formulating a theory that something magical connects the two victims."

"You think the assailant is magical rather than Unnatural?" A curious glint lit his friendly grey eyes.

"Yes. Both men's remains emitted a very faint magical trace. I don't know how it might have come to be there. It is almost as though it resided in their bones. Is such a thing possible?"

At first, Kitty had suggested Mr Perdith might have eaten food prepared by an aftermage with a touch of wizardry, or come in contact with a magical device. But that would not account for the same tingle rising from Mr Grove. Five years in the ground would have washed away anything in his stomach or that had brushed against his skin. The finger bone Hugh had removed for her tended to confirm that whatever was responsible resided within the porous material.

Lord Pendlebury rested one elbow on a shelf and stroked his smooth chin. "Was either man an aftermage?"

That idea had rolled through her mind, but she didn't know if any trace of magic remained after death in mages or aftermages. Perhaps she should ask Hugh to accompany her to dig up a few mages and conduct their own study on that. Or she could just ask, which wouldn't be as much fun, but would deliver an answer faster.

"Do you know if magic lingers after we have passed? I've not been near a recently deceased mage or aftermage."

"On that, I can satisfy your curiosity. Yes, surprisingly, the remains of a mage will continue to release a faint trace of magic even though their power has passed to a new form. As to aftermages, I believe a trace is almost indiscernible to any but the strongest amongst us." His gaze wandered off to the left, and then he gestured with one hand. "There is a book in our history section that explores several theories about why our magic remains detectable. The author believes that a shadow or echo of magic remains in these earthly vessels, even after the source of our power is transferred to a newborn."

Blast. That might indeed account for the faint tendril that tickled against her palm. Although that raised another issue—if both victims were aftermages, had the assailant targeted them for what flavoured their blood and flesh, rather than for their parentage?

"I haven't been able to discover whether either man possessed gifts. Both were foundlings and did not know the identity of their parents. But from what their friends and family said, neither exhibited any after-mage traits."

"Is it not unusual for some aftermages to keep their gifts secret. Or they might have been so many genera-tions removed and with such a slight trace that they didn't recognise any particular ability as coming from a mage ancestor. If they were aftermages, the mage genealogies will hold such information. Not that the book is much help without knowing their parentage. You would have many generations to search. You might be ensconced in the library for some weeks and unable to prowl the poorer suburbs in the evening." He huffed a quiet laugh, probably imagining how pleased Lord Ormsby would be if she were engaged in study and off the streets.

If either man were a sixth- or seventh-generation aftermage, she could just imagine all the offspring of each generation to search. The tight script of the book formed a dense spiderweb of names in her mind. She could start with the volume that covered 1753, the year Horatio Valentine was born. But the problem was, she didn't know if he was an aftermage, what generation, or who his trace flowed from. She couldn't afford to lose that much time on what might possibly be a fruitless endeavour.

But the more she thought about it, the more she doubted either man had magic flowing in their veins. A certainty dwelt within her that whatever she felt came from their bones. "I doubt searching the genealogies could be any worse than reading all those reports. I feel sorry for the poor scribes who had to write them all down. They must have had numb fingers by the end of the week."

"They did work in shifts." He winked, then with a satisfied noise, pulled a book free. When he waved it at her, the title read *Kelpie or Hippocanthus: A Guide to Aquatic Creatures*. Then he nodded, about to take his leave.

"Lord Pendlebury," she called, beckoning him back. "When we created the remembrance spell together, did you notice anything... odd... about my magic?" The murmured comment from Lord Rowan festered in the back of her mind.

A frown pulled his eyebrows closer together. "Odd? In what way? I find you a most capable mage. There is something very fluid and intuitive about the way you wield your power."

She didn't want to say outright that Lord Rowan considered her magic tainted. It might simply have been a comment thrown in frustration at her refusal to bend to his commands. "Do you remember Lord Dewlap?"

His frown deepened. "Only slightly. He had withdrawn from public life while I was still a lad. I understand he was quite ill in his last years. Why do you ask?"

She clutched the book on large cats tighter to her

chest, unsure what to say. It could be nothing, or it could be something. "I recently worked an enchantment with Lord Rowan to freeze the round pond in Hyde Park. He made a comment about Dewlap's *shadow* having settled over me and that it affected my magic. I wondered what he meant by that."

Lord Pendlebury stilled and pursed his lips. "I only ever met him twice, and as a youngster at the time, I was never privy to any high-level discussions of anything concerning him, so have only my speculations to offer. I believe there were... whispers... that Lord Dewlap did not always follow the code laid down by the council."

Sera bit back a snort. If Lord Rowan meant that Dewlap ignored their rules, then that *taint* most certainly ran in her veins, too. She was guided by her own principles—especially when the edicts of the council either made no sense or were designed solely to hamper her. That might be what Lord Rowan meant— that like the previous vessel containing her line of magic, they both operated somewhat independently from the council.

"So your curiosity never scratched at those whispers to find out what lay behind them?" she asked.

He tapped one finger against the cover of the book in his hands. "I think in many ways we mages are like chickens."

"Chickens?" Laughter welled up in Sera at the mental image of twelve fowl around the council chamber table. Lord Ormsby would be a grumpy rooster with ruffled feathers and a comb at a distinct tilt.

Lord Pendlebury nodded with enthusiasm for his analogy. "With only twelve of us in this coop, we all like to know where we are in the pecking order. We size each other up, stamp, and ruffle a few feathers to find our place each time a mage comes of age."

She had certainly ruffled Lord Tomlin's feathers and placed herself higher than he in her mental order. "You wanted to take Lord Dewlap's measure when you reached your majority."

He nodded. "I was eighteen and convinced I was the greatest mage ever to walk this earth. I was mistaken, of course." A wry smile crossed his lips, and his eyes became unfocused as he stared at the ceiling.

Sera wondered what event stirred in his memory. Had an arrogant youngster overreached and learned his boundaries in spectacular fashion? Somehow she struggled to see the calm and in control Lord Pendlebury doing anything rash. Or he might have suffered such a harsh lesson that he remembered it for the rest of his life.

"I wanted to gauge the extent of Lord Dewlap's magic, although I was certain I was more powerful. At every opportunity I tried to find a reason to descend upon his country bolthole. Then one day, Lord Rowan pulled me aside and told to leave him in his isolation— that I didn't want to meddle with his sort."

His sort. How familiar that phrase was to her. "What did he mean?"

He coughed and cleared his throat, as though the words he tried to say tasted foul and wouldn't make their way out. "There was the faintest whisper about dark magic, Lady Winyard. That Lord Dewlap performed rites and castings that were forbidden. Nothing was ever said in the council, nor was there ever any proof. I suspect Lord Rowan referenced those rumours when he mentioned a *shadow* having settled over you. Although, I would hasten to add, I sensed no such thing when we worked together."

His words did little to reassure her, but she took what comfort she could from them. "The previous vessel to hold my magic may have dabbled in dark magic, and now I have chosen the persona of Nyx. By doing so, I may have confirmed those long-ago rumours that our vein of magic is laced with the depth of night."

His expression lightened, though a hint of concern remained in his eyes. "But as you often remind us, Nyx is not evil. Just as light is not inherently good. How many people have been killed in Holy Crusades, all in the name of God? That one always perplexes me. How can any supposedly peaceful and loving religion condone the slaughter of others?"

Hugh had once warned her that she walked a dangerous line to openly embrace the goddess of the night, and ran the risk that people would come to fear her. "Odd that Lord Branvale never mentioned any such taint in Lord Dewlap. I can imagine him taking delight in telling me my line was fouled."

"Or he never knew. I am sorry I mentioned it now.

210

It was a most tantalising rumour to a young mage. How I longed for Lord Dewlap to storm into the council chambers one day and do something—I don't know—forbidden. But he died not long after, and I never got to see any grand showdown across our table." His shy smile returned for a moment, then he dropped his gaze.

If Sera had heard that one of their kind engaged in dark magic, she would share a similar curiosity to see how it differed from a normal casting. "Lord Dewlap did do something forbidden in the end—he passed his magic to me. A woman now sits in the chamber."

Lord Pendlebury barked a quick laugh. "Ha! An excellent point. Now, if you have no more need of me, having found what I need, I can depart for my Highland adventure. I wish you luck, Lady Winyard, in tracking down your monster."

She murmured her good-byes, then took her book to the reading table. Flicking through the pages, she concentrated on the pictures, hoping one that fit the description given by young Daniel Grove would leap off the page at her.

None of the cats were winged, nor did they hunt heavily inhabited regions. When the clock struck twelve, she abandoned her fruitless research. There remained enough time to return home to change for the afternoon visits.

On the stroke of two, Sera waited near a front window for Lady Abigail to collect her in the Crawley family carriage. Her friend hoped the crest on the side would be their entrée into many a parlour that afternoon. Only a handful of people on the list remained in London. The rest had already departed for their country homes. Abigail absolutely refused to let Sera visit unaccompanied or with Kitty. Her friend was terrified of some imagined *faux pas* Sera might commit, so she insisted on being present for every visit.

At their first call, Abigail handed over both their cards. They stood in the foyer while the butler hurried to present them to the mistress to see if she was *at home* to them.

Either curiosity or etiquette made Lady Delamere remember she was in the parlour and available to visitors. The butler gestured for them to follow.

"Best behaviour, Seraphina," Abigail whispered as they were announced.

After the introductions, curtsies, and social niceties, the older woman turned a curious eye upon Sera. "I admit I am mystified as to the reason for your visit. I do not believe we are acquainted."

"I am investigating two deaths and believe they may be related to certain events some thirty-five years ago." Sera edged around the topic, mindful of Abigail's watchful gaze.

The noblewoman chuckled and leaned back on the settee. "Well, I would only have been a young woman then. Why, that is even before I married his lordship."

"Both victims had been given up by their mothers, and I am trying to identify the latter." At a startled gasp from her friend, Sera hurried to add, "Do you recollect if perhaps a maid in your household might have left after finding herself in such a condition?"

Lady Delamere shook her head and pressed one hand to her chest. "Goodness, not under our roof. Father would never have tolerated such scandalous conduct among our servants."

While they chatted, Sera let her magic ripple through the house, trying to find anything that resonated with the tingle she'd found on both corpses. Then she slipped a hand into her reticule and pulled out one of Mr Perdith's drawings. "This is the token left with one child at the Foundling Hospital. Do you recognise the work?"

Sera kept her attention on the older woman, watching for any reaction to the sketch. The only impression she received from Lady Delamere was one of perplexity and some boredom. Sensing the conversation wouldn't bear fruit, Sera rose and thanked the woman for her time.

Out in the carriage, Abigail glared at her. "How could you be so rude? A call lasts a quarter of an hour, Seraphina. Honestly, all this running around at night is turning you quite cross."

"Lady Delamere didn't react, and at this point, I do not think she knows anything. We still have nine other women to call upon while they are still in London. I cannot afford to waste time chatting about balls I never attended."

Abigail's gaze hardened. "If you attended the

events that your status dictates you patronise, you would have more to contribute to the conversation."

Sera bit back a retort. She couldn't imagine a more pointless existence than to attend boring social events with narrow-minded nobles, unless it was to be forced to talk about them afterwards.

"Really, Seraphina, this is the world you inhabit. You will simply have to bend to society's rules." Abigail tapped on the roof for the carriage to move on to their next call.

"I will not bend," she murmured. Why was it that lately she was clashing more than ever with Abigail?

"Then you will break. And you will have only yourself to blame."

A frosty atmosphere descended over them and before she said something she couldn't take back, Sera turned to study the pedestrians out the window.

EIGHTEEN

They managed three more visits in quick succession (with no reaction to either questions or fabric) before they returned to the Crawley family home. One person on Sera's list had married well and become a duchess. Since the Featherstones had a town house across the square in Mayfair from that of the Crawleys, Abigail deemed it acceptable to walk. One of the Crawley footmen would walk behind to accompany them home again, when an early twilight descended on the city.

They stepped out the front door and glanced heavenward. The clouds darkened and a misty drizzle fell. Sera crafted an umbrella above their heads and, once warm and dry in their cocoon, they linked arms for the short walk through the park.

"Remember, she is a duchess, Seraphina," Abigail murmured as the Featherstone butler opened the glossy black door.

"So am I," she murmured in reply. "And I can do magic."

Abigail handed over their visiting cards and whispered in the butler's ear that their visit was of a discreet nature. When he returned from consulting with his mistress, he showed them through to an elegant parlour decorated in cream and gold, with an accent in the drapes of a deep yellow that bordered on orange. Abigail curtseyed and Sera inclined her head politely.

"Thank you for seeing us, your grace," Abigail said on rising.

The duchess was in her mid-fifties, with fine lines radiating from around her eyes. Her hair was powdered a pale cream to match the room and was piled high in the current fashion. Lady Featherstone had maintained her youthful figure and made an elegant impression. Or perhaps she had more practice at being a duchess and over the years, poise had seeped into her very bones.

"Yours was an unusual request, Lady Abigail, that aroused my curiosity. While I am friendly with your mother, I have little to do with young people."

The duchess invited them to sit, but there was no offer of tea. Since the subtle clues indicated they were not to stay long, Sera thought she may as well jump straight in. In as polite a fashion as she could manage.

"I am investigating a death that occurred on the south bank, Lady Featherstone. It seems the man was a foundling and held a belief that his mother had some long-ago association with a noble family." Sera reached into her reticule for the sketch.

"It is possible his mother worked in your parents' household some thirty-five years ago, before you were wed. A kitchen maid, perhaps, who might have got herself into trouble," Abigail added.

Sera passed over the sketch. "Do you recognise this drawing? It is the strip of fabric his mother left with the baby boy. We suspect the pieces of fabric stitched together by the mother reflect a particular set of heraldic arms."

Lady Featherstone stared at the sheet of paper for a long time, and a slight tremble ran through her wrist to her hand. Then she drew a deep breath. "No." She thrust the paper back at Sera. "Why are you trying to find this unfortunate woman? Surely you do not think she had anything to do with the death of the man?"

Sera took the paper and tried to hold back her frustration. "I am trying to find any clues as to why he met his fate. No one deserved to die in such circumstances, which you may have heard were violent. Indeed, there are now two men who met a similar horrid death. Neither knew their mothers and I suspect something connected them. Something magical."

The duchess glanced at her hands and twisted her wedding ring. "Well, many children are given up every day in London. I understand the Foundling Hospital is practically overrun with them. Sadly, finding oneself in the family way, unwed and alone, is hardly a remarkable thing in this city."

"As you say, many women find themselves in such a situation. No woman, whatever her circumstances or station, should have to give up her child simply because she conceives and the father refuses responsibility." Even more ridiculous that a noble woman was considered *ruined* because of a man's behaviour. Sera's palms itched as magic pooled beneath her skin. How she would love to mete out a little justice to a few such bucks, who had their fun and left destruction in their wake.

The duchess huffed. "It is all well and good to hold these ideals, but they seldom do much to help a woman in distress. Particularly if, because of expectations upon her, she—" Lady Featherstone broke off as two spaniels ran into the room and rushed to her. One jumped onto the sofa beside her and she stroked a silken ear.

"Horace! Valentina! Where are you, you naughty dogs?" a voice called from the hall.

Horace? Valentina? It could be no coincidence. Not with such a similarity to the names scrawled at the bottom of the sketch. Sera turned to the duchess and arched an eyebrow, waiting for the admission that would surely flow from her lips. The woman was obviously feigning that she knew nothing.

A young woman in a dark grey gown covered in a white apron appeared in the doorway and froze. "I am sorry, your grace, they got away from me and I did not realise you had company."

"It's no bother, Penelope. My guests were just leaving." The duchess rose and Abigail jumped to her feet.

Sera stood more slowly and wondered if she could

fling out an arm and shout *liar!* Would that be a breach of etiquette?

"Thank you for your time, Lady Featherstone." Abigail dipped at the knees.

"Yes, thank you. It was charming to meet Horace and Valentina. I am sure I have read similar names somewhere else, fairly recently." Sera tapped the folded sketch against her chin and then glanced from the two spaniels to the duchess. Would she now say what had happened when the drawing had appeared in her daily mail, sent by Mr Perdith?

A frosty stillness descended over the duchess's features. "Penelope will show you out. I seem to have developed a headache." With that, she glided from the room without a backward glance.

Sera's feet were stuck to the carpet. There might be evidence in the parlour, or Lady Featherstone's study, that would connect her to Harvey Perdith. Unless the duchess had thrown the drawing upon the fire. The writing desk in one corner of the room caught her attention, but as she made a move in that direction, Abigail took her arm.

"Come along with me, Lady Winyard. It is dark outside, and the rain has begun to fall." Abigail escorted Sera from the parlour.

Outside, the Crawley footman waited for them. Sera cast the protective bubble around them all for the walk back across the square. She cast one last look at the house, to find the duchess at an upstairs window, staring down at her.

"She's lying," Sera said, hoping the duchess could read the words on her lips. Certainty that she had found Mr Perdith's mother took up residence inside her. When the duchess had taken the drawing, her hand had trembled. And she had called her dogs by names nearly identical to those given her son long ago.

"If she were indeed the mother, can you blame her for maintaining her silence? She has much to lose and nothing to gain. For all you know, this man might have been trying to extort money from her." Abigail set a brisk pace as the weather continued to deteriorate.

"Even if he had, did he deserve to be murdered?" The *how* bothered Sera. No human assailant had taken Harvey Perdith's life. What creature did the duchess have at her beck and call? A loyal shifter, who perhaps served tea or answered the door when not needed in winged cat form? But what offence had Mr Grove committed against the Featherstones? Sera could not see any connection between the late printer and the noble family.

"Promise me you won't do anything rash. I can ask Mother to call upon her in a few days," Abigail said as they reached her home.

"I promise." Sera crossed her fingers behind her back as she spoke. She would allow the duchess a few days to stew upon their visit. Possibly, one did not admit during an afternoon social call a matter as serious as a child born out of wedlock and given up.

"It is quite horrid how Lord Ormsby has you, a woman both young and unmarried, investigating such inappropriate crimes. But all that will change shortly." In the foyer, Abigail shook off her cloak and let it drop. The quick-thinking maid scooped it up before it touched the tiles.

"What do you mean?" Sera's mind was occupied, thinking of how to lure the duchess into an admission of the truth, making her slow to grasp the change of topic.

"Why, once you are married to the earl, the council will assign you tasks more in keeping with your station and situation. I thought garden parties would utilise both your interest in horticulture and your ability to entertain society." Abigail drifted towards the parlour.

Sera snorted and rolled her eyes as she followed her friend. "I'm sure the earl will decide against such a rash course of action once he considers my many faults."

Abigail seated herself close to the fire. "I have it on the best authority that he intends to propose before he leaves shortly for his country estate. Given the ruinous conduct in which you insist on engaging, I do not see any point to a long engagement. Don't you think a late winter wedding would be rather pretty? Then, once you are wed, you may be my matron of honour! Oh, how marvellous everything will be!" Excitement bubbled in Abigail's words.

Sera's limbs froze as she dropped into a chair opposite. "He intends to propose?" The words rasped from her dry throat.

How could he have reached such a conclusion already? It was too soon. She had thought to follow the example of Queen Elizabeth and keep potential suitors circling hopefully around her while she dithered for years. Decades, even.

Her friend gasped and covered her mouth, then lowered her hand. "I had promised not to say a word, but I can't see any harm in telling you in advance. Now you have time to consider an effusive acceptance, for it is the most perfect match. The earl has such a lovely townhouse not too far from here, and his staff are impeccable. You will be able to fire that horrid footman. He always looks like he's come in late from a night at the pub, and has a most insolent way of speaking." Abigail shuddered and pursed her lips.

Move out of her little house? Fire Elliot, to say nothing of the others? It had never occurred to Sera that marriage could so alter her life. "I do not see any great need to rush into matrimony. I had thought to get to know Lord Thornton better, before any proposal was made or needed to be considered."

"How much time do you need, Sera? You have had your fun, scandalised society, and defied king and council by refusing to accept the wisdom of a guardian. It is time to grow up and accept the responsibilities of your position." Abigail turned to stare at the flames.

Grow up? Sera dug her nails into her palms to stop her from blurting out some hurtful truths to her friend. "I have been confined and controlled my entire life, Abigail. It has been only a few short months since I threw off Lord Branvale's shackles and stepped into my rightful place in the world. I had not thought to marry for some years, if at all."

Abigail turned and narrowed her gaze. "You think this a game, to thumb your nose at society. But you do not understand that we must all abide by the rules, Seraphina. That is how we maintain order."

An argument surged up her throat—it was society that needed to change. It was no one's business to whom she decided to give her heart. But one look at the tight set of her friend's shoulders and the pursed lips made the harsh words wither on Sera's tongue. On this matter, she and Abigail stood on opposite sides of a wide chasm. While they had both been raised in captivity and groomed to obey, Abigail had moulded herself into the expected shape. Whereas Sera had torn the door off her cage and flown free with no intention of ever being captured again.

Mr Napier had taught Sera that there were times to pursue an argument, and times to leave it alone. She was not willing to sacrifice her friendship with Abigail for this one.

"I am sorry, Abigail. I admit that hearing Lord Thornton intends to propose shocked me. You are right. I need time to consider his generous offer and to prepare my response. It was kind and thoughtful of you to give me notice." She rose and moved to her friend to say good-bye, waving her back down when she would have risen from her cosy spot before the fire.

Mollified by the apology, Abigail took Sera's hands and squeezed. "While you're a duchess in your own right, you will gain legitimacy in society by taking his title on your marriage. Not that it should bother you, given the circumstances of your birth, but some have muttered you aren't a real duchess. When you become a real countess, no one may deny it. Do notify me the instant he comes to call." She winked and indicated the mage silver ring on her finger.

Sera returned home in a daze, her thoughts swirling in a multitude of directions at once and picking up debris like a small tornado blasting through a forest.

"Any plans for tonight?" Elliot asked as he held the door open for her.

"Yes. We're going out after supper." She could have stayed at home, curled up in the parlour, and spent time thinking about what to say to the earl. But that wouldn't be a productive use of her time. Besides, she needed a distraction. The idea of upending her life for a man she didn't love filled her with dread. If she were honest with herself, Sera needed to find a fight to release the pent-up frustration rushing through her veins.

Once again, Sera changed into her long coat that hugged her torso and was open at the front to reveal her breeches and boots. When she did up the silver buttons, it felt as though she donned the night goddess's persona. A sense of calm filtered through her limbs and settled her turbulent thoughts.

Elliot waited at the bottom of the stairs, a mischievous gleam in his eyes. "I'm glad I let you hire me. I'm good at this job—sitting in a pub and drinking."

Elliot might be impertinent, and he refused to wear livery anymore, but he was someone she trusted with her life. Besides, she enjoyed his company. Not that Sera would ever admit it to him.

Instead, she swatted him in the stomach on her way past. "Remember, you are not to drink too much. I might need you. Plus, I think all that beer makes a man run to fat."

"You know just where to cut a fellow," he complained as they left the house.

Sera had asked Kitty if she could examine the ensorcelled ring she'd used to remove the alcohol from ale and had crafted a similar item for herself and Elliot. Utilising the spell enabled them to fit in better among other patrons and not draw attention to themselves by failing to spend coin at the bar. Everyone looked with suspicion upon the person drinking water in a tavern, especially when water was notorious for making people ill.

They spent a rowdy couple of hours in first one tavern, then another. Sera kept her ears open for whispers of trouble or for anyone who had known either of the deceased men. Then she decided to prowl the streets with Elliot at her side. Darkness wrapped the district in inky velvet. There were fewer street lamps here, unlike the better lit, wealthier enclaves. Even what light escaped from behind tightly drawn curtains seemed of a lesser quality.

"You're going to get us killed," Elliot muttered as he breathed into his clasped palms to warm them.

"I will find another pair of eyes." Sera closed hers and reached out across London, looking for a particular kind of helper who had accompanied her before.

"Are you doing something, or should I be looking for smoke coming from your ears?" Elliot muttered.

Sera hushed him. "Give it a few minutes to work."

Soon a rustling came from above and a large black bird swooped down to perch upon Sera's outstretched arm. It uttered a single hoarse cry and peered at her.

Elliot pointed to the bird. "That's a raven, not a crow, and no relative of mine."

"There are a number of these intelligent creatures living at the Tower of London. I simply asked if one could assist. The others are tucked up asleep, but this one was willing to join us. She will fly overhead and alert me to any... situations." Sera crooned to the bird and stroked its breast, giving thanks for its time while its fellow ravens slept at the Tower.

The large corvid croaked, then took flight. Its wings stirred the mist as it kept pace above them, hopping from building to building.

Elliot stared at her, then winked. "You've figured out who you are, haven't you?"

Sera considered his words and glanced at the raven. "Yes. I'm the terrifying night witch, who protects those she cares about."

Nineteen

The next morning, after an uneventful night, Sera set off to talk to Kitty about a number of things. First was how to tackle a deceptive duchess. The second was more personal. As much as she loved Abigail, her friend was prejudiced towards the Earl of Thornton because he was noble. She assumed that Sera secretly pined for a husband, as she had, or like any other young woman.

There was much to gain by securing a well-placed husband. Even Sera could see that. But there was also much to lose. Kitty would objectively work through the advantages and disadvantages of such a match.

In the Napier parlour, and in a move that would have horrified Abigail, Sera pulled off her shoes and tucked her feet under her. The footman handed her a hot chocolate, and she leaned on the rolled arm of the chaise as she discussed her case with Kitty. "The duchess lied. I am absolutely certain she is the mother of Harvey Perdith. That is why he thought his fortunes were about to change. His mother is wife to one of the highest peers in the land. Abigail thinks he tried to blackmail her, but that doesn't matter now. I want to know what she did after receiving the sketch and any accompanying letter. We must find out whether she instructed some creature to permanently silence the poor man."

If the duchess had pursued such a course, it was more likely blackmail had been involved. Mr Perdith might have said he would turn up at some social occasion and announce himself as her illegitimate child, unless she paid him off.

Kitty took the armchair opposite and settled on the brocade seat. Her shoes remained on her feet, which were evenly placed on the floor. "Even if we assume she ordered his death, that does not explain how Mr Grove met his end five years ago. The Duchess of Featherstone could not have been involved in that as well—unless you wish to posit that she bore twins and had them separated at birth. Then, independent of each other, both men tracked her down and wanted a slice of the duke's fortune?"

Sera considered the idea for a moment. It would be most convenient if the duchess had birthed twins. But from what she'd seen of the remains of both men, they did not appear to have been of similar stature or build. Not that all twins were identical. But she agreed that revenge-seeking twins was rather an improbable stretch of the imagination.

"If not twins, then perhaps two noblewomen had access to an Unnatural assassin? The greater a woman's position and finances, the more likely it is that she can access magical solutions to her problems. Perhaps such intelligence is whispered one to another behind their fans."

"I've attended many a social gathering and can assure you that nothing close to intelligence is whispered by those women. You are also overlooking the fact that Mr Grove never sought to find his mother. Indeed, he seemed content with his life. Why would his noble mother need to employ a beastly murderer when he was no threat to her?" Kitty seemed to enjoy picking holes in Sera's arguments. "By the way, Master Daniel Grove visited my father's offices the day after our visit. Father is most pleased with him. He's a smart and capable lad and will go a long way in the profession, should he wish it."

The news made Sera smile into her cup. There was one small glimmer of hope in the horrible situation. "I am glad he has a chance at a better life. Returning to possible mothers, I still have more names on my list. The problem is that most of them have already left town. While I know the duchess is the mother of Mr Perdith, I wonder if the woman who gave birth to Mr Grove might be among those who have gone. Some event five years ago must have triggered his death."

"It would be a remote possibility if her name was on your list. Even if she were a noblewoman, we do not know if she even appeared in the gazette, let alone whether her family crest shared any common elements with that of Lady Featherstone." Kitty sipped her drink.

Sera wanted to throw up her arms in frustration. There was still one person she wanted to talk to—Miss Pearson. Her curiosity about the woman who had removed herself from society thirty-five years ago had less to do with the case, though, and more with how the spinster had withstood the constant pressure society exerted on women to marry. Miss Pearson might have some valuable counsel to impart about how to weather the oncoming storm of censure awaiting Sera should she take the course of action she wanted most.

"There is also a magical resonance that clings to the remains of both men," Sera mused aloud. "It seems familiar to me for some reason. A tickle at the base of my neck leads me to believe it is what connects these men to each other and who—or what—killed them."

"Can you discern the source of the magic from the remains?" Kitty asked.

"In time. It is a slow process to tease out the ensorcellment responsible." Sera told her friend how Hugh had removed a finger bone and presented it to her. Kitty replied that most men gave women flowers or chocolates, not bone fragments prised from skeletons.

She sipped her chocolate, needing to move the conversation in a different direction. "While we are alone, I need your advice about a... delicate matter. And I want you to be utterly objective. Please do not let your personal opinions sway your counsel."

"Oh, now I am intrigued." A keen glint sparkled in Kitty's eyes. "Start at the beginning. I shall weigh in with any pertinent questions and deliver my verdict at the end."

Sera floated her empty cup towards the low table between them, then drew up her knees to her chest, and laced her hands around them. "Abigail informs me that I will shortly receive an offer of marriage from Lord Thornton. I am urged most strenuously to accept it. I have to admit that, on the face of it, he is a good match."

Kitty stared at her for a long, unblinking moment. Then her friend pursed her lips. "Lord Thornton? Not Hugh?"

"Hugh has already said he does not dare aim so high as to ever ask for my hand." Sera locked her hands together more tightly, trying to contain the sparks rippling over her skin as she thought of Hugh. If he did pose the question, how would she respond? Warmth flowed through her at the thought of being wedded to the surgeon.

Odd that the idea of his attic room appealed more than the fact of a large country estate. As well, Hugh wouldn't make her move from her comfortable Soho home or fire her staff.

Kitty arched one brow and made a noise in the back of her throat. "If there is to be no offer from Hugh, then you are right. The earl is an excellent match. He possesses a fortune, a title, and an education. I have not heard any rumours that he beats his servants, nor does he appear to have any excesses of drinking or gambling that would give you pause."

Sera's shoulders slumped. If Kitty agreed with Abigail, then her becoming Lady Thornton was inevitable.

"But what do you know of his politics?" Kitty leaned forward in her chair.

"Why, he—um—" Sera replayed each conversation she had had with the earl. They discussed tea, gardening, literature, music. But not one word about politics. "I am sure he shares our views. He told me that he funds a school in the village near his estate."

One eyebrow arched high. "What do you know of his views on suffrage for all? Or a system to care for the most vulnerable in our society? Or the redistribution of property? For that matter, on a more basic level still, is he Whig or Tory?"

Sera now understood how a witness on the stand felt when the prosecution fired questions at them. A worry itched at her. Everything her friend asked led to some conclusion, but she couldn't yet discern what. "You must speak plainly, Kitty, please. This is my future, and once a decision is made, it cannot be undone."

Kitty leaned back in the chair and rapped her fingers against the arm. "Arwyn Fitzfey murmurs in my ear that Thornton belongs to a group, led by the Duke of Harden, who are most intent on keeping power and property in the hands of the upper echelon. His philanthropic work to educate his villagers is only because it benefits him, producing a higher quality worker for his estate and businesses. Likewise, he believes a woman should be able to read, write, and do arithmetic, but only so she can keep house more efficiently and balance the household budget."

Sera squirmed. "The night we went skating, I asked whom he supported for the Regency, and he changed the subject. But how reliable is Arwyn, Kitty? I could likewise caution you about him. His politics are extreme. If not for his gentle nature, I suspect he would happily depose his father, round up the aristocracy, and imprison the lot."

"I admit that for the son of two monarchs, he is quite the revolutionary at heart. I am fully aware that his opinions cause alarm among many in society. But my point is, Arwyn is open about his politics and his desire to see all men treated as equal. Is the earl also open about his opinions on the topics we both hold close to our hearts? If he cannot talk freely to you about something as commonly discussed as the Regency, what other conversations might he also keep secret? I could not wish my dearest friend wedded to a man who kept a large, and important, part of himself locked away." Kitty rose and poured more hot chocolate from the silver pot being kept warm over a magical blue flame. She handed Sera her cup and then joined her on the chaise with her own.

Sera managed a sip as she considered Kitty's words. "I admit to knowing very little of what he believes. But perhaps he simply does not discuss such things outside of his home, or with those he does not know intimately?"

That raised another question—did she want to marry the man and only learn whether their views were compatible after the wedding? They needed to at least broach the topic before she accepted any proposal.

Another face rose before her, one with warm hazel eyes and lips she longed to kiss. A man with strong arms who ran towards adventure beside her. Someone who never held back his opinions, but who discussed everything with an open mind and heart. In that moment, the certainty burrowed into her bones that her heart belonged to Hugh.

Sera tugged on the chain around her neck and held the misshapen silver kiss that dangled close to her skin. Tears misted her eyes, and she wiped them away with the back of one hand.

"Abigail insists that I accept the earl, but I love Hugh." It was the first time she'd said the words out loud, and they tasted sweet on her tongue.

Kitty patted her knee. "Well, of course you love him. I have known that for some time—I am relieved to hear you finally acknowledge it. But you must engage your mind on the subject, Sera. Just as you can have a marriage without love, so too can you love someone without marriage."

Sera followed her friend's line of thought. "Do you think I should marry, or not marry, Hugh?"

"Neither king nor council will let you marry the man of your choice. But they cannot dictate whom you love. Will you really let a bunch of crusty old men steal all the joy from your life?" Kitty's keen gaze peered at Sera over her cup.

Let men meddle in every aspect of her life? A snort burst from Sera's throat. "Of course not."

But could she truly love Hugh with every part of her, outside the sanctity of marriage? Imagine the scandal. Abigail would swoon and it would likely be the end of their friendship. Lord Branvale had fathered children without marrying their mother, even after his original match had been erased by Lord Rowan. Many mages chose not to marry, but they all had one thing in common: their gender.

"I'm not saying it would be an easy path. You would be heavily sanctioned by society. But I don't think you have ever shied away from what is difficult in life," Kitty murmured.

Sera sipped her hot chocolate in silence. Having made her declaration, even if only to Kitty, decisions locked into place in her mind with the rigidity of a stone wall built by gargoyles. She thrust her cup at Kitty and stood.

"Where are you going?" Kitty enquired.

"To find Hugh." As she left the parlour, the tinkle of laughter followed her.

Sera couldn't wait for a carriage, despite the gloom of the day. Instead, she strode along the pavement, intent on her destination. Occasionally she stopped to perform small acts for those on the street who had hailed her. To fix holes in a child's boots. To repair a broken wheel on a barrow. To move a heavy crate for an old woman. It took her some hours to reach the building where Hugh lodged and climb the stairs to his attic room.

Only to find it empty.

Even the potatoes were gone, the temperature was too cold for them to grow. Idly, Sera dug her hand into the soil and found the seed spuds nestled under the earthy blanket, waiting for warmer weather to sprout once more. She spun a cloche from the air, to protect the vegetables from the chill radiating off the window and to create an environment that would see them flourish.

With nothing more to do, she stretched out on the oversized settee and closed her eyes. Peace enveloped her, and she surrendered her tired mind and body to sleep. Darkness had fallen outside when a soft tread awoke her.

Hugh knelt by the settee and took her hand, kissing her knuckles. "What are you doing here? Not that I am complaining about finding Sleeping Beauty in my little home."

She opened one sleepy eye and caressed his face with the other hand. "I came to tell you that I love you."

A grin broke over his face. "And I am most gladdened to hear it."

Leaning forward, he kissed her, one hand stroking a loose strand of hair from her face.

He paused. "What has brought on this sudden declaration?"

"I have decided that no one can dictate to whom I give my heart, or my body." She pulled his head down and kissed him again.

A confused look pulled his brows together. "Body?"

She tried to school her features into a serious expression, but love and mischief burned in her eyes. "Yes. You're a surgeon and, I am told, one who is rather skilled at anatomy and familiar with the female form."

His eyes widened and his mouth opened and closed, but no words came out. With a soft plop, he sat on the floor near her. "But I cannot marry you. The council will never allow it," he rasped.

"You love me, and I you. That is all we need. Besides, what can they do? I am a mage and throughout history, others of my kind have sought companionship for love with no interference from either king or council." Sera took his hands. "Unless you do not want me, because your abilities have been greatly exaggerated..."

He huffed through his nose and quietly rose to his feet. His tall, broad frame blocked what little light the feeble moon offered.

Hugh swept her up in his arms. A serious and heated light shone in his eyes. "I will show you what I remember of my anatomy lessons. Then my lady can make her own decision as to my skill."

Sera laughed and wrapped her arms around his neck, as he carried her to the shadowy corner where his bed waited.

TWENTY

The next morning, Sera woke filled with a sense of peace and warmth. Peace, because she knew she had made the right decision. Warmth, because Hugh had pulled her close to his chest and curled his larger frame around her. Sera nestled against him, luxuriating in the sensations running over her limbs and swirling deep inside her.

The rain clouds had drawn back as sunrise lit the large round window at the end of his garret, and sunlight crept across the floor. A chill in the room made her breath frost, so Sera crafted a warming spell around the bed to chase away autumn's bite.

Hugh stirred and stretched without letting go of her. "Could you find a way to make this room warm throughout winter, please? I swear I can ice skate up here when the roof leaks and droplets freeze on the floor."

"If I can craft an efficient warming method, I will

ensure the entire building benefits. And then the next building, and the next, and the next... until the entire neighbourhood has warm homes and the nobles are left rubbing their hands in their chilly parlours."

While she could mend leaking roofs and cracked windows, how to channel heated air throughout a home eluded her. There would be a way. She simply had to find it.

Hugh stroked a hand up her arm and caught his thumb under the chain around her neck. Tugging, he revealed the lump of silver. "What is this, some magical talisman?"

"Of sorts." She rubbed the uneven circle with a fingertip. "This was a kiss you placed in my palm. I curled my fingers over it and my magic turned it into a physical thing. I have worn it ever since. As a reminder of your touch."

He placed a kiss on her bare shoulder. "If you turned every kiss into silver, we could accumulate quite a fortune."

"But I could never part with a single one. They belong only to me." She rolled onto her back and clasped her hands around his neck.

How easy it was to be with Hugh. To give and accept love. Sera wondered why she had tormented herself for so long over what to do, when all she had to do was trust herself. Of course, Abigail would have a conniption if she caught even a whisper of what had transpired the previous night. But she would most definitely be sharing the details with Kitty.

"I must go. I still have a murderous beast to track and I need to extract the truth from someone who wishes to keep her silence." With great reluctance, Sera left Hugh's bed and found her clothing scattered on the floor.

"Will I see you tonight?" Hugh lowered his feet to the bare floorboards.

"If your patients allow it. I know how important your work is." Sera shrugged on her gown and twirled her fingers in the air to magically tighten and tie her laces.

"Would it be permissible to come to you?" A trace of worry lingered in his words. "You can still maintain your reputation if no one knows you stayed here overnight."

Sera snorted. "I no longer care who knows. You are more than welcome in my bedchamber this evening. Be warned—Elliot will have a few jokes to make about it. But we will be more than amply compensated by breakfast from Rosie."

Having tugged on her shoes, she went to Hugh for one last, lingering kiss. "Until tonight."

He touched his forehead to hers. "I'm not sure how much use I will be to my patients today. I might be somewhat distracted."

She touched his smile. "No, you won't. You are too good a surgeon not to give them all your attention. But afterwards, well, I shall see what I can do about being a distraction."

His hearty laughter curled around her as she took

the steep, ladder-like stairs down from his garret. When Sera turned into her street, she took the outside stairs down to the kitchen. Once in the homely warmth, she dropped into a chair at the pine table.

"And what hour do you call this to be coming home?" Elliot arched one eyebrow and pointed to the clock on the shelf.

"I was busy." Sera reached for the teapot.

Elliot huffed. "Too busy to make it home to your own bed?"

Sera sipped the hot tea but couldn't keep the good humour from her eyes as she winked at the footman.

He burst into laughter. "Like that, was it?"

"A lady never reveals, and a gentleman should never ask," Sera murmured as she took the bowl of porridge from Vicky and poured a dash of cream over the top.

Elliot nearly choked on his breakfast. "There're no ladies or gents at this table, but don't tell me. I don't want the picture in my head of what you and the surgeon got up to that put that wicked grin on your face."

Sera ate her breakfast and even though Elliot teased her the whole time, she wouldn't have traded a moment of it for any fancy home or legions of stuffy, silent servants. Once she had washed and changed her gown, Sera retreated to her study.

She removed the finger bone of Mr Grove from a tiny box, and laid it in the middle of the desk. For an hour, she wrapped tendrils around the bone. They filtered through the porous material to collect every speck of the casting held within. Then she coaxed the residual spell from where it resided. A pale grey mist seeped from the bone, and she gently encouraged it into a waiting vial.

When Elliot rapped on the door, she had captured a fragment of magic the same size as a fat raindrop. Would it be enough? Setting the corked vial next to the bone, she turned to the footman. "What is it, Elliot?"

"Visitor for you. It's Lord Thornton. He's waiting in the parlour." He gestured with his head back along the hall.

Sera's pulse raced and her palms moistened as she stood. Abigail had not exaggerated when she'd said it would be soon. "Fetch tea for the earl, please."

In the few seconds it took to walk down the short corridor, she gathered her thoughts and steeled her nerves.

"Lord Thornton, what a lovely surprise," she said on entering the parlour.

The earl rose from the leather armchair by the fire and nodded in greeting. "Lady Winyard, I hope you will forgive the early hour, but I came to take my leave of you. My household departs later today for my estate in Norfolk. I much prefer the solitude of the ocean and fens. I have been overlong in London this season."

Sera gestured for him to return to his seat, and lowered herself onto the settee. "I can appreciate that. I have purchased myself a modest parcel of land in West-bourne Green, so I might build my own retreat from the noise of the city. Can you see the ocean from your house?" A thrill shot through her at the thought of having a cosy spot where she could tuck her feet under her, clasp a hot drink, and watch waves pound against a cliff.

"Oh, yes. The sea is visible from the top of the corner tower. Dreadfully cold spot, though, and buffeted by the wind." He fidgeted with his top hat, running the brim through his fingers.

A sigh escaped her, and Sera leaned back. How marvellous to have a tower with an ocean view, far away from the bustle of London and the demands of both king and council. "You are most fortunate. Perhaps I might be able to visit one day?"

He smiled and nodded to himself. "I very much hope so. On a related subject, I have a boon to ask of you, Lady Winyard."

"Oh?" Her heart skipped a beat, and she thanked Abigail for the warning of what this visit might entail.

He tossed his hat to the low table and edged forward on the seat, leaning his elbows on his thighs. "I have a question to pose to you, but before I say the words, I ask that you please do not reply immediately."

Nervous ants skittered over her skin, and she cast around the room to check that the exit remained unhindered. After the previous night in Hugh's arms, how could she ever contemplate an offer from the earl, ocean, and towers notwithstanding? If would be dishonest to all parties involved. "Lord Thornton—"

"No. Please," he interrupted. "I can see the refusal on your lips already. Let me at least present my case."

They fell silent as Elliot entered, bearing the tray. The footman set out the teapot and cups in awkward silence. Sera poured and passed a cup to her visitor. Then she sipped the special blend of tea the earl had gifted her. How she would miss the floral brew once things ended badly between them.

Without tasting his tea, Lord Thornton set it aside, left the armchair, and knelt before her. He took her cup from her chilled hands and placed it on the table. Then, holding both her hands in his, he met her gaze. "I am aware there is no grand passion between us, but we do have friendship and a mutual regard. Many marriages are built on less. I also believe we share some similarities and appreciate the value of a sanctuary far from politics and people. I would be honoured, Lady Winyard, if you would consider becoming my wife."

A thousand words crammed themselves into her throat. First among them—*I cannot, I love Hugh!* She could never marry another, not when the surgeon held her heart in his strong hands. Others might be able to set aside love and marry for duty... but Sera had known since last night that she couldn't.

"My lord, you do me great honour in asking such a question." Sweat slicked her palms. "But may I ask a question of my own, before I give yours the serious consideration it deserves?"

"Of course. Do you wish to negotiate the amount of land I will make available to you for a new garden?"

Humour lit his eyes. He let go of her hands and resumed his seat. Only now did he pick up the teacup and drink.

Sera clasped her hands and called on a measure of Kitty's caution. "No, I would discuss a more serious matter. I would know if our politics are aligned. Whom do you support for the Regency—Queen Charlotte or the Prince of Wales?"

His gaze narrowed, and he shifted in the chair. "I hardly see the relevance of such a question to my proposal of matrimony."

"I believe it is exceedingly relevant, my lord. I am a champion of Queen Charlotte's cause, and if we differ in our political views, it must cause as many ruptures in our home as it does in Parliament."

He placed his cup on the table with a slow and deliberate care. "I support the Prince of Wales for the Regency. There are many reasons why Queen Charlotte is unsuitable. Our differing opinions could, in my view, make for intelligent discussion during cold winter evenings. Do we not learn by having our beliefs challenged, and by exchanging ideas with others we admire?"

She had to concede his point. Encountering others who held alternate views was a way to expand one's world and understanding. But did she want to stare at such a man every morning across the breakfast table, if there was a chasm between their perspectives too deep for discussion to bridge?

"What of emancipation for all? Do you think the

vote should be extended to all Englishmen and women, regardless of their station in life?" These were questions close to her heart.

He huffed and replaced the teacup so abruptly it rattled on its saucer. "There is a reason the vote is limited to landowners. A man needs to be educated to know what is best for this country. You cannot think that the man gutting fish over a barrel has any concept of what is needed to grow our economy or to protect our interests abroad?"

Sera edged forward on the settee and settled a keen gaze on him. "Then is not the answer to educate everyone? Which brings me to the matter of how women are treated in society. Would you support women taking charge of their lives and careers, if they wished to work instead of raising a family?"

Colour crept up his neck, and one hand curled into a fist. "You are deliberately provoking me, my lady. Are you testing me to see if I possess a temper? I tell you now, I am a most even-tempered man."

"No, Lord Thornton. I do not tease or provoke. These are matters dear to me. I would have a husband who likewise champions the humble workman and the downtrodden woman. Who sees that educating every child will ultimately lift them out of poverty and allow them to change the course of their lives. I require a husband who believes every man and woman should be allowed to have their say in the governance of this country and cast their vote."

His eyes widened, and then he laughed. "You have

had your little joke, Lady Winyard. You cannot seriously believe a working-class man like your footman—" He waved his hand at the hall beyond. "—should be allowed to have any say in who sits in the House?"

"I do. And my cook and maid should also have a vote. As should I."

He shook his head. "You are young and idealistic. Lord Ormsby was quite right. You need guidance. Your views will settle with time and experience, and become more rational."

Rational? Oh, no. He had not just implied her beliefs were *irrational*?

Sera rose to her feet. "No, my views will not become *rational* with time. In fact, I am now coming to the conclusion that there is no need for a woman to marry at all. For too long we have been but chattel." Tiny silver shackles formed around her wrists. "Passed from our fathers, to our husbands, then to our sons. It is time women stood shoulder to shoulder and said *enough!*" She slammed her fist into the opposite palm with the final word and the shackles were crushed, falling to the carpet like dust motes.

"Enough? You are truly naïve, Lady Winyard, if you think you would last more than a year in society without the calming influence of a steady—and influential—husband. Together, we could build a fortune and create a legacy that would last for centuries." Lord Thornton stood and picked up his top hat.

"I am sorry, my lord, but I do not require a husband to tell me how to think or act. Nor will I ever become any man's chattel. I seek a *partner* in this life. One who will listen with an open mind and support my beliefs because they are mine, even if they differ from his own. I would see girls aspire to careers in medicine, the law, or even politics, if such is what they desire."

"A woman who does not marry? The very idea is monstrous and unnatural." His eyes widened behind his spectacles and he drew back from her.

"I also support any legislation that would see Unnaturals legally recognised as English citizens." She stepped towards him.

Lord Thornton gasped, the pink flushing his face turning to deeper red as he retreated. "The rumours about you are true, then. There is a monster lurking behind that plain face. I rescind my proposal. Good day to you."

He spun on his heel and stalked straight out the front door, which an obliging Elliot was already holding open for him. Elliot pushed it closed and let out a low whistle. "You certainly know how to turn down an offer of marriage. The entertainment is better here than at the music hall."

Sera let out a long-held sigh of frustration and slapped her hands together. The *crack!* sent a bolt of dark lightning from floor to ceiling, and her anger dissipated as the sound echoed through her. "I could not face a man at the breakfast table every morning who believed he was morally superior to ordinary men and every woman—including his wife. Besides, if I married him, I would have to fire you and move house."

Elliot clutched a hand to his chest. "You did that for me? It was nothing to do with how you crept home at sunrise after spending the whole night—"

Sera held up one hand, and the words were stolen from Elliot's still moving lips.

"All things considered, that didn't go too badly. He left in the same condition in which he arrived, and I didn't even consider using my magic to change the prescription in his spectacles to make him think he's gone blind. Nor did I damage his carriage."

Yes, all things considered, that abortive proposal had gone rather well.

Then a speck of concern nibbled at her satisfaction. What would Abigail think? Or Lord Ormsby?

She straightened her spine. Words said could not be undone. There was no point worrying about the consequences of her harsh questions, not when she had a beast to catch.

To say nothing of a lovely pot of tea to savour.

TWENTY-ONE

After the horrible visit with Lord Thornton, Sera rushed to Mayfair and her friend's home. Kitty stood in the foyer, pulling on gloves in anticipation of going out. "Where do we go this morning? Do tell me I get to cross-examine this duchess."

"No. At least, not today. I think I have done enough to foul my relationship with Abigail without interrogating yet another peer." By afternoon teatime, whether Thornton had departed for Norfolk or not, all of society would be whispering about her abhorrent behaviour, and her declaration that she would rather remain unwed than become any man's chattel.

"Another?" Kitty quirked one eyebrow and interest shone in her gaze. "What have you done now?"

"Lord Thornton called on me this morning, and asked me to be his wife." Sera paced as she recalled their exchange.

Kitty's lips thinned, and she smoothed the leather gloves over her fingers. "May I assume it did not go well?"

"I may have asked him one too many probing questions such as the ones we discussed yesterday, and he withdrew his offer of marriage. I also told him I would never be any man's chattel." Theirs had to be the shortest engagement attempt of the season. The prospect had hung between them for less than fifteen minutes.

Kitty stared at her with wide eyes. "Truly? You told him you would be no chattel of his?"

At a nod from Sera, soft laughter escaped Kitty's long throat. "While you will never hear the words from Abigail, let me say how proud I am that you stood up for what is important to you. You can regale me with all the details in the carriage." Kitty linked arms with her, and they stepped out the front door to the waiting conveyance.

After they had dissected the horrendous aftermath of the marriage proposal, Kitty peered out the window. "Who are we calling upon in Knightsbridge?"

"A Miss Pearson, for personal reasons of mine. Lady Crawley said she withdrew from society thirty-five years ago and has remained unwed. I am curious how she weathered the storm of disapproval that must have created. I am hoping she might have some advice to help me through the next few days and weeks." Perhaps they could start their own society for determinedly single spinsters. Their goals might include supporting one another in their careers. Or helping one another fulfil life aspirations that in no way required a husband. None of them would ever be a mere appendage trotted out at dinners to display the family jewels to good effect.

"Wealth would have given her the freedom to remain unmarried," Kitty said as the carriage rolled to a stop.

"But it would not have filled her life with love or companionship, once her peers turned their backs on her for breaking their rules." Sera took Kitty's gloved hand and squeezed. How she appreciated her friend. Whatever path they trod in life, they would be there for one another. Neither of them would ever be alone so long as they had their friendship.

Their rap on the forest green door was answered by a butler of advanced years. He bowed politely, revealing a bald head surrounded by a mere trimming of clipped grey hair, and gestured for them to enter.

He showed them through to a comfortable parlour decorated in warm, verdant colours that made Sera think of a forest glade with filtered sunlight playing through the leaves. Miss Pearson rose from a settee covered in a deep green brocade the same colour as the front door. Of average height and a trim build, her greying hair was pulled back in a severe hairstyle, and gold-rimmed spectacles hung on a chain around her neck. She had the appearance of a strict schoolteacher, but then she smiled and it softened her face.

Miss Pearson bobbed a curtsey to Sera and nodded

to Kitty as one gentleman's daughter to another. "I am honoured, Lady Winyard, that you should call upon me. I am curious how I might be of service." She gestured for them to be seated.

Sera and Kitty took the settee opposite their hostess, the seat well padded and comfortable.

"I have an odd request and a very old one. I wish to discuss somewhat delicate matters that occurred some thirty-five years ago," Sera said.

Miss Pearson clutched her hands together. "Oh? I'm not sure my memory is what it used to be. Might I ring for tea, ladies?"

At a nod, she crossed to the butler, who lingered in the doorway. "Tea, Monty, and that lovely cake Mrs Smythe made yesterday." She spoke loudly enough that Sera guessed the butler was hard of hearing.

Miss Pearson returned to her seat. An eerie silence enveloped them, as though the staff all crept around on their toes.

"Do you share your home with anyone?" Kitty asked, peering out the open parlour door.

Miss Pearson shook her head. "No. I never married and since my father died, I am alone in this world. I keep only a small staff, sufficient to meet my few needs. And I treasure what visitors come to my door."

As they chatted of inconsequential things, a footman much younger than the butler, so probably only sixty years old rather than a hundred, coughed discreetly on the threshold before entering carrying a tray. He set it down on the table between the settees and then retreated.

Miss Pearson poured and handed them teacups in a pale green with curling ferns painted on the side. Once they all had a drink in hand, she tilted her head to peer at Sera. "You say a delicate matter brought you here?"

"Yes. I understand you withdrew from society after the season of 1753." Sera took her cup and inhaled the aromas drifting from the tea. The scent wasn't as floral as Lord Thornton's special blend, but there was more to this cup of tea than the leaves of *Camellia sinensis* alone.

Miss Pearson's cup rattled on its saucer. "My father once said that secrets do not stay buried forever. I did not believe him at the time," she murmured.

Kitty shot a glance at Sera over the rim of her teacup.

Sera wondered if the older woman's status as a spinster was too delicate to discuss, but it was hardly a long-buried secret. All of society knew she remained unwed. "I am aware I may dig up events from your past that might stir uncomfortable memories. If I trespass too far, I will, of course, respect your privacy. But there are things you might know from that time that would greatly assist me today."

The teacup in Miss Pearson's hand clattered to the saucer, and she placed it on the table. One pressed her temple. "If there had been any other way, I would have kept my child. But I thought—well—things did not go as I planned them in my head."

Sera nearly choked on her mouthful of tea. She had called on Miss Pearson to discuss how to keep a steady course when all of society wanted to haul one down the aisle. The conversation had taken an unexpected and very welcome turn. Could Miss Pearson have been the mother of Mr Grove?

When Sera couldn't think what to say, Kitty took control of the conversation. "A man died in Southwark recently. Killed by some form of beast. He was a foundling, left by his noble mother at the hospital to be raised by strangers. We believe the manner of his death may have been triggered by his search for his mother."

Sera adapted to the swing in the conversation. "Another died under similar circumstances five years ago. He was another foundling, this time left by his noble mother with a family in Winton. If we could find her and ask if she had attempted to locate him, it might aid our search for the killer."

A weak smile touched Miss Pearson's lips as she picked up her tea once more. "I assure you, I was neither man's mother."

Sera knew that to be true for one victim—the son of the Duchess of Featherstone. "How can you be certain?"

Miss Pearson's gaze dropped to the cup in her hands. "Because I gave birth to a girl."

Blast. They'd finally found a noblewoman who admitted to secretly giving birth years ago, only to discover the child was the wrong gender. That set Sera to wondering how often such a thing occurred. They now had *three* young women from one season, who had all quietly handed off their children so they could be offered up to prospective husbands as blushing maidens.

"What became of the father?" Kitty asked.

Miss Pearson closed her eyes, and a heavy sigh shook her torso. "Oh, how I loved him. But his family did not approve of me. He said they needed time to learn to love me, but I needed no time to know my heart. When my womb quickened—well, I would never have been acceptable as his bride then. We agreed to place the child with a family for a few years. Once we were wed and settled, we could reclaim her."

"What happened?" Sera couldn't drink her tea, too intent on the tragic tale. Something must have gone horribly wrong for Miss Pearson to have spent decades alone.

"My father's fortunes improved as theirs declined. I rose in their estimation and our engagement was announced. Then Henry died. Thrown from his horse. Only too late did I realise the consequences of my actions." Miss Pearson rose and walked to the writing desk by the window. She stared out at the empty street and the gathering clouds. "If there had been a way, I would have reclaimed her to fill this empty house. I could have said she was the child of a cousin and no one would ever have known."

"Why didn't you?" Sera asked. Perhaps the foster family had moved and left no forwarding address. Or worse, perhaps the girl had succumbed to one of the many diseases that all too often snatched infants away from their families.

Unshed tears glimmered in Miss Pearson's eyes when she met Sera's gaze. "Because I did not wish to harm my child. At the time, I thought it was mere puffery, meant to scare me into remaining silent. But as I sat at this window and stared out into the street, I did not dare risk testing the ensorcellment. He said that any attempt to find my child would result in the removal of all concealment of what I had done."

Sera's interest sparked into flame. Such a declaration dripped with magic. "What ensorcellment?"

A shake of her head. "I am no mage. All I know is that Lord Dewlap promised that the spell he cast would drape my actions in such a dense cloud of secrecy that even my own father and those who lived under this roof would not know that I carried and bore a child."

The name exploded in Sera's brain. "Dewlap," she rasped.

Miss Pearson nodded. "I sought his help to keep my condition a secret, never realising that the spell was more like a curse."

Sera let out a sigh and leaned back on the settee. What had Dewlap done? His involvement explained why the faint trace of magic seemed so familiar.

It should be. It was hers now.

"Can you tell me more of the spell he cast?"

"Sadly, no. All I can tell you is that five years ago, and then more recently, I... felt something. Here." She tapped a spot on her chest where her heart resided. "A

257

sharp pang, as though a knife were driven into my chest. Monty, my butler, thought my heart was going to give way. It was what took my father, you know. But I had felt such a hot agony before, on the day my child was taken from my arms and the spell settled over us all."

"You're connected to the other two mothers. You experienced the spell activating and removing the physical trace of their indiscretions." Ideas whirled in Sera's mind as to how on earth her predecessor could have bound the women and their children.

"Is there anything that can be done to remove this curse? I know it is too late, but I would like to see my daughter, if it were possible." Tears glistened in Miss Pearson's eyes.

Sera finished her tea and stood. "If there is a way, I promise you, I will find it."

THAT EVENING, as Sera stared out her window, a shape detached itself from the side of the building across the street. Her senses came alert. Could this be the longed-for messenger with her key to the Fae realm? The man glanced around him, ensuring the street was empty, before approaching her door. He was shrouded in a cloak the same colour as darkness. He knocked and without waiting for Elliot to answer, shoved something into the slight gap at the edge of the frame.

Curiosity aroused, Sera rose to see what he had left. Part of her hoped it was the key she needed to cross Shadowvane. As she opened the door, the envelope fell into her outstretched hand. She shut the door and slit the plain seal with a narrow shaft of magic. The note clung to anonymity, with no signature at the bottom.

Come out, alone, and hear my words.

How could she refuse an invitation like that? Alert to danger, she grabbed her cloak and left the safety of her home. Sera stuck to the shadows and called her magic to the surface of her skin, ready to strike.

"Lady Winyard?" a masculine voice murmured.

"Yes." She turned towards the sound.

The courier stood in the shadows of the neighbour's stone wall, his hood pulled over his features. "I am instructed to say the following to you. *I was present at his birth, but had no hand in his death. Dewlap cast a spell of anonymity so that none would ever know of what transpired. I swore to abide by the vow on a silver figurine. He promised that if anyone tried to find the truth, all evidence would be destroyed.*"

The man slipped away without saying another word.

Sera didn't have to ask who the message came from. The duchess had finally admitted what was obvious that afternoon in her parlour. But she had ensured nothing was ever written down or could be used as proof of her youthful indiscretion. Committing the brief message to memory, Sera returned home.

The strands were drawing tighter around Lord Dewlap's involvement. With the same sort of spell cast over two women, even Kitty would now consider it a safe assumption that Mr Grove's mother had made a third, seeking the same veil of anonymity over her delicate condition. It also explained the familiar tingle Sera had felt from the remains of the two men, for it was the same magic that coursed through her veins.

On repeating the last sentence of the message, a shudder worked down her spine. *All evidence would be destroyed.* If no one knew what had happened because of the spell, there was only one piece of evidence—the remaining child. Two men killed by the same monster confirmed that Miss Pearson's fears were justified. Any attempt to find her daughter would invite the creature to enact its decades-old promise.

"What nightmare did you unleash?" she murmured to her predecessor.

To meddle in the minds of people, to wipe all trace of the woman's pregnancy from the lives and memories those involved, was a violation of the Mage Council's protocols. But would that stop a mage who ignored the rules and dabbled in dark magic? What price had he demanded for such a silencing spell for the noblewomen? Had the gold lining his pockets assuaged his guilt over the lives his magic took?

Mr Perdith sought his mother and had found her.

That event must have triggered the magic residing deep in his bones. Mr Grove had lived content, without knowing anything of his mother. It was possible that the noblewoman had tried to find him, and perhaps had questioned his foster family about her child's whereabouts.

"What a horrible spell." She leaned back on the settee and stared at the ceiling. It acted more like a curse—or possibly the dark magic twisted it into a thing of nightmares. That was the warning taught to every mage from the very beginning. Dark magic could not be trusted. It perverted a mage's intentions and took its own malicious path.

That still didn't explain the *manner* of the men's deaths. Some creature must have been bound in the casting that sought out the child when the certainty of discovery arose. She let out a sigh. What to do now?

Two men were dead, but a woman went about her life somewhere, unaware of the curse hiding in her bones. Sera recalled the loneliness in Miss Pearson's eyes and her own promise. If there was a way to reunite mother and child, she would find it.

As she had found Meredith Hillborne and Hannah, and reunited them.

Sera stared out the window without seeing the children playing in the street. Her thoughts splintered in different directions. What creature had attacked the men? Did the propensity for dark magic flow in her own veins?

When she considered the spell she had cast over

Lord Hillborne, she had the answer as to the sort of magic required to burrow into someone's bones. She had created her curse to disperse throughout the viscount's body in order to remain untraceable. What if Dewlap had deliberately cast his curse to remain in the babes?

"As a marker," she whispered. Then another idea burst into her head. "As a way for the beast to find the evidence that needed to be removed!"

If she had an Unnatural creature at her beck and call that she could command to kill, the easiest way to ensure it found the right target would be a touch of magic to identify them. Something buried deep inside their body that they couldn't wash away or cut out. She still needed to find a creature with wings, teeth, and claws. But the shape it took mattered less than the fact that she now had a way to trap it.

All she had to do was find the bait.

TWENTY-TWO

The first thing Sera did was dash off a note to Kitty, telling of her plan. Then she tackled the main problem—understanding the spell Dewlap had cast and how it transformed into such a horrible curse. Only then could she untangle the mess he'd made. When she found Miss Pearson's daughter, Sera wanted to be sure she could remove all trace of the marker so that the two could be reunited. It wouldn't do to find her, only for the beast to descend first and tear her flesh apart in front of her horrified mother's eyes.

In her study, Sera fetched the finger bone and the vial containing the raindrop trace of the spell. Seated at her desk, she held one item in each hand, then closed her eyes and concentrated. For as long as she could remember, she had made a game out of picking apart Lord Branvale's spells and trying to determine how he cast them. When she'd reached her majority, she kept doing it every time she encountered castings by one of the other mages, due to her fascination with the way all their gifts were different, each taking a unique route to achieve the same ends.

The curse before her was thirty-five years old and faint. But she had a secret advantage. Her magic had cast it—or her line, at least. She pushed concerns over the association with dark magic to one side. She refused to believe that she was tainted because of something her predecessor had chosen to do. Actions dictated whether a person was good or evil. Sera only cast to benefit others, and to ensure monsters did not escape punishment. That did not make her a fiend.

She set the bone and vial holding the tiny drop of curse on her desk. Then she fetched a bowl. The next part was tricky—turning the blob into a liquid so she could distil it to an even more concentrated form. Would there be enough? She would try first. If she failed, she would engage Hugh in another spot of grave digging to fetch larger bones from Mr Grove.

First, she added lavender and rosemary oil to the bowl for remembrance. Then she drew the droplet out and immersed it in the oil. This created a small, malleable blob the size of a pea. At a wave of her hand, purple flames erupted under the bowl. The substance coalesced and simmered, and then shook as though the pea now contained a tiny creature that wished to escape.

When she judged its activity had reached a peak, she blew upon it as though it were an ember, letting it flare into life. The pea popped, and released a flash of inky navy mist. Sera held out her hands and let the substance soak into her palms. When she turned her hands over, runes in an arcane tongue were inscribed across her flesh.

In a flash, her magic recognised the spell and the full casting slammed into her brain.

"Oh, Dewlap, what did you do?" she whispered as she stared at the curse written on her skin.

His hex touched many lives—surely in ways he had never anticipated.

Fetching a clean sheet of paper, Sera held her palms out once more and allowed the runes to detach from her skin and settle on the page. Then she wiped her hands free of any residue.

"The problem with dark magic," Lord Rowan had once lectured her, "is that it deceives the one casting it. Evil often seeps out and infects others in ways the mage never intended. That is why we shun its use. One dark spell gone awry can have devastating effects on many people."

Sera leaned back in the chair, the hex laid out before her, and sorted through what she had discovered. In casting a spell to cover the noble mothers in a blanket of silence, Lord Dewlap had drawn upon dark magic to manipulate the minds and erase the memories of family, friends, and midwives. Memories had been the target of his casting, but the taint had fed upon the desperate situation of the women and transformed itself into something wicked.

Her predecessor had intended to remove any memories should someone seek the truth. But in its malice, the curse had targeted the tangible *evidence*—the child.

The only missing piece was how the creature featured in the original ensorcellment. To befuddle someone and pluck out what they recollected didn't require a winged beast with sharp claws and teeth. It only needed a mage to ignore the rules set down by the council that governed their magic—to say nothing of the lack of any conscience in calling forth forbidden ways to tamper with a person's mind.

She picked up the page and studied the spell, and a chill shuddered through her body. It was worse than she'd feared.

"Blood magic," she whispered.

THE NEXT DAY, Sera and Kitty once more found themselves seated in Miss Pearson's comfortable parlour with its stacks of books. The spinster must have sought companionship among the fictitious characters of novels in their many pages.

Hope burned in Miss Pearson's eyes. "Did you find a way to break the spell?"

Sera trod carefully. They had a dangerous path to walk and while she remained optimistic, she couldn't be certain she could find and save the other woman's daughter. "I believe so. But I am trying to ascertain how the spell warped over time, and resulted in the deaths of Mr Perdith and Mr Grove. They are the two other children born to noble mothers after the season of 1752. Can you tell me exactly what happened when you visited Lord Dewlap?"

Miss Pearson waited until the butler had set down the tray, and they all had a cup of tea. She did not touch a drop, only warmed her hands around the cup. "I had asked a friend, discreetly of course, where a young woman in a difficult situation could seek a solution. The child was wanted, but the timing was unfortunate." One hand dropped to her stomach, and she stared into the fire. With a sigh, she continued. "Lord Dewlap's name was mentioned as a mage who could provide any remedy a wealthy person required. He was known to frequent a certain bookshop at a certain time and day of the week. Anyone needing his services could find him there. Such things as could never be spoken of in a parlour were whispered among the stacks with only books as witness."

Sera admired his cunning. Anyone could enter a bookshop. Their business had no doubt been conducted in a hushed conversation encased in a silence spell to be absolutely certain no one overheard.

"I told him no one could know. I had to maintain my position, after all, as I hoped to make myself agreeable to Henry's family so we might wed. Dewlap said he would contact me when the solution was ready." Only now did she pause to sip her tea.

"Weren't you afraid?" Kitty asked.

"Yes. But I was more afraid of the scandal if it became known I was with child. I would have been ruined and we would never have been able to marry. Henry desperately needed his parents to approve the match, which meant we could not elope. As it happened, life played a cruel trick upon us and I lost everything." Her head bowed, she stared at her hands. On the right she wore a ring with a plain red stone, which she rubbed as she spoke. "A week later, a note was slipped into my hand while I browsed parasols in a shop. It gave an address and a time, then the note dissolved like wet tissue paper until only a clump remained on my glove."

Dewlap certainly ensured that not a word of his activities escaped. Probably so that no evidence could be presented to the council as to how he violated their rules.

"At the appointed time, I knocked on the door of a boarding-house. The room was sparsely furnished, but I assume he only used it for such meetings. On the table stood a silver statue, about eight inches in height. Next to it, a silver goblet. In his hand, he held a needle. He confirmed that I wished to carry the child to term, but needed to ensure no one ever knew of my indiscretion. I whispered my agreement." Her voice fell, as though she lived the moment again in her head.

Sera knew what had waited in the goblet: a potion

that connected the woman's condition to a person's memory. A spell so powerful that anyone who touched, or even *stared* at, the pregnant woman would find the memory of her state snatched from their minds. Even the midwife who delivered the babe would never remember doing so.

What she wanted to unpick was how the casting had deformed into killing the children of the women who sought help.

"He told me to hold out my hands. In one, he placed the goblet. He took the other and pricked my fingers with the needle. Then he told me to wrap my bleeding fingers around the statue. I had to drink the potion and repeat my vow of secrecy." A shudder worked through her body.

"Blood magic. The strongest kind we can cast." Sera blew out a breath through clenched teeth. That was what she had suspected when she'd studied the form of the hex. It needed a potent activator, and blood was the strongest. The women had, unknowingly, tied their life-force to the spell, which was why it endured. The magic filtered through to their unborn children and settled into their growing forms, and their lives also fed the curse.

If each woman had, in turn, placed her bloody hand on the statue, the blood magic would have been absorbed by each of them. That would explain the faint connection they shared. The women had been bound in a terrible pact, with results all of them felt but none of them would have wanted.

"What was the statue?" the ever curious Kitty asked.

Sera assumed it to be some talisman of the mage, used to complete the casting.

Miss Pearson hummed and stared into the fire. "Oh, some mythical creature. An odd thing, like several animals stitched together. It had a head like a bird, but the body of a large cat with a long tail. What was it, now?"

"A gryphon." Sera knew with a terrible clarity that dark magic had twisted the blood vow and made the gryphon its guardian.

"Part eagle, part lion." Kitty's horrified gaze found Sera's. "Can all mages summon such beasts to do their bidding, even long after their deaths?"

"Dewlap died, but his magic that crafted the spell lived on in the children—and in me." Her very existence might have played a role in the deaths of two men. Now, Sera would bring the curse to an end.

"Can you break it? I would give anything to be able to hold my child in my arms once more." Tears glimmered in the older woman's eyes.

"By trying to find her, we call forth the guardian of your secret. I have no idea how much time elapsed between Mr Perdith's finding his mother and the creature ending his life. Mr Grove never sought his mother, so we must assume she decided to find him." Sera hated to say it, but the mother had to be fully informed. "There is a chance I might not be able to locate your daughter first. Indeed, we could have triggered the curse already."

Miss Pearson let out a cry and her teacup tumbled from her hands. Sera caught it with a net of magic and carried it to the low table. Then she sent tendrils to remove the puddle and stain from the carpet. The older woman's shoulders heaved as deep sobs wracked her body.

The elderly retainer appeared in the doorway, drawn by the sounds of distress. He glared at Sera, as though she was personally responsible. Which, in a way, she was.

"Do you need anything, ma'am?" He ventured farther into the room on unsteady legs.

"Only a few moments, Monty. Do not worry about me." She found a weak smile for her butler and waved him away. The distraught mother blew her nose and met Sera's gaze. "Events have been set in motion. Better we try to save her, please, than do nothing, only to grieve at her graveside. Do you require anything from me?"

On the cusp of saying no, an idea occurred to Sera. She grabbed her satchel and felt around in the bottom for an empty vial. Then her attention lighted on the glint of a needle in the pincushion atop a workbasket. "A little blood, if you don't mind?"

A few minutes later, the red liquid stoppered in the vial, they took their leave.

The two young women returned to the Napier home. Sera paced the parlour as she ran through what she needed. "Could you summon Hugh, please, Kitty? I need to find Miss Pearson's daughter. Even now, the gryphon could be flying above London, searching for the trace of the curse. I must reach her first."

How would she battle a gryphon? Her obsidian dragon might come in handy. Or would it be as simple as unpicking the spell and watching the gryphon dissolve?

"Of course. But... why?" Kitty yanked on the bell pull to summon a footman.

"I need you to watch my body." Sera tossed the pillows from the chaise and lay down. Crossing her hands over her chest, she said, "I have to seek the trace of the curse that lingers in the daughter's bones. Let us hope she lives in London, and not somewhere far away, like York."

Drawing deep breaths through her nose to steady her nerves, Sera closed her eyes. Then she gathered her magic to her and summoned the curse crafted by Dewlap. Holding the shape and taste of it tight, she sent her mind soaring free of her body and searched for an avian accomplice. One of the Tower's ravens answered and signalled its willingness to assist.

Sera experienced a moment of falling, as though her body plummeted off a cliff as her mind and magic merged with the bird. Then she found her balance as the crow made space for her.

What do you require of me?

Something lesser birds never asked. She conveyed her request, and the corvid circled higher over London.

As the raven flew, Sera let loose drifting tendrils of magic, seeking those who would answer her call. More birds joined them, and each was given a piece of the spell and a sliver of her mind, to spread their search wider. She didn't know how much time had elapsed. Her mind splintered into thousands of shards, like a shattered mirror, as she commanded an army that blanketed the sky.

On and on they flew. Skimming over buildings, swooping through skeletal trees, darting low over pedestrians braving the weather. After what seemed a thousand miles... an answering tug. Sera cried out as she pulled the strewn parts of herself into the strong raven to focus on the tingling thread of magic. With her power burning through her veins, she directed the midnight-feathered bird to find where the woman resided. Seconds ticked by as the neighbourhood narrowed down to a building, then the creature found the particular window that called to them.

Placing her own marker on the glass, since a bird's view differed greatly from a street view, Sera thanked her legions of helpers and let her mind sink back to her body.

She woke with a gasp, her skin slick with sweat, her limbs burning from exertion and a throat so dry she struggled to speak. Hugh grasped her shoulders and shouted for water.

"How long?" she rasped. Even in her exhaustion, his worried face gave her joy.

"Five hours. Night has fallen. We were debating

273

trying to wake you—you burn with fever." He held a glass of water to her parched lips and Sera drank, too weak to hold the glass.

She let cool water dribble over her lips. "I found her, but we must move quickly."

"You are in no state to battle a gryphon." Kitty placed her hands on her hips and glared at her.

Sera waved away their concern. "We cannot wait for me to fully recover. A cup of tea with plenty of sugar and something to eat on the way will help. None of us know how much time she has, now that we have called forth the curse's guardian by seeking her out."

Hugh and Kitty exchanged worried glances. Then Kitty strode to the bell pull and gave it a good tug. "Well, a gryphon hunt it is. I shall bring my lucky sabre, since you don't like me carrying firearms."

Hugh's eyes widened and he raised both fists. "I shall rely on my size and boxing skills."

Sera grasped his arm and rose on unsteady legs. "With you both beside me, we shall defeat it. I am its master after all, and even in a weakened state, it must obey my command."

She didn't know that to be true at all.

But it sounded logical.

TWENTY-THREE

Within the space of a few minutes, Sera found herself bundled into the Napier family carriage. Hugh spread a blanket over her knees, as though she were an elderly patient. Both Hugh and Kitty regarded her with worried eyes.

"What direction?" Hugh asked.

"The East End," Sera murmured.

Hugh stuck his head out the window and instructed the coachman. Kitty clutched a flask of sweet tea and made Sera take frequent sips.

"It's not too hot, as I didn't want to scald you if we hit a bump. Nor did I want it to slosh around in a small teacup. This seemed a good compromise for drinking in a moving vehicle," her friend explained.

The tea helped revive her while Sera let her mind drift. Like a musician with a tuning fork, her thoughts were tuned to the sign she'd left on the building. At intervals, she called out left or right. Between the tea from Kitty and the pieces of hot buttered scone fed to her at Hugh's hand, she felt restored by the time an internal alarm pinged through her body.

Sera shot forward in the seat and yelled, "Stop!"

Her senses tugged her towards the tenement. Glancing at the grimy facade for a moment, she raced up the front stairs. Inside, she paused for a moment, swinging her head like a hound after a scent. She schooled her senses to ignore the damp, unwashed odour and concentrate on the magical tingle.

Kitty and Hugh raced into the building after her. Glancing up, Sera fixed a location in her mind and then bounded up the staircase, jumping over a rotten spot where a roof leak had ruined the timber. At the first landing, her magic pulled her along the narrow corridor. Abruptly, her feet stopped at one door. From behind came the faint trace of the old spell.

Sera rapped on the faded wood, bouncing on her toes with anxiety about what they would find within.

A woman holding a grizzly baby on her hip answered the door. "Yes?" Brown eyes like those of Miss Pearson widened in surprise at their number and their dress. Worry lines were etched in her brow and her plain gown was worn and repaired in a number of places.

Without a word, Sera wrapped a hand around the woman's upper arm. Like reached for like as her magic plunged into the woman and touched the hex buried deep inside her bones. "It's her."

"I haven't done anything. You're not taking me in!"

She wrenched free of Sera's grasp and turned to slam the door.

Hugh shoved his foot in the gap and pushed it open again with both hands.

Kitty crossed her arms. "Oh, for goodness sake, we're not the constabulary. This is Lady Winyard, the mage. We're here to save your life."

Sera pushed across the threshold and surveyed the sparse room. Apart from the baby, there were two more children sitting on a sofa—a boy of around five and a girl slightly older. Both children possessed dark colouring at odds with the auburn-tinted fuzz on the head of the baby. She didn't want to alarm the youngsters, but nor could she wait for a convenient time.

"There is a curse in your bones and I need to get it out. Now." Sera waved towards the door.

The woman scoffed and stuck her head out into the hall. "Bloody neighbours, thinking they are funny. Which one of you put this lot up to it?"

Sera stuck close to the woman's side and made faces to distract the crying babe. "This was placed inside you while your mother still carried you. Your *noble* mother, who had to give you up." Sera let her magic tangle with the trace inside the woman and tried to yank it out. But the hex refused to budge, just like Elliot in a bar nursing a half-full tankard of ale. The spell wouldn't go easily. It had spent thirty-five years nestled inside the woman's bones.

The baby screwed up its already wrinkled face and screeched. The mother jiggled her hip while making soothing noises. "If this thing has been inside me since I was born, why bother me about it now?"

"Because she wants to meet you, and cannot while this trace of magic is inside you." Hugh stepped forward and took the fractious child. Leaning the baby over his broad shoulder, he rubbed her back. After a loud burp, the crying was replaced with giggles. "I'm sure she would be delighted to meet her grandchildren, too."

Ripples raced over Sera's skin, as though she had brushed against a stinging nettle. "We need to go."

She took a firm grip of the mother's hand and pulled her out into the hall.

"Here! Let go. I can't leave my children." She dragged her feet, but a slip of magic under the mother's heels made her skate along the wooden floor as though it were ice.

"Surely one of your neighbours will mind them for an hour or two?" Kitty gestured to the nosy residents of the tenement.

Resigned to her fate, the woman gestured to a neighbour with bright red hair. "Daisy! Watch them for me, will you? You know I'd do the same for you."

Daisy stepped out into the hall and knelt, opening her arms to the young boy who had followed his mother. "Come here, Hamish. You can go play with my lot." Then she took the baby from Hugh and the hand of the older girl before going back through her door.

"What's your name?" Sera asked as they ushered the woman down the stairs.

"Olive Draper. What's this curse do? Will it hurt my children?" Olive glanced back over her shoulder, resisting Sera's onward urging.

That comment made Sera's feet slow. She hadn't thought of the children. Would the same dark magic have burrowed inside their small bodies?

"No," she replied.

Mr Grove had children, and the creature had not pursued them. Perhaps the melding with their other parent's blood diluted the ensorcellment enough that it put the beast off the scent. Or could it make a difference if the father, not the mother, contained the curse? Olive's children had grown inside her, surrounded by the old curse, and it would have seeped into every part of them. Whereas Mr Grove had a rather... small... contribution to the process of creating his children.

Sera pushed aside those concerns. Once she had undone Dewlap's spell, she could satisfy her curiosity about how the gender of a magically touched parent affected their offspring. That dovetailed with her studies about a Nereus.

"Your mother consulted a mage to cast a web of secrecy over her pregnancy. Unfortunately, it has deteriorated over the years, with fatal consequences for two men whose mothers sought the same solution."

"Fatal? You mean it'll kill me?" Olive paused and tugged her shawl higher up her shoulder with one hand as Sera kept hold of the other.

"Yes." *And most likely tear out your flesh and consume it.* But there was no need to impart that gruesome detail of the gryphon's devotion to erasing all evidence of a pregnancy.

"Where do we go?" Kitty asked once they reached the street.

Sera stared up at the dark sky and a chill of premonition washed over her skin. "It's close. We need to be somewhere open, with less chance of anyone else getting hurt." The tenements and streets of Whitechapel were crowded, and she wanted to reduce the risk of the beast striking an innocent person.

Hugh gestured to the east. "Just behind these tenements is an open field."

"We shall face the beast there." Sera steeled herself for the battle ahead. She had wanted to test herself against a charging enemy. Now she might have her chance.

Ignoring the carriage, they dashed between tall buildings to the moonlit space beyond. Autumn grasses parted around them as they strode out to the middle of the field.

Sera closed her eyes and grabbed a tendril of Dewlap's casting. Tethered at one end to Olive, she sent the thread high into the sky. As though she were an angler, she cast her line this way and that, teasing the creature to rise to her bait. Her whole body knew it was there, lurking behind the clouds. Then, a heaviness reverberated back along the line.

The gryphon had caught hold of her summons.

"Make ready!" she called out to Hugh and Kitty.

A piercing scream rent the night and made gooseflesh pop up along Sera's arms. The moon was obscured by the flurry of creamy feathers on beating wings. Swooping down with the speed of a kestrel, the creature dropped to the ground before them. The ground shuddered under their feet.

Olive screamed and ducked behind Sera. Hugh and Kitty closed ranks to either side of her. Kitty pulled her sabre free of its scabbard and stood ready to defend her friend and the innocent woman. Hugh removed a pistol from under his jacket.

Sera had a moment of surprise—the surgeon had claimed to have no weapon—before turning her concentration to the fierce beast.

The size of a small horse, the mythical creature snapped at the cowering woman. When it reared up on its back legs, it was taller than a man and more powerfully built. Its front half was covered in soft feathers, its front feet clawed. Its eagle's head possessed a deadly curved beak and staring black eyes. Then feathers gave way to soft, tawny fur and the powerful hind legs of a lion. A tail like a length of rope with a tufted end whipped back and forth.

The protector of secrets reared up on its powerful legs and lashed out with its clawed front limbs. Spreading its wings, it held itself steady to attack. It screeched at Olive and snapped, its beak clacking like nails banging on tiles.

Sera threw up a shield as it leapt, claws raking against her magical barrier.

It shrieked again, perhaps in surprise that its usual attack didn't work.

Sera planted herself in front of the frightened women and raised her hands. "No! Down!" she commanded, lacing her words with magic and letting their weight press its form to the ground. Would it obey her?

A deep-throated warble came from its thick neck, and it bunched its hind legs before jumping into the sky and breaking free of Sera's attempt to harness it.

"I seem to have annoyed it," she muttered, and rethought her plan.

It soared above them, then flew low, lashing out with its claws. They instinctively ducked, even though Sera's shield held. She grunted with the force of its attack, its massive weight thrown against the barrier, hitting her like a physical blow. Each time it changed position to launch a fresh attack, the friends thwarted its attempts while Sera tried to subdue the thing.

Creating a hex was easier than undoing one. Especially when she hadn't created it in the first place. Sera had nearly exhausted herself trying to find the elements used to cloud mother and child under a blanket of secrecy so tight that no one ever suspected she had given birth out of wedlock.

"Any time you want to banish the thing, or do whatever magic you need to, Sera," Kitty called out as she lunged and thrust her blade into the creature's side. A bright dot of blood spread over its pale feathers. The gryphon spun to face the new threat, its beak snapping at Kitty. "Now we know it is a physical thing, and not entirely magical."

"A mere scratch to it, though." Hugh stretched out his arm, aiming the pistol. He would have one shot, then must reload.

"I am trying my best!" Sera reassured her friends and the terrified Olive. Again, she sought to bind the gryphon with her magic and have it recognise her mastery over it. All the while, another part of her mind picked at the spell, trying to find a loose end to pull that would unravel the original casting. But time had changed it. The hex had festered and morphed into a knotted mass.

Kitty dodged a kick and stabbed at its haunch. With a howl, its tail lashed out and, since she'd stepped outside Sera's shield, it swept Kitty's feet out from under her.

"Kitty!" Sera yelled. For a split second she agonised over whether to throw the shield over her friend or to keep protecting Olive.

Then a loud *crack!* made Sera inhale a sharp breath, but she held her position. Hugh had fired, spinning the gryphon off balance and giving him time to help Kitty to her feet and pull her inside the shield.

The creature dropped to all fours. Blood flowed over its feathers and fur, but none of the wounds slowed its attack. The gryphon screamed. Confused perhaps, that the magic that had summoned it lingered inside Sera and prevented it from achieving its objective.

Then an idea burst into Sera's mind.

"Leave her be. Your duty is done," she called out. Rather than trying to undo the spell, she needed a way to end it.

Reaching into her pocket for the vial, she pulled the stopper free with her teeth. Using a swirl of magic, Sera lifted the drops of blood donated by Miss Pearson from the glass. Swiping her hand through the air, Sera brushed the blood on the gryphon's feathers.

Words appeared in her mind as though she had read them long ago. She infused each syllable with every ounce of magic she could muster.

"The secret is no longer yours to hold.

The mother wishes it to be told.

You are free, no longer bound.

This child, shall be found."

An unsteady cry warbled from the animal's throat, and it shook its head. In refusal? Or confusion?

Sera kept up her chant, repeating the rhyme over and over as she brushed her magic over the beast. Soothing it, praising it for a job well done, but telling it that it was no longer needed. Its decades-long vigil was now at an end.

The warble turned to a croon, and the gryphon's front legs buckled. Lowering its body to the grass, it curled up on its side like a house cat in the sun.

Sera crouched beside the gryphon and stroked its head. "You did as you were told, my friend. You can rest now."

With one hand on its side, Sera exhaled a deep

breath and recalled the curse to her. A snap vibrated through her bones, and her magic smothered a dark ember.

Olive gasped. "What was that? It stung."

"It's done. I have finished the purpose of the spell and brought it to an end."

At Sera's side, the gryphon closed its eyes and emitted a massive sigh. Then, bit by bit, its body shimmered, then turned to insubstantial dust and scattered over the soil. Only a silver glint remained. Reaching out, Sera picked up the silver statue of the mythical beast.

She turned to face Olive. "There is no longer any danger to you or your children. Would you like to meet your mother?"

"But she's a noble, you said. I was raised good, but I ran away with a fellow who died and left me with two little ones. Then I had rotten luck with the next one, who took off as soon as he heard I was pregnant. She would surely be ashamed of me." Olive wiped her hands down her skirts.

Kitty linked arms with the older woman. "I think you might have more in common with your mother than you realise. Besides, I suspect she will be delighted to learn she has grandchildren."

They returned to the tenement and collected Olive's children. Then they all piled into the carriage, somehow, with each of the adults holding a child. Hugh had the boy on his knee, Sera the older girl, while Kitty peered at the baby as though she had discovered a new species.

In Knightsbridge, Sera rapped on the door and old Monty answered it. "Is Miss Pearson still up?" she asked.

The hour was late, and she had probably roused the entire household. Monty blew out a sigh and gestured to the parlour.

Olive paused in the tiny foyer. "I'm not dressed right," she whispered.

Sera took her hand. "It's not your clothing she wants to see, but you."

As the group entered the parlour, Miss Pearson rose, and one hand went to her heart. "Olive. Oh, my dear. Is it really you?" she whispered. She reached out, but didn't move.

Olive stopped in the middle of the room and hugged the baby close to her chest while the other two children clung to her side. "Pleased to meet you, ma'am."

Miss Pearson took one step forward. Her gaze dropped to the children. "Are these yours?"

Olive rested one hand on Hamish's head. "I've had a hard time the last few years. My man died. Then when I found another to love... he up and left us."

"I have grandchildren?" With a sob, she rushed to Olive and touched the baby as though she expected her to dissolve into mist. Then she stroked Olive's cheek. "My child. Oh, my child..." she murmured as tears ran down her face.

"Hot chocolate and cinnamon toast, Monty, then ask the maid to make up two rooms. One for Olive and the baby and another nearby the older children can use." Kitty was an old hand at issuing instructions.

Once everything was sorted to Kitty's satisfaction, they left the two women to become acquainted.

"That was quite a night. Shall we return to Mayfair for a well-deserved nightcap?" Kitty gestured to the waiting carriage.

Once they settled inside, Sera took the hand of each of them. "I couldn't have done it without both of you." Then a question flared bright in her mind. "Where on earth did you get a pistol, Hugh? Surely a surgeon shouldn't be shooting at things?"

Hugh grinned and tapped his coat pocket. "Captain Powers gave it to me. Said I might need one if I was to stand at your side. Turns out he was right."

Twenty-Four

Hugh had accompanied Sera home and slipped from her bed early to start his rounds. Mid-morning, she was penning her report for Lord Ormsby when a man trotted up the steps and knocked on the door. Intrigued, Sera wondered if Lady Featherstone had sent another mysterious messenger.

After a murmured conversation, Elliot put his head around the parlour door. "Chap for you. It's your watcher, but he won't come in."

"Oh!" Sera pushed back her chair and hurried to the front door. A cloaked figure stood on the top step, the hood pushed back to reveal a genial-looking man in his late thirties. She had hoped to find one of the Fae. This man appeared... ordinary.

"I am Lady Winyard," she said.

"My lady, my master instructed me to give you this. Said you would need it when crossing the field." He held out his hand and slipped her something small and fragile.

Her heart pounded in her chest as she took the item without looking at it. "Who is your master?"

He grinned and shook his head. "I cannot say more." Then he nodded and walked away.

Sera opened her hand. In her palm rested an autumnal leaf no more than three inches long. Made of metal, it was mottled in tones of red and dark orange, as though a spell had captured it at the height of its autumn brilliance and cast it in a permanent material.

She held it by the stem and twirled it before her eyes. Finally, her unknown correspondent had given her the key. Now she could leave for Shadowvane. Winter wasn't the best time to journey to Somerset, but she would not wait any longer. Once she returned, she would hand over the bracelets to Lord Rowan as he wished, and then she would finally know all the secrets of her origins.

One edge of the leaf had a tiny hole, as though it was meant to be worn. She threaded it on the chain around her neck and let it dangle next to the silver kiss. Tucking the charms under her bodice, Sera wandered thoughtfully to her study. From a shelf, she took down a rosewood box and set it on her desk. Then she stood before it. Modest in size, the container was barely eight inches long by six inches wide. The honey-coloured wood was inset with brass detail in a swirling pattern. Magic vibrated from every inch and when she held her hand over the surface, her palm tingled.

The box was empty, yet it was warded like a castle.

For a quiet minute, she focused on the spellwork infused in the box's construction, which would hold its contents secure from all but the most determined mage. With eyes closed, she examined the casting and tried to identify the unique touch that formed Lord Rowan's signature.

A tickle at the base of her brain made her open her eyes.

"How odd," she murmured to the pretty container.

What in the spell created an itch in her brain? Perhaps it was merely the complexity of the binding. Lord Rowan had created layers that would lock tight once she placed the bracelets inside and closed the lid. Yet here, in her small study, it seemed a needle swung in her brain and pointed in another direction.

"Everything all right?" Elliot asked from the doorway. "You've gone awful quiet. Standing in that spot for ages, like you've forgotten how to work a chair."

Sera shook her head and tapped the box with one finger. "Something is bothering me about this, and I don't know what."

"You don't like the box? It's rather fancy. I think you're getting spoiled by the gifts these suitors keep dropping on our doorstep." He crossed his arms as he lounged against the door frame.

"This isn't from any suitor. Lord Rowan made it as an impenetrable safe for the two magical bracelets. Once inside, they cannot be removed except by the mage who ensorcelled the container. I need to ask

Hugh to fetch them from wherever he hid them." Her attention wandered over the shelves. With each day, each task, she added more ingredients, potions, and herbs to her collection.

A whisper in her brain pulled her attention to a particular shelf.

"That's good, though, isn't it? Then no one else can use them?" Elliot had become far more than a footman. He was her right-hand man. Especially when mischief or nocturnal exploits were afoot.

"I suppose so." It still bothered her that Lord Rowan should have the final say over what happened to the bracelets just because he was old.

In her exploration of the shelves, a small vial with a tiny swirling teal mist inside caught her eye. The mass rolled like a ball tumbling down a hill and the colour seemed more vibrant than usual. Sera plucked the vial from its shelf and held it to the light.

"You are rather animated today," she said to the wisp captured inside.

As she moved to be closer to the light shining through the window, her hand passed over the box and the wisp shot up to the cork and lightened a shade in hue.

"What was that?" Elliot moved closer, the antics in the small bottle drawing him farther into the room.

"This is the essence of the spell I extracted from the poison that killed Lord Branvale. I have never seen it do this before." She turned the vial this way and that. The essence reacted to something, but what?

Then she looked down and gasped. "The box!"

"The vial thinks the box is pretty, too?" His brows drew together.

"Nothing so shallow. The vial is connected to the box." Curling her fist around the vial, Sera laid the palm of her other hand on top of the box. With a horrid suspicion growing in her mind, she sent a trickle of magic from one object to the other. Searching for the signature, rather like squinting at a painting for the scrawl hidden in one corner.

A cold chill dropped down her spine. "They're the same." She turned to Elliot and held up the vial. "Lord Rowan brewed the poison that killed Lord Branvale."

Elliot blew out a silent whistle. "Do you think the old mage has a sideline in brewing poisons?"

That was one option—that he brewed fatal potions and sold them with the utmost discretion and perhaps a disregard for who might have purchased it. Or he might have concocted the spell, knowing exactly who would ingest it.

"It's possible, but—" A loud rap at the door interrupted her train of thought.

"I'll see who it is." Elliot tugged the corners of his waistcoat, smoothed his hands through his hair, and left her study.

"Did you know you would be used to kill a fellow mage?" Sera whispered to the essence in the vial, imagining the hand that had crafted it. With questions spinning in her mind, she placed the object back on the shelf.

A familiar voice came from the foyer—Abigail.

An unexpected visit after their falling-out. She left the study with a backward glance at the box. While pretty, was it merely another poisoned chalice touched by Lord Rowan? The logical part of her brain said it was mere coincidence. Lord Rowan most likely supplied a number of dark potions to a shady individual, who had then sold the poison to Jake, Lord Branvale's valet, in some dark alley.

But what if he had brewed it knowing exactly who would drink it, and why? Had there been some feud between the two mages that bubbled over with such deadly consequences?

Elliot appeared in the doorway and Sera glanced at the parlour door. She put a hand on his arm and whispered, "Whatever happens, Lord Rowan is not to have those bracelets. Not until I figure a few things out."

Sera paused by the parlour door and took a deep breath to calm her wild thoughts. Then, with a demure smile in place, she entered the room. "Abigail. What an unexpected treat to see you." Sera clasped her hands in front of her, waiting for the admonition for her behaviour.

Abigail kissed her cheek. "All of London is talking about how you refused Lord Thornton. You probably expect me to lecture you, but I am here as your friend. I have bought a special blend of tea to try to mend the breach in our friendship."

Sera's shoulders relaxed. How could she refuse

such an olive branch? "Of course. Elliot, fetch some hot water and the tea things, please."

They sat and stayed on safe ground by discussing Abigail's forthcoming wedding. Sera had some ideas about how to turn it into a magical and memorable day. Elliot brought the tray and Abigail poured hot water over the leaves of her tea blend. While it steeped, Sera conjured an array of magical rose petals to see which tint of pink her friend preferred. The correct shade had to be neither so pale that it appeared washed out, nor so deep that it was garish. It took Sera five attempts before Abigail declared herself content with the shade that resembled the faint blush of a sunrise.

Abigail poured the tea and passed over a cup.

Sera had never imagined that conjuring rose petals would be such thirsty work. She gulped a few unlady-like mouthfuls and then frowned at her cup. The new brew didn't have the subtle floral notes of the marvel-lous blend from Lord Thornton.

"Do you not like your tea, that it warrants such a look?" Abigail asked as she nibbled a slice of cake.

"It seems rather sweet." No, that wasn't it. She took another sip. What was it that niggled at her about the flavour?

"Oh, I do like a sweet blend. This contains honey. Then I might have put sugar in yours as well as mine. I have been so distracted lately. If you do not like my blend, let us call your man to bring an ordinary pot of tea." Abigail reached for the offending brew.

Sera smiled at her friend. Abigail was trying to

mend the holes in their relationship, so Sera should make some effort, too. Although as time passed, the cracks in their friendship grew larger. They had different views on matrimony and the role of women in society. Now it seemed even their taste in tea was at odds.

If Sera told Abigail she had taken Hugh to her bed, that might be the fatal blow to their acquaintance.

"No need to summon Elliot. He would say I need sweetening up, anyway. I will become accustomed to it." To demonstrate, she took a larger sip and swallowed. Her brain pulled apart the ingredients contained in the liquid. The blend of tea she particularly enjoyed had orange peel and rose petals. This one seemed to be mainly black tea, honey, and then... a hint of something else?

She drank a little more. "What else is mixed in here, Abigail, apart from honey and then sugar?"

She tapped one elegant finger against the side of her cup. "Let me think. A little camomile. I find it very soothing."

Sera took another sip. Yes, there was the slight taste of apple from the camomile. But there was something lingering under it.

Abigail put her cup on the low table and clasped her hands. "I am going to sing after the ceremony. It is a song of my own composing. I would value your thoughts on it, as I have never performed my own piece before."

"Oh, yes, please." There was a treat. Abigail's

singing held a trace of magic inherited from her grandfather.

Abigail sang in a low, soft tone.

The words rippled over Sera and she closed her eyes as she tried to decipher the language. Was it Italian? It had a lyrical cadence to it. She had expected a song about love, devotion, or even doing one's duty. But this one conveyed a dreamlike, lullaby quality.

Her limbs grew heavy and then a stinging thread of red alarm wove its way through a descending mist in her mind.

Mentally, Sera tried to bat the thread away. She wanted to listen to the song. Abigail would expect fulsome opinions, so it required all her attention. The darting red arrow shot back and forth through the mist, which grew thicker until it turned into a pea-soup fog. In a final burst of activity before the murk enveloped it, the line transformed into the loops of a single word.

Poisoned.

"Abigail, what have you done to me?" Sera struggled to form the words. The teacup fell from her hand and clattered to the floor. Her body, no longer able to remain upright, slumped to one side on the settee. Her limbs refused her commands. More terrifying, when Sera grasped at her magic to counter the poison... she found no trace of it within her veins.

Abigail bent down, picked up the broken pieces of porcelain, and set them on the tray.

"Grandfather brewed a special potion to send you to sleep and to put your magic into hibernation. We had to be ever so careful. He said you are so clever that we needed a way to ensure you wouldn't detect the spell until it was too late. He had a brilliant idea—to make one that wouldn't be activated until I sang."

"I thought you were my friend." A tear formed in her eye and rolled down her cheek as her vision faded.

Abigail knelt by the settee. "No. I was never your friend. We could have been, once. But despite my best efforts, you refuse to do what society expects of you and you defy both king and council. Parading around in breeches, Seraphina, really." A shudder ran through Abigail's form. "The final straw was refusing Lord Thornton, to instead become a common whore. Throwing yourself at a penniless surgeon. Did you think no one would know?"

Sera's heart split in two. Her friend had betrayed her. As had Lord Rowan, when she had worked so hard to gain the approval of the old mage. Another piece of information managed to push its way through the darkness in her head. "Your grandfather brewed the poison... that killed Lord Branvale."

Her former friend nodded. "I delivered it to his valet that day. Remember? I paid my last visit to you at his house."

None of it made any sense. "Why?" The word rasped from her throat.

"Branvale had to go. He wanted to extend your guardianship and Grandfather needed you out of his clutches. Our friendship has provided me with some benefits. Delivering you to Grandfather means I will become a duchess, and much sooner than I ever expected. Even now my fiancé's father sickens. I should thank you for that."

"What... now?" Sera's whole body struggled to form the two syllables as the spell stole her consciousness. Already the room was fading to black. Yelling and scuffling came from the hall, and she was vaguely aware of Elliot shouting her name.

Abigail leaned closer. "Grandfather was most insistent that I tell you what awaits you. The Repository of Forgotten Things."

Fear surged through Sera and, for an instant, peeled back the dark. Two large men held Elliot at the doorway while a third pummelled her brave footman. Then the curse tightened its grip and her lungs struggled to draw breath.

A wave of darkness crashed over Sera and swept her away.

Will Sera escape her predicament?
You can find out in book 5:
CASTLE MANOEUVRE
https://tillywallace.com/books/tournament-of-
shadows/castle-manoeuvre/

History. Magic. Friendship.

I do hope you enjoyed Seraphina's adventure. If you would like to dive deeper into the world, or learn more about the odd assortment of characters that populate it, you can join the community by signing up at:
https://www.tillywallace.com/newsletter

Also by Tilly Wallace

For the most complete and up to date list of books, please visit:

https://tillywallacebooks.com

Available series:

Tournament of Shadows

Manner and Monsters

Highland Wolves

Grace Designs Mysteries

About the Author

Tilly drinks entirely too much coffee and is obsessed with hats. When not scouring vintage stores for her next chapeau purchase, she writes whimsical historical fantasy novels, set in a bygone time where magic is real. With a quirky and loveable cast, her books combine vintage magic and gentle humour.

Through loyal friendships, her characters discover that in an uncertain world, the strongest family is the one you create.

Email: tilly@tillywallace.com
STORE: https://www.tillywallacebooks.com

facebook.com/tillywallaceauthor
bookbub.com/authors/tilly-wallace
goodreads.com/tillywallace

Made in United States
Orlando, FL
19 March 2025

59607403R00178